PEACOCK BOOKS

*Editor: Kaye Webb*

# THE BUSHBABIES

'What will happen to the bushbaby when you are gone?' asked Tembo the African headman, and that was how Jackie discovered she was leaving her home in Africa for ever. Of course she was miserable for herself, but she was even more worried about Kamau the bushbaby, her funny little pet with the face of a fox, the ears of a bat and the eyes of an owl. And when she lost her export licence for him she decided that there was only one solution – to slip ashore at night and release him in the dockyard at Mombasa.

But her plan went wrong and, as if in a bad dream, she heard the ship's propellers begin to turn, saw it move away from the quay, and found herself alone with Kamau and Tembo. So Jackie sets out on a perilous journey through storms and floods and the haunts of wild animals to take her pet back to his birthplace. And to make matters worse the police believe Tembo has kidnapped her and have given orders to shoot him on sight!

Besides being a moving story, this book is full of the sights and sounds of the wilder parts of Africa, where there are still more lions and crocodiles and elephants than houses and people.

*William Stevenson*

# THE BUSHBABIES

*Illustrated by Victor G. Ambrus*

PENGUIN BOOKS

Penguin Books Ltd, Harmondsworth,
Middlesex, England
Penguin Books Australia Ltd, Ringwood,
Victoria, Australia

First published in the U.S.A. 1965
Published in Great Britain by Hutchinson 1966
Published in Peacock Books 1971

Copyright © William Stevenson, 1965

Illustrations copyright © Victor G. Ambrus, 1965

Made and printed in Great Britain by
Cox & Wyman Ltd,
London, Reading and Fakenham
Set in Intertype Baskerville

# Contents

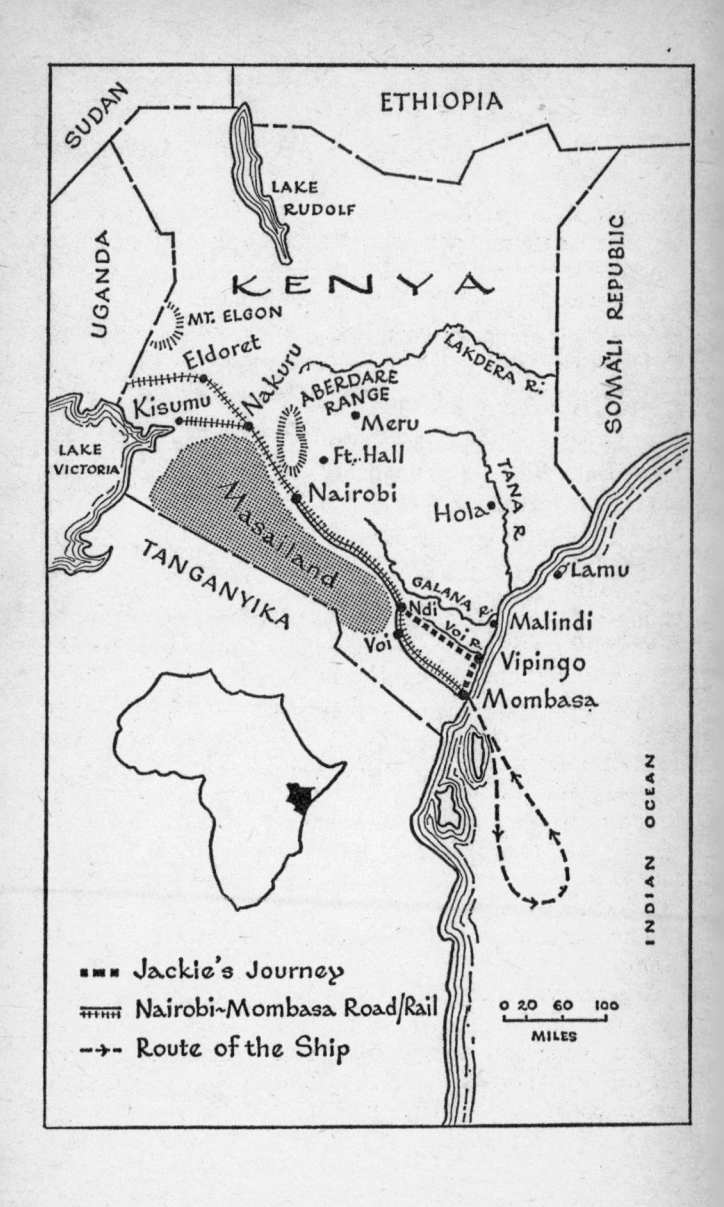

## Author's note on bushbabies

There really is an African named Tembo. The girl, Jackie, is my eldest daughter. She and Kamau, the third bushbaby (and the only true one), live with the rest of my family now in Malaysia.

Kamau is an African lemur. Between Africa and Malaysia, he lived in Scotland, in Jackie's Latin room at school. *Life* magazine called him a Latin-loving lemur who 'experienced' every extreme of heat and cold, and changes of diet that would give ulcers to most humans. His only indulgence: mealworms from the fashionable London store of Harrods.

He flew to Malaysia hidden in Jackie's basket. Here he found relatives, the big-eyed Asian tarsiers. Yet between here and Africa there is no wild creature to link them, unless you count Abominable Snowmen. They survived unchanged, as a tribe, through forty million years because they are night prowlers; they can look through 180 degrees backward into the jungle; their hearing is radar-sharp.

Kamau is a primate, the closest relative to man. He differs from his Asian cousins in many ways. He can jump thirty times his own length in a split second, and he keeps upright whereas most primates 'fly' horizontally. He makes each tree his castle by leaving his odour on every branch. Jackie first met Kamau one Christmas morning on a Kenya farm. He had fallen into a bowl of soap powder and looked like a snow-white dwarf.

The third of this trio, Tembo, remains in his beloved Kenya.

It seems far from Jackie's Malay garden. Spider orchids spill over the trellis. We swoon in the fragrance of frangipani. A nightjar swoops through the jungle creepers, crying *tok-tok*, a language foreign to Kamau. Still, mysteriously, his Asian cousins are all around him.

w. s.

## 1. Good-bye to Africa

'What will happen to the bushbaby when you are gone?' asked Tembo.

The African headman put the question so cautiously that Jackie continued to stalk the grasshopper perched on a blade of grass at her feet.

'Gone?' She flicked a duster, and grabbed the stunned grasshopper. 'Where are we going?'

A tiny creature popped out of her shirt and took the insect.

'It is said you are leaving Africa soon.'

She stiffened. 'Leaving Africa?'

'I am sorry, baba, I thought you knew.' Tembo dropped his hands to his sides, aghast.

The girl's face had gone white. She said: 'But Africa is my *home*.'

Instinctively she closed her hands around the bushbaby, who gripped the grasshopper as if it were a stick of celery.

Tembo turned away, embarrassed to see the moistening of the girl's eyes. He became absorbed in the task of catching more grasshoppers for the bushbaby's breakfast.

'Where did you hear this?' The girl shook his arm. 'Where?'

Still he avoided her. He was stripped to the waist and when he bent forward she could see the ribbed welts slashed across his back long ago by a leopard.

'Please, old friend.' Her voice caressed him. 'Please tell me what you know.'

He glanced uneasily at the stone bungalow on the hill above them. Her father was the game warden, known far and wide as Trapper Rhodes, a man to be respected.

'It is all over the camp.' He spoke in Swahili, lowering his voice. He paused, torn between loyalty to Rhodes and affection for the girl he had known since infancy.

'Daddy's busy building a rhino pen,' she said impatiently. 'The rest of the family's at church. Come on, Tembo! Nobody will know you told me.'

He shoved back his neat little bead-edged cap, fashioned from a sheep's stomach, and revealed stiff black hair that sprang up around his unruffled forehead.

'By the time of the short rains your father is to be replaced.'

'And then . . . ?'

'And then you will go away.' The lines around his nose and mouth deepened. She saw him swallow, trying in vain to find more words.

'Thank you for telling me, Tembo.' Her hands flew up to the bushbaby hiding under her pony-tail of corn-gold hair. She stroked the long curling tail and fondled the creature's big cup-shaped ears.

Finally she said: 'I'm taking Mandarin to the top of the ridge.' She pointed her chin at a small pony grazing nearby.

'Yes, baba.' He followed her in silence.

She walked with long loose strides, and he thought sadly that the girl had already ceased to be a child. By his reckoning she must be eleven or thereabouts, although Tembo had never been able to figure age by the counting of years. But he knew that white children grew like bean-poles in this alien climate. Jackie had sprouted as fast as any boy, and behaved like one. She had a sleepy boyish grin, a wide mouth that stretched under a slightly crooked nose, and quietly observant eyes that matched the blue jacaranda blossoms.

He helped her into the worn English saddle. 'You will not tell what I have said?'

'Of course not.' Both took refuge in the elaborate courtesies of formal Swahili. 'Please forgive me that I go now. It is to give myself time to think.' She circled him once and then spurred Mandarin into a fast trot. When she could no longer see Tembo's mournful figure she broke into a canter. The bushbaby had already moved to his favourite position between the pony's ears, flattening his small body against the mane.

They moved between trees that were flat and horizontal, through thorn-trees that whistled softly in the morning wind. Dew still lingered on the sweet crunchy grass and the sky was filled with the white galleons of clouds peculiar to the Rift Valley. The Rift cut across this part of Africa like a knife wound. On either side of the gash, for hundreds of miles, the bronzed earth peeled back to expose the blue bones of the mountains.

The girl sat astride the pony and tried to understand the news she had just heard. She saw her world with sharpened senses, the yellow fields of wheat and maize, divided by spinneys of Australian gums and the weeping blue jacaranda. She looked down to where her family worshipped in the simple Anglican church, its lichened stones touched by the early sun. The parson visited only once a month now so many of the white settlers had gone. The church stood on the floor of the valley, and cacti protected the graveyard filled with the bones of pioneers.

The hot air of the plains shimmered like fire, and plumes of white dust followed the kicking heels of wild herds. Here, more than six thousand feet above the sea, the air was so clear that it seemed you could reach up and touch the sun; a sun that cast no shadow at its zenith, for this was the Equator. The ridge overlooked a narrow strip of cleared land where a windsock stirred lazily. The girl brought the pony's head round, laying the rein against his neck, and gently urged him along the edge of the elephant grass.

'Hush, Kamau.' The bushbaby had jumped back to her shoulder and now blew out his cheeks and made soft noises in her ear. She gathered the reins in one hand, and with the other she scooped the bushbaby into her shirt. He was the size of a small squirrel, with black-rimmed eyes like elder-berries and an expression of sharp intelligence. He nestled against her, chirruping absent-mindedly to himself, and fell asleep with the ease and speed of a dormouse.

She had slowed to a walk. Mandarin had been nothing but a poor ill-used pony when she rescued him from a passing caravan. His flanks were branded, his mouth hardened by the brutal frontier bits, and his body was scarred and dumpy. But her imagination transformed him into the fleetest of Arab chestnuts.

'*Pesi! Pesi!*' she whispered in his ear and the pony jerked into a shambling trot.

A man appeared at the door of a shed near the wind-sock.

' 'Morning, Cranky!' The girl waved.

The man who responded to this unflattering title was small and old, and tough-looking. He leaned back, hands on hips, grinning. He had a cocky little red beard and mutton-chop whiskers. His bared head was bald and freckled by the sun. Like the girl, he wore bleached shorts and shirt and ankle-boots.

'Hullo there.' Professor Crankshaw waved a stiff, gloved hand. 'What brings you out this way?'

'I was catching grasshoppers for Kamau.' The girl said this as if it were the most normal of occupations. She slipped down from the saddle.

'Some folk go hunting lion. Others hunt grasshoppers. Each to his poison, eh?' The little archaeologist tapped the bushbaby gently. 'I thought Kamau would take a lot of taming. He seems to be taming you.'

Jackie forced a smile. 'Cranky!' She faced him squarely. 'What's all this about Daddy going away?'

'You've heard?' He raised his artificial hand so that the black leather covered his mouth.

'It is true then!'

He tried to retreat. 'True? Depends what you've been told.'

She stroked Mandarin's soft nostrils and, without looking up, she said: 'Why does everybody want to hide the truth?'

'I'm trying to hide nothing,' Professor Crankshaw said sharply. Too sharply. He stopped and rubbed his beard. 'Look, young 'un, you shouldn't hear these things from other folk. Have you spoken to your father?'

'He never tells me anything.'

'That's not true.' The archaeologist wiped his good hand across his shirt, leaving a smear of grease. 'There's been a lot of pressure to put Africans into jobs like your father's. He's been hoping to change this – or at least be allowed to stay on as an adviser.'

'The Africans all like him.'

'I know, young 'un.' He shrugged, screwing up his eyes. 'It's all politics, you see. I don't pretend to understand 'em.' He dismissed the entire subject with a vague gesture. 'Now you're here, come and look at *Mother Goose*. Got the old lady fixed and ready to fly again.'

Glad to push aside her anxieties, even for a moment, the girl followed him into the shed. A powered glider, resting on one silver wing-tip, was dimly visible inside. 'Did you get the motor working?' she asked with quickening interest.

'Just about.' Crankshaw ran his gloved hand over the polished nose. 'I want to fly over the new diggings near the crater. One of my men found a fossilized bone – piece of vertebrae.' He fumbled in his shirt and unfolded steel-rimmed spectacles with tinted lenses. 'Thought I'd make an aerial reccy. Surprising what you see from above . . . mass graves . . . buried villages.'

The girl sighed, trying to find words to explain that she knew the archaeologist was trying to distract her. She said: 'Dear Cranky. I'm just too worried to concentrate.'

'I always hoped you'd help me on these digs.' He hooked the spectacles over his ears with one hand, regarding her solemnly. 'I even planned to turn this old crate into a two-seater. Teach you to fly. You're almost big enough. You could get away with it here in Kenya by the time you're fourteen.'

She saw his enthusiasm mounting and bit her lip. For twenty years Professor Crankshaw had been digging up bits of Africa, burrowing so deep into the past he seemed like an old fossil himself. He even talked in phrases that went out of fashion in the thirities.

Her sense of doom returned with renewed force. 'I must be off and tackle Daddy,' she said abruptly.

'Well, remember I'm always here if you need advice.' Already his attention had wandered back to the glider, reminding her that the professor's world was perfectly adjusted to the sudden arrivals and abrupt departures of small girls.

Jackie's father was a hard man to catch alone that Sunday. He was utterly absorbed in the mechanics of moving an injured rhinoceros to another game reserve. This meant building a pen where the two-ton beast would be kept until it was fit enough for the long journey. His job was to catch animals in need of protection, moving them to remote but safer regions. This had earned him the somewhat misleading nickname of 'Trapper'.

Late in the afternoon he came bounding into the bungalow. 'Penny my love!' he trumpeted to his wife. 'Gather up
the kids and we'll have a picnic at the Hippo Pool.'

There were squeals of delight from the other three children. Picnic teas were a Sunday ritual that had been
neglected in recent weeks.

They were driving through a wild bit of country inhabited by baboons when Jackie decided she would have to put
the question in front of everyone. 'Is it true we're leaving
Africa?' she burst out, and watched the back of her father's
neck go red.

'Who said we're leaving?' challenged Andrew. At fourteen, he rather expected to be first with any family news.

The station-wagon jogged along the washboard road,
trailing clouds of red dust. Trapper Rhodes let the speed
drop away and fumbled with his pipe. There was a com-
motion in the back from Kevin and Sally, the younger children.

'They've been listening to gossip,' said Penny accusingly.
She leaned against her husband's burly shoulder. 'You'd better tell them.'

He stopped the car. 'It's very simple. My job finishes in a
few months and then ...' He forced cheerfulness into his
voice. 'And then, why, we start a new life together.'

'But in Kenya,' said Andrew hopefully.

'No.' The warden opened his window and emptied his
pipe. 'Not even in Africa.'

As he spoke, a pair of giraffe cantered down the road and
halted, rubbing their long necks together.

'I'm sorry I couldn't tell you before.' The warden
wriggled round in his seat. 'I really hoped for an extension of
contract – '

Sally interrupted him. 'Look out! Baboons!'

Three of the coconut-headed animals were vaulting along
the crest of the road like nimble old men on crutches. Jackie
wound up her window hastily, and watched the bushbaby
press his nose against the glass.

The biggest baboon leapt on the hood and peered through the windscreen. He had a black pointed muzzle and tiny golden eyes in a sharply receding forehead. When he saw the bushbaby he bared his teeth. As if giving a signal, the big baboon uttered a short dry bark. At once the surrounding fever trees came alive. Baboons dropped from the branches, dodged out from behind gnarled trunks, and converged upon the car. There were mother baboons with beetle-brows and up-curling tails like whips, and pink babies who rode pickaback or swung from adult bellies. Dozens of youngsters tumbled over each other and sprang on the backs of elders.

'See how Kamau attracts them?' Trapper Rhodes dodged a long furry arm that reached through a small opening in the driver's window. Leathery fingers groped for his ear.

'Do they eat bushbabies?' asked Kevin.

'Like jelly beans.'

Jackie squeezed Kamau. 'If we do go away . . .' She stopped. 'If we go, can we take the bushbaby?' She held her breath.

'Lord yes!' Her father tipped back his wideawake hat, leaving a white line across his tanned forehead. He massaged his temples, twisting to watch her. 'I'll get a game permit,' he said.

'And permits for Mandarin and the dogs and – ' chorused the boys.

'Hold on!' Penny Rhodes had to shout to be heard. 'We can't take *all* the pets.'

Andrew said quietly: 'Better keep Kamau with us, though. He'd never survive by himself.'

Jackie knew it was true. The bushbaby had grown up under her protection. He was only a year old and knew nothing about danger.

The baboons were among his worst enemies. A grizzled old grandad came sailing into the windscreen and began tapping the wiper impatiently against the glass. Another inspected himself in a wing mirror. Youngsters danced on the metal roof, creating a terrific din.

Trapper Rhodes judged this a good time to shake them off. He reversed a few feet and then propelled the car forward. When he braked, five or six baboons cascaded from the roof, skating over the hot metal of the bonnet and bouncing into the road. They glared back at the car, rubbing their rumps with injured dignity. The two giraffes sauntered lazily out of the way, flapping maidenly eyelashes.

The incident deepened Jackie's resolve to guard the bush-baby closely. She would never abandon him.

In those last few months she carried him everywhere, even taking him to bed with her. He was like a gnome, hopping always in close company with her, or curling up in a ball under her shirt. His species was known to Africans as 'the tree dwarfs', and Kamau, especially, seemed to possess an almost human sense of mischief. He was the one fragment of Africa that Jackie felt she could keep with her always.

He made it easier for her to pull up roots. With him, Jackie said good-bye to the lonely bungalow above the Rift, in the season when the red waxen trumpets of the flame trees were exploding into their richest crimson colour.

They caught the train that travels from Uganda down through Kenya to the sea, to the East African port of Mombasa where a cargo ship would be awaiting them. Trapper Rhodes had booked all the freighter's accommodation, three two-berth cabins. With them on the train came Tembo, who insisted that he must supervise the loading of baggage.

Tembo was a former *askari*, a soldier of the King's African Rifles, and he had served with Trapper Rhodes, who dreaded the moment when they must part.

'It has not rained here for seven months,' said the headman as the train moved down into the parched Athi Plains. 'The farmers are lost.'

'Why?' asked Andrew. He was playing with his pet chameleon whose rough cold fingers groped along his bared arm.

'Because the farmers measure time by the short millet rains and the long bean rains,' said their father. 'Now the rains are all mixed up. People are frightened of another year like '61 when there was a long drought followed by terrible floods.'

Tembo tickled the chameleon. 'See how he turns green. Some say it is a sign the rains will come before long.'

The chameleon plodded slowly along the seat, eyes swivelling in baggy sockets as if looking for the rain.

In another hour the African night would fall with the swiftness of an extinguished lamp. Now all the animals were on the move, faintly visible from the train. Plump zebras kicked their heels near a saltlick. Streams of gazelle sprang through the tall yellow grasses, and lyre-horned impala sailed against the red sunset. Eland with swaying dewlaps grazed on the verge of the lion's haunts. Tall giraffes rocked through veils of evening mist.

Andrew, watching through the window, grew pensive. He understood why the bushbaby could not be released. It would be like throwing a small child into an arena of lions. But he felt sorry now about dragging his chameleon away from Africa.

Next day, when the train stopped at Ndi to take on water, he jumped out and raced across the station yard to place his pet in a safe branch of the local sacred tree, a fig. The horned chameleon turned yellow and red like a small dragon. His long forked tongue lashed out and whipped a fly from a distant leaf. He, at any rate, knew how to fend for himself.

'Good-bye,' said Andrew. When he boarded the train again he marked the spot carefully on his map and then blew his nose very hard.

Jackie frowned. Would Kamau ever again enjoy the freedom that was *his* birthright? Was she, after all, right to take him away like this?

The train jerked forward. She saw the high silvered tank that fed water into the locomotive through a long flexible pipe like an elephant's trunk. The scene impressed itself upon her mind: the tall water-tank, the small flat-topped concrete station, and the steep embankment. She would need to remember these details very clearly many days later.

## 2. 'When the Saints go marching in'

'Are you the little girl with the bushbaby?' asked the second engineer of the United States motor vessel *Thoreau.*

Jackie, picking her way between coils of tarred rope, said: 'Yes. Want to see him?'

She lifted the lid of the basket, displaying Kamau asleep in his nest of old sweaters.

'That's a rare 'un,' said the engineer. 'Worth his weight in gold, I bet.'

He stood in front of her, face red against the brilliant white of his starched shirt and shorts. 'You've got a game permit, of course.'

'Of course,' Jackie replied quickly, and flushed.

'Good kid.' The engineer let her pass. 'It'd be a bad thing if all the rare animals of Africa were taken away, eh?' he called after her.

But Jackie was already running, gripped by the sudden fear that she had forgotten the vital permit with the impressive words: GRANTING PERMISSION HEREBY FOR THE EXPORT OF ONE BUSHBABY TO WIT: *galagos senegalensis zanzibaricus*. She could remember even the Latin name. Where had she put the permit?

She flew to her cabin and hooked the door shut. Then she threw open her suitcase and whirled through its contents.

The permit was nowhere to be found.

She searched Sally's bag on the adjacent bunk. She went carefully through all her own pockets. She combed her memory. She had no recollection of packing the permit. With growing certainty and alarm, she knew she had left it behind. Of one thing she was sure. It would be illegal to keep Kamau.

There was a knock at the door. Trembling, she unhooked it.

'I come to make bunks ready.' It was the Swahili steward. He moved to the two-tiered bunks and saw the basket.

'Little missie has a *galago*, a bushbaby?'

'You know?'

'All the ship knows.'

In that case it would be impossible to keep Kamau as a stowaway.

'Does the captain know?'

'The captain?' He paused, crouching over the coverlet, eyes dark and expressionless. 'The captain will find out, missie. He is not liking animals on board. One time he makes the ship's carpenter leave a pet monkey behind in Madagascar.'

This was worse news still.

'Please don't tell him.'

'Why for should I tell the captain?' The steward gave her an indignant look. 'I do my work. Captain does his.' He turned and busied himself with the blankets.

Jackie picked up the basket and took it into the small shower-room. She closed the door and lifted Kamau gently out. He disliked being disturbed and drew back his ears, blowing between sharp little teeth with a sound like a muted roar.

From outside came the whine and screech of cranes. Soon the ship must sail. She had to think fast. If she tried to keep Kamau hidden the captain was bound to find out. Even if she deceived the captain, there would be Customs men to face later. Either way she would certainly lose her bush-baby.

She let him leap to the rail of the shower-curtain, where he clung upside down, head twisted so that he could watch her. Her father had gone to some trouble to get Kamau's export licence from the Kenya Game Department.

And now she had forgotten to bring the permit with her.

She remembered, too, going to the public library and reading: 'These are among the strangest animals in existence. Their relatives of the *tarsier* family are found only in equatorial forests of Asia. The animal commonly called the bushbaby, however, has been known to survive in cold climates.'

Jackie winced. Here she was, planning to expose Kamau to the wintry blasts of a northern climate. Yet she could not even preserve the piece of paper that protected his life.

She heard the outer door clunk open again.

'Daddy!' She rushed to meet him.

'What is it?' He caught the urgency in her voice and looked at her with such frank eyes that she faltered.

'Nothing.' She was suddenly afraid to mention the permit. Her father was a square sort of man, square of shoulders and with a face that seemed to be chiselled from stone. He had an old-fashioned square-dealing approach to life. She could see no way of enlisting his help in breaking regulations.

'Come on deck and join the others.' Trapper Rhodes took her arm in the belief that her evident distress was due to the tension of recent days. She let him lead her to the main deck, her mind working furiously. There was only one solution that she could see. Kamau must be released here in Mombasa dockyard.

Shrinking from the thought she took her place at the rail. The dock was almost deserted. The last of the cargo had swung aboard. Big arclights swayed in the humid night breeze, casting an eerie light on the greasy concrete below. Chains rattled. Davits creaked.

A voice behind her said: 'We'll be another coupla hours before sailing.' It was the second engineer talking quietly to Rhodes.

'In that case,' said Penny firmly, 'we'd better get some sleep.' She herded the children together. 'It's been a long day. And, truth to tell, I'd sooner not be here when we cast off. We'll say good-bye to Africa tomorrow, at a good long distance.'

Later when they were all bunked down, Penny said to her husband: 'Did you see how upset Jackie was?'

His answer was lost in the metallic whir of the fan.

'You know,' Penny continued, 'that girl has changed a great deal since we gave her the bushbaby. She's still awfully clumsy. And forgetful. She breaks cups and trips over her own legs, which are certainly too long for her age. She's awkward and dreamy, and moves like a young colt. But she's a gentle child.' Penny closed her eyes. 'A kind heart's worth a ton of cleverness.'

In the next cabin Jackie waited until she heard Sally's breathing deepen into slumber. Then she crept into the shower-room. Kamau squatted beside the dish of milk and cornflakes she had smuggled from the cook's galley. He was clasping a mint candy, licking it with rapture in his eyes. She knew from long experience that mints had an almost hypnotic power over him, glueing his attention just as firmly as his twig-fingers were glued to the candy itself. With a movement so swift it was scarcely perceptible, she scooped him up.

'Kek-kek-kek!' His screech was somewhat muffled by the mint. She bundled him into the basket, crammed down the lid, and pegged it into place.

She checked again that Sally was asleep and slipped into
the clothes she had worn in the train – riding breeches, a
yellow shirt, and a brown whipcord jacket. Into a pocket of
the jacket she stuffed a paper bag full of Kamau's remaining
mints. She tied her long golden hair at the back hastily,
using an old piece of blue ribbon. She donned her favourite
chukka boots made from the ear of an elephant. Finally, on
impulse, she bent and kissed Sally.

The gangway was down and still unattended. Men scurried about the decks. Jackie was grateful that nobody had
come to see them off. All farewells, except Tembo's, had
been made up-country. And Tembo, once he saw the baggage safely stowed away, had not lingered to drag out the
agony.

Jackie slipped down the gangway and stood for a moment
in the shadows. A stumpy locomotive of the port railway
fussed along the gleaming metal of the line. Stevedores,
bared backs glistening in the artificial light, stood arguing in
a group. She waited, and when the way seemed clear, she ran
to the shelter of a nearby godown. There, in the thick smell
of diesel oil and coffee, Jackie took stock.

She could let Kamau out of his basket now and pray that
somehow he would find his way safely back to the highland
forests that were his natural home. But then she thought of
all his enemies. The hooting owls. The giggling hyaena. The
fish eagle whose harsh cry sounded across the marshes. The
baboons who worked in teams, so clever and ruthless they
could tear a leopard to pieces, never mind a bushbaby.

She remembered the very first time she had seen the basket she now clutched in her arms. It had been their last
Christmas Day in Africa.

The African workers and their children had gathered
under the tall pine tree growing outside the bungalow. The
tree had been decorated with lights and gifts scattered on
the grass below. The straw basket was tied with red ribbon.

'How do I open it?'

Her father had bent down and freed the ribbon. 'It will open itself.'

The lid of the basket had lifted a fraction, making her jump. And then, for the first time in her life, she had seen a bushbaby. A tiny hand had groped along the basket's edge, followed by a face like a furry walnut.

'What is it?'

'Galago.' Tembo's deep voice had boomed in her ear.

She had clapped her hands. 'What a super, super surprise.'

At the sound of her voice the bushbaby had jumped clean out of the basket and into her lap, tail thrashing like a propeller.

'His name is Kamau.' Again it had been Tembo who spoke. 'The sprite who lives in the jungle. Kamau.'

Now, as Jackie peered out of the darkness of the godown, she smiled at the recollection. Kamau had been comforted by the warmth of her body, and made a permanent haven inside her shirt. She had had to teach him to give up his nocturnal habits, for he was by nature a night animal.

*He's got the face of a fox, the ears of a bat, the eyes of an owl,* Jackie had written to a distant uncle. *He's the colour of a squirrel and he grins like a monkey and he's got the fingers of an old man. And he jumps like a kangaroo.*

She could hear him now, stirring inside the basket.

She stood alone on the dockside in an agony of doubt, and heard the locomotive come clattering and clanging down the line again. It stopped and there was a moment of silence.

Away in the distance she heard the faint notes of a toy harmonica. At first she thought the sound came from the ship. She heard Kamau scratching to be let out of the basket, and she lifted the lid. The bushbaby scrambled on to her arm and stiffened, his big paper-thin ears pricked forward, his head twisting in every direction to pick up the sound.

Tembo!

She knew it must be Tembo, for the bushbaby had recognized the same harmonica notes.

Long ago, her father had said: 'The most constructive thing the Army ever taught Tembo was to play the mouth-organ.' And he had given the African headman a big old-fashioned German harmonica made of engraved metal and carved walnut. In camp, at night, Tembo would play this impressive instrument while the women husked coconuts or pounded the evening meal of *posho*, made from maize-flour.

The sound was lost again in the deep and sudden thunder of the *Thoreau*'s siren. It reminded her of the foghorn near the family cottage, a few miles along the coast from Mombasa. Its desolating thunder made her think of shipwrecks and storm-tossed seas. When it stopped, and the echoes dwindled away, she listened again for the notes of a mouth-organ, but heard nothing.

Kamau slipped under her shirt and, hugging the basket, she ran the length of the godown. Part of her mind insisted that she had imagined the mouth-organ. Deep down inside herself she was not so sure.

Again the ship's siren blew. She stopped running and looked back.

There was a great deal of activity now around the *Thoreau*. She saw figures moving about the stern and on the fantail. A rope snaked astern and fell with a clear splash into the murky water.

She stood, breathing fast.

A loud clatter drew her attention to the gangway. It was moving away from the ship's hull. Mesmerized, she saw more ropes curl through the air. Her legs were rooted to the ground. Common sense told her to shout, to run back to the trundling gangway. She felt the furry warmth of Kamau against her skin.

The ship's propellers began to churn. She heard small waves slap against the wharfside.

As if in a bad dream she saw the ship detach itself from the black density of the docks. Lights twinkled along the hull. The gap between the *Thoreau* and the quay began to

widen with surprising speed. The ship had moved so slowly
at first. Now it surged forward in a great hurry to be free
from Africa. In the wake came a stench of fuel and tar, of
stale cooking-pots and sacks of coffee. A stream of garbage
shot through a chute in the stern, and again the siren
blew.

The girl stared at the black and deepening gulf between
herself and her family. The basket in her arms, however, was
like an anchor. Her head span with the enormity of her
situation, but her legs still refused to move. Then she heard
the notes of the harmonica again, and she was certain it
must be Tembo.

She followed the sound, half sobbing, until she came to
the end of the main wharf. There she saw him, seated on a
bollard, silhouetted against the city's glow.

'Tembo!' He was playing a mournful African song. Jackie
had heard it many times when he crouched over the charcoal brazier at night. It was a song of his own people, made
long ago when Arab slavers laid waste this part of the con-
tinent. The song was a lament for the lost freedom of the
chained African slaves, and for the slaughtered children
they left behind. It was a dirge that recalled the endless
march of the slaves, and in it were echoes of the wide hor-
izons and the great forests they would never see again.

Moving softly, anxious not to alarm him, Jackie whispered: 'Hullo, old friend. It's me. Do not be disturbed.
Tembo?'

She spoke in Swahili.

The man jumped to his feet. His eyes shone, whites
gleaming. He was on the very edge of the shifting pool of
light cast by the swinging flood-lamps, and he peered dubi-
ously into the surrounding dark.

'Baba?' His voice was a hiss. 'What are you doing here?
*Wafanyajee?*'

'Come quickly, Tembo, out of the light.'

He took a firm grip on the short club hanging from his
wrist and moved towards her.

'Is it really you?'

'It is me, Tembo. I want your help.' She touched his arm.

When his eyes had adjusted to the dark, and he saw truly that the girl stood there, the man sucked his breath. 'What have you done?' He dropped to one knee and pressed her face between his calloused hands. Then he saw the basket.

'Kamau?'

'Yes.' She began to explain.

The African groaned. 'You have done this thing for the galago? You have left the ship?'

'There was nothing else I could do,' Jackie said simply. She hesitated. 'I must get him home, to the place where he was caught. To the Place of the Hippopotamus.'

Until this moment she had given no thought to such a plan. It rose unbidden to her mind. At once, however, she saw what a sensible solution it would be. Among his own family, he would be safe.

'That is a long way,' Tembo was saying. 'It is beyond Ndi.' He added slowly: 'Your father will be angry.'

'He will understand.' She spoke with more confidence than she felt. 'If I had stayed on the ship Kamau would die.'

Tembo nodded slowly. He had never pretended to share the Rhodes' curious love of animals. As a young Kamba warrior, one of the fleetest hunters in his village, he regarded animals as either a nuisance or as a source of food. He passed no judgements on white-skinned foreigners who took a different view. He regarded them quite simply as mad. There was no telling how far they might go in their craziness.

He fingered the bracelet on his scarred wrist. It was made from the hairs plucked from a lion's tail, and it was the most powerful of his charms. He turned it slowly between his thick fingers, standing there in the darkness while the girl waited patiently at his side.

'How will the bushbaby make such a long journey?' he asked.

'With your help.'

His friendship with Trapper Rhodes went back a long way. He had not expected to have it tested so severely by the daughter.

'You will help?' she persisted.

She was interrupted by a long blast from the ship's siren, and she waited, head cocked, watching Tembo's face. He was wearing the old desert kepi, with a neck flap at the back, that he used on safari. Over his thin shoulders he had flung an army greatcoat, worn like a cloak. His feet were thrust into black boots that were several sizes too large. The leather was cracked and the boots lacked laces. In these clothes he had gladly suffered the most acute discomfort, considering them to be appropriate to the sad occasion of parting.

The siren echoed across the harbour, and faded. Again it reminded the girl of the foghorn, and her father's cottage.

'I know!' She seemed to explode with the idea. 'We will go to the cottage at Vipingo. It's a short bus journey from here. And tomorrow, when the post office is open, I will send a telegram – a letter by radio – to the ship.'

She saw the doubt lingering in his face.

'You have not seen the cottage, but it is beside the farm of Major Bob.'

Tembo's face cleared slightly. He knew about Major Bob and felt less apprehensive.

'Is it not possible to take the northern train?'

'No.' She spoke decisively, detecting from his voice that the battle was half won. 'In the cottage at Vipingo we shall be safe tonight. Major Bob will tell us what to do in the morning. If we go to the train there will be questions at the barrier. There will be white policemen.'

She knew the beefy red-faced police. They seldom understood small girls as her African friends did. The red-faced whites were too busy blustering around. The cottage was far off the beaten track. There she could plan her next move.

Tembo wiped his harmonica across the knee of his torn pants. Perhaps if he humoured the girl now she would see sense in the morning. 'You are sure this is what you wish?'

'I am sure, old friend.' She slipped her free hand into his
gnarled fist. 'Remember when we all went climbing on Kilimanjaro?'

Tembo chuckled softly.

'And we got lost in the mist, you and I?' She grinned up at
him. Behind her, the *Thoreau*'s lights twinkled in the harbour mouth. 'We had such fun, just the two of us, singing
and shouting down the mountain. It will be like that,
Tembo, like climbing a mountain together.'

The African smiled and hunched his shoulders under the
greatcoat. It was far too big and much too warm but he wore
it with pride. He wore it as he had once worn the skin of the
colobus monkey, in days when he carried a spear and shield,
before he went to war in the service of a foreign king. The
coat was a link with those distant days.

His days as an askari in the King's African Rifles had
taught him many things. His days as a tribal warrior had
also taught him much. He had learned to accept the passing
of these days – the great days of hunting the lion, and other,
more bewildering, days, marching against an unknown
army. Time had taught him never to grieve over his lost
youth, never to look back in sadness at what had gone beyond recall. Despite this he had been sitting on the dockside
in great despair as the ship sailed away with those he had
served with loyalty and affection. Foolishly he had nursed a
secret hope that Trapper Rhodes would take him away too.
But the ship had sailed, with no word said. A few minutes
ago the world had seemed a forlorn and lonely place. He was
a failure, and age came creeping into his bones.

Now, as he held the girl's hand, he felt a warm surge of
joy. Jackie's mother had once said he would follow the girl
to the ends of the earth, and he himself had believed this.
Now fate was giving him the opportunity to prove it.

He laughed, the deep booming laugh that Jackie knew so
well. He was a religious man, respectful of tribal gods, and
devoted also to the biblical figures he had learned about at

mission school. He released the girl's hand and cupped the harmonica between his horny palms.

There was a marching song they both remembered, played on ceremonial parades by the King's African Rifles. It was called 'When the Saints go marching in'.

He squared his shoulders. 'Come, then, baba. You will be my captain-bwana and give me orders.' He blew out his cheeks, the wooden club dangling by a thong from his wrist. 'Let us go.' He sucked in a lungful of air and began to play.

'Forward!' cried Jackie, falling into the spirit of the game. 'To the bus for Vipingo.'

On the hot sticky night of 24 October a puzzled Sikh policeman patrolling the Kilindini dockyard in Mombasa heard the strains of a familiar military march float down the tarmac road by the ferry. He thought he saw an African in flowing robes, accompanied by a slender blonde girl, flit in the shadows between the street-lamps. He was sure the tune he had heard was 'When the Saints go marching in', when the record was played several days later. By that time the unusual spectacle had assumed an importance that even the most efficient Sikh officer could never have foreseen.

## 3. The empty cottage

An old country bus carried the man and the girl through the sisal plantations along the coast road to Vipingo. The bus bulged at the sides and its roof sagged under a pile of hampers stuffed with vegetables and ducks and chickens. It rattled and bounced over pot-holes and the body was badly twisted from years of misuse so that the beam of one head-lamp shone upwards into the midnight sky.

In its light glistened the ebony faces of the sisal workers; plump women in frocks printed with bright colours, and men in torn vests and faded khaki shorts whose muscles rippled under black skins. They were thrown into the air each time the bus jogged over another hole, but this did nothing to stop their chatter. They were silent for a brief moment when Jackie and Tembo stumbled down the aisle to an empty seat in the back. Someone steadied the girl when the bus jerked forward, and the conductor in his flat peaked cap looked surprised when he saw the bushbaby's tail hanging out of Jackie's shirt. Then the chatter resumed, like a chorus of tropical birds in an aviary, and the newcomers were quickly forgotten.

Tembo balanced at the very edge of the slatted seat. He sat very erect and his face seemed to be carved from mahogany. It was a good strong face with deep lines on either side of a scarred nose. Once he glanced down at the girl and smiled, revealing dazzling white teeth of which several had been filed to sharp points.

Jackie held the bushbaby's basket in her lap, and felt Kamau breathing as he slept under her shirt. Sometimes his body trembled as if he dreamed.

The conductor swayed between the rows of nodding heads and gesticulating hands, pinging his ticket machine. The springs of the old bus creaked and twanged. The warm salt air flushed through the glassless windows and Jackie leaned her forehead against the iron bars and watched the palm trees glide past.

Tembo hauled a long knotted string from his topcoat. The string was threaded through a number of East African coins. Each had a hole punched in the middle for this purpose. He detached a few to pay the fares. Then he slipped his hand under the coat, and felt the purse that hung from a thin chain around his neck. In the purse were ten Maria Thérèsa dollars, heavy silver coins which had been the unofficial currency of East Africa for many years. This was the sum total of Tembo's life savings, and this he intended to spend if necessary to make sure the girl beside him should achieve her goal.

He was well armed against trouble. A religious medallion also hung from the chain, but to make doubly sure he wore around his left ankle a wooden cylinder filled with dust and powdered leaves from seven different trails, given him as a child by the family witch-doctor.

Finally there was the club. It was made of close-grained smooth Cape walnut, the same red-orange colour as the African soil. It had a large polished knob at one end. The narrow neck was bound with leather and secured with beads of white, green, blue, and red. The leather was also looped around his wrist. Properly swung, the club could split open a man's skull.

Wrapped in their private thoughts, the man and the girl rocked gently side by side until the bus stopped with a final jerk at Vipingo. By then most of the passengers had gone. It was so late that even the Indian traders had left their tin-roofed stalls and gone to bed.

'Where now?' asked Tembo.

The girl blinked sleepily. 'This way, about a mile.' She noticed for the first time a small canvas bag he carried over one shoulder. She was too tired to question him about it. Instead, she led the way down a rough track. She knew every foot of the way to the cottage. On one side were African *shambas* of maize and sugar-cane. The other side was straggly forest. The moon, three-quarters full, lit their way.

A breeze rustled the palm-fronds high in the slanting coconut trees. The boom of the surf grew louder. It was a strange wild sound, a roar that came in waves, starting as a distant rumble and ending in a thunderous volume of noise that quickly receded again.

Tembo was not familiar with the sea. He came from the open plains near the snow-capped peaks of Kilimanjaro. When he heard the thundering surf he gripped his club and looked about him with sharpened senses. He had never seen the cottage. It was one place where Trapper Rhodes insisted upon being alone with his family.

They reached a bend in the track and Tembo stopped. Jackie, impatient to get on, tugged his arm and then saw his face in the moonglow and slowly removed her hand.

'That's the reef,' she said.

It looked like a long smudge of white chalk drawn clear across the inky sea, half-way between a foreshore of white sand and a slate-grey horizon. The reef extended for mile upon mile, a barrier between the Indian Ocean's long swell and the calm of the inner lagoons.

'Reef.' He repeated the English word. He had neither seen nor heard anything like it.

They had to pass Major Bob's place to reach the cottage. Jackie paused to whistle softly to the farmer's dog. The two-note whistle got no response, and no light shone in the tumbledown farmhouse. It was too late to call on the old man, she decided. Major Bob kept a shotgun and might use it if surprised.

'I'll see him in the morning,' she said.

Her father's cottage stood alone near the edge of a great cliff. It had whitewashed walls and a roof made from heavy kavirondo cane and papyrus. Wind and rain had hammered this roof into a thick swooping mass that resembled an old felt hat.

When Jackie saw the cottage so solid above the sea her heart leapt. Trapper Rhodes had brought the children here in all seasons. He called it the family's 'glory hole', a place for fishing gear and old clothes and the leftovers from safari – canned food and torn tarpaulins and frayed ropes. He had left it, just as it stood, to Professor Crankshaw. 'It was the family hideaway if ever things got bad,' he had told the archaeologist. 'It's full of rubbish that might be useful in emergency.'

The cottage was built, in the ancient Arab style, from coral rag and red earth. The mortar and plaster came from the lime of burnt coral and provided a fierce resistance to the powerful vegetative forces of the tropics. There was a concrete reservoir to catch rain-water. Paraffin for the lamps was stored in a stone shelter. Shiny brass bolts secured the shuttered windows and there were big padlocks on the doors, back and front.

Jackie stretched up, ran her fingers along the lintel above the massive teakwood front door, and found the key. Her parents had treated the cottage in the way an African used his mud-and-wattle hut, without much regard for the danger of human intruders. She knew exactly where everything was. She unbolted the door and groped her way into

the larder. There she located the oil lamp, always kept
ready, and matches that were soggy from exposure to the
warm humid air. She found a dry Swan Vestas and struck it
on the concrete floor. She lit the lamp and trimmed the wick.
Then she checked the level of the paraffin and turned the
flame low. She made a mental note to locate the matches
that her father always kept sealed in candle wax, and took
the lamp into the main room and set it upon a big refectory
table.

'Come and help me find food,' she called to the man who
hesitated outside.

Tembo crossed the threshold. The room was central to the
cottage, with openings that led off on either side to angled
wings. There were no ceilings and he could see the long
knotted mangrove poles that supported the thatched bark
leaves. The cottage was built in the form of a 'V', open
towards the sea.

'Quick! Close the door!' Jackie flapped her hands. 'All the
*dudus* are coming in.'

The light had attracted a swarm of flying insects. They
danced in a cloud above the smoking lamp. The man
slammed the door shut with a faint look of unease.

Jackie was flinging damp cushions from the long window-
seats. The seats were really big storage lockers and as she
raised each lid, Tembo saw blankets and utensils packed
tight in the coffin-shaped boxes.

'The bedding's damp,' said the girl, 'but it's something to
sleep in.'

She started to range cans of food on the table and then
noticed Tembo's silence.

'What is it?' Her voice was sharp.

'Forgive me, baba.' Tembo shifted his feet. 'It is not good
to be in a white man's house like this.'

'But you came into our house in the Rift all the time!'

'It is different. There I am serving your father. Here, I
feel like one who comes secretly at night . . .' He stood with
his big hands clasped, looking at the floor.

Jackie said with swift understanding: 'Please, make a fire. A big fire! There are stones here, near the door outside. You will guard me beside the fire, and I will sleep near it.' She used an imperative form of Swahili that brought a smile to his face.

'It is not necessary for you to sleep outside,' he said. 'I will keep watch.'

'I know I can rely upon you,' she replied with quiet deliberation. 'You are the *mlinzi*, my protector.'

Tembo's shoulders snapped back and he lifted his chin. The moment he was outside he kicked off the city boots and his toes curled gratefully into the soft white sand. He walked across the dry water catchment and found a place on the low surrounding wall. Here he spread his army greatcoat and placed the boots carefully inside before folding it.

He untied the neck of the canvas bag he carried and tipped out a fibre cloak. It was wrapped around a razor-sharp *panga* in a protective sheath of barksin. The panga was an all-purpose weapon with a long metal blade and a short wooden handle. The edge of the blade was honed to a sharpness that would slice through flesh and bone.

In his singlet and torn trousers, with his red-fibred cloak slung over one arm, he looked a different man. He swung the panga, feeling the good weight of it, and moved off in search of firewood. The girl had said that he was to be her guardian. He began to slice into the nearby undergrowth with hearty swings.

Jackie listened to the thud of steel on wood. It was a comforting sound and she knew from Tembo's rhythmic grunts that he was well content. Now it was Kamau's turn to claim her attention. She was worried about feeding him.

The bushbaby was spoiled. This she knew. He seldom had to find his own insects. These were brought to him. His peculiar tastes had been refined by his regular attendance at the dining-table of human beings. He took marmalade at breakfast, and was partial to an avocado pear for lunch. He was perfectly capable of stealing someone's brandy after the cheese at dinner. It seemed high time to teach him to hunt alone.

'Come on, let's catch the dudus.' She used the African word for insects, prodding him out of her shirt. First his snout appeared, followed by ears crumpled from sleep. The white streak down the ridge of his nose gleamed in the yellow lamplight.

A large insect fluttered to the table.

Kamau moved down her arm, assuming the crouched position of a white hunter stalking his prey. He leaned forward on the knuckle of his hands, knees bent, and his head began to move up and down and sideways in sudden excitement.

This movement of the head was quite extraordinary and as she watched Jackie realized that she had little cause for fear. Kamau could certainly hunt. He was twisting his head now in order to get a three-dimensional picture of his target. He did this because his eyes would not swivel. They were placed instead so that he looked straight ahead in the manner of a man – 'binocular vision', Jackie had heard it called, rare among the lower animals.

The insect on the table was a praying mantis with large translucent wings and a fat succulent body like a chewed matchstick. Jackie stifled the urge to catch it for the bushbaby. 'I've only got  a few days,' she told herself, 'to teach him to be independent.'

Kamau leaned back, clasping the girl's arm with his cold padded hands, tail slightly curled as a sign that he was now keyed up.

The praying mantis reared on its back legs, the serrated forelegs bent as if in prayer. Its flat heart-shaped head moved slowly in every direction like a radar bowl.

With a faint rustle, Kamau jumped through the air, his back straight and his powerful legs stretched forward. He landed lightly as thistledown on the table and froze.

The praying mantis swivelled its head and clicked its jaws. Jackie shivered. Those microscopic green eyes seemed to pierce the darkest corners of the cottage. Kamau moved his body up and down by folding and unfolding his legs, nostrils quivering as he measured the range.

The two creatures were quite unevenly matched. Yet it seemed to Jackie that the praying mantis ought to terrify Kamau. Those flat eyes, the curious attitude of prayer, and the robot pincers, left an impression of evil. The lamplight flickered over the lacquered wings that drooped like a magician's cloak.

Jackie had focused her eyes so closely on the praying mantis that it seemed to grow until it filled the room, an illusion that was assisted by the long shadows it cast in the flickering light. Each detail was thrown into high relief – the four legs, the claw-like arms, and the big pincers in place of hands. In a moment of panic she put her hand out to stop Kamau, a fraction too late.

He bounced on to his victim, his long pink tongue lashing across the insect's head. He rebounded on to the floor, and using his legs like pogo-sticks he sailed to the top of a clay water-jar. There he held the praying mantis between his twig-like fingers and slowly and deliberately bit off the head.

Jackie winced and then laughed. Her nightmare fears vanished. As Kamau crunched his way through the insect, she wondered if she was not exaggerating a good many of the dangers that faced him.

Soon nothing remained but whiskerish bits of leg that protruded from either corner of the bushbaby's mouth. He hopped to the girl's shoulder and stood up to lick her cheeks.

A voice outside called: 'The fire is burning, baba.'

She joined Tembo beside logs blazing between three big stones in the sandy soil.

'What time *chai* tomorrow?' he asked with a shy grin.

'Tea? Where did you get tea?'

'I carry it with my *chakula*.'

'You've got food with you?'

'Of course.' He stood awkwardly, one foot rubbing against the other. 'Only it is African food, mostly.'

'Why did you carry food?' asked the girl, full of curiosity. She knew he had planned to catch the upcountry train.

'I did not tell your father,' he said. 'But he gave me money for the train – and I kept it.' He looked at his feet, wriggling his toes.

'Why, Tembo?' She moved nearer the fire.

'I have other ways to spend so much money. I had nothing to do when I got back. So I was going to walk to my village.'

'How long would it take?'

The man raised three fingers. '*Tatu*.'

'Three days.' Jackie bit her lip. 'That would take you perhaps as far as Ndi?'

'Further. To the Place of the Hippopotamus.'

Jackie's hand automatically stroked the bushbaby on her shoulder. 'That is Kamau's home.'

'Of course.' He nodded and laughed. 'I took your father there to trap this galago.' He clicked his long fingers. 'First we put beer in tin saucers around the bottom of a baobab tree.'

She knew the mysterious baobabs with their fat trunks like radishes and branches that reached high into the sky like crooked white fingers.

'The bushbabies drink the beer during the night,' Tembo said. 'It is an old African trick. In the morning they lie fast asleep in the grass with aching heads.'

Again he laughed. Jackie saw her opportunity. 'Will you take me there?'

Tembo's jaw dropped.

'I *must* return Kamau somehow. Otherwise he will die. It is certain.'

The man looked away. He wanted to tell her that an armed Kamba warrior could easily walk upcountry for those hundred miles and inside three days. For a white girl it was different.

'Better you should wait and talk with Major Bob tomorrow,' he temporized.

He watched her stir the fire. He had no fear of wild animals. They lived in a state of mutual respect, killing only if necessary or when attacked.

'I'm worried about the drought,' he said. 'There are reports of big herds of elephant on the move. The elephants search for water-holes, and the other animals follow. The way to Ndi crosses the route of the elephants.'

She knew that behind the mass migration of elephants would come the poachers, the quick darting pygmies of the forest who worked with bows and arrows dipped in poison.

'We will see Major Bob tomorrow,' said Jackie. Everything seemed to depend on Major Bob.

'I have a thing in which to make the tea,' he said, making himself busy. 'It is an army *birika*.' He used the word for kettle, being unsure how to describe a billycan.

'Where will you get water?'

'From the well,' he said, surprised. He felt a sudden guilt. There had been no rain. So there would be no water in the well.

But the girl was already scrambling across the water catchment. It was shaped like a shallow dish with a reservoir in the middle, covered by a wooden hatch. Jackie found the hooks to unlatch it. Together they raised the lid.

'Do you see water?'

'No,' he said sadly. 'No water. You will think me a fool, baba.'

'You're not an elephant, that smells water.' She laughed. 'There are rusty cans of milk in the cottage. We shall live like royalty on milk and cream buns – and no water.'

Their voices boomed in the hollow of the tank. The man scratched a match. In its brief light they saw only concrete walls and slime.

Something slithered from the hinged side of the lid, between Jackie's feet. She saw a dark slim shape that hissed through the dry leaves and she glimpsed two close-set eyes. The bushbaby screeched.

Tembo moved so swiftly that the girl fell backwards. He

snatched the snake by the tail and cracked it like a whip. The snake was a good six feet long and looked like a cobra. When the man flicked his wrist the snake lashed through the air and Jackie heard the awful crunch and snap of the neck vertebrae.

The snake was dead when Tembo stretched it full length and severed the head with a quick blow of the panga. Blood pulsed from the headless body and stained the ground with oily darkness.

'I might have been killed.'

'No,' said Tembo. 'The snake was harmless. Look.' He turned the head over with his big toe, and struck another match. 'It is brown like a cobra but the mouth has black bands. It is a rat snake.'

'Did you know when you picked it up?'

He shook his head. He had thought it a cobra. The muscles in his arm still ached from the violence and speed with which he had moved.

'Then you did mean to save my life, anyway.' Jackie cupped her hands around the hump in her shirt where Kamau still cowered. 'Suppose it had been a cobra and bit you?'

Tembo chuckled. 'That is why I took him by the tail. He could not twist and bite.' He seemed surprised that she was unaware of this, and added: 'There are many things I must teach you about the bush, baba.'

'And you will?'

He hesitated, suspecting a trap. 'Perhaps,' he said.

'On the way to Ndi, and the Place of the Hippopotamus?'

'Now, baba, I did not say such a thing.' But his protest sounded thin.

Later, curled up in her makeshift bed inside the cottage, the girl listened to the crackling fire and watched its warm glow projected through the open window. She had a curious sensation, like the first time on a ski slope. She seemed to be sliding unwillingly into one adventure after another, without really trying.

## 4. 'We call it Do-you-remember'

The rain-bird awoke the girl with his plaintive call on three notes. She stared at the sunlight filtering through the roof's thatch, puzzled. What was she doing here? She propped herself on one elbow. She was alone, in an African cottage she had never expected to see again.

Her family? She shivered despite the sticky heat. They were probably in a panic. She must have been crazy to leave them. She wiped her face with grimy hands. She must think clearly and fast.

Kamau. She remembered putting him in the lock-up larder before going to sleep.

'Tembo?' she called out the name.

'*Jambo!*' His cheerful voice came through the window. '*Habari?* What news?'

Her confidence began to return. 'Jambo!' She returned the traditional greeting. '*M'zuri!* Good news.'

The first thing, she decided, before she did anything else, was to find Major Bob.

She thrust a toe from her nest of damp-smelling blankets, wrinkling her nose at the sight of a squashed millipede. Warrior ants scurried around the messy remains. They marched implacably in a solid file from a crack under the door. She knew these ants. They destroyed any living thing that remained in their path. Once, at home, her favourite brown hen had been found with half its stomach eaten away. The chicks had been stripped to the bone.

She thought of Kamau again and rushed to the larder. He was curled into a ball, in the corner of a shelf. He stirred when she touched him, blinked an eye, and dozed off again. Things were never as bad as they seemed.

She tugged open the cottage door with rising spirits. 'Did you see the *chungu*?'

Tembo, crouching over the fire, glanced at the flood of black ants. 'Another sign of rain.'

'Thank goodness.' She sniffed at a row of roasting corn-cobs. 'Where . . .?'

The man raised a black-pointed stick in the direction of Major Bob's house. 'There's a maize patch over there.'

'That's stealing,' she scolded.

'The house is empty.'

His words struck dully in her mind.

'Major Bob's *always* lived there!' she said, reaching for a cob. 'He cannot be far away.'

She handed the cob to her friend and took another. They squatted side by side, chewing with relish.

'Perhaps he's gone fishing,' she said suddenly. 'Of course. He keeps a boat on the beach.' She wiped her mouth with the back of her hand. 'That was good.'

'It was not much.' He felt apologetic. He had conjured many better meals out of three stones and some sticks.

'I'm going to look for the boat.' She got to her feet.

'Kamau's fast asleep. He must have been up all night inspecting his quarters.'

She was back from the cliff's edge within five minutes. 'Major Bob's out on the reef.'

'You saw him?'

'No. But his boat's there. Come on. We'll swim over.'

Tembo hung his head. 'Baba, you must surely know I cannot swim.'

'The tide's going out,' she said quickly. 'You can wade in the shallows. There are spearguns in the cottage. We can spear some fish. The raw flesh is good to chew when you have no water.' She added gently: 'Of course you cannot swim if you were never near the sea.'

She had already decided that some of the urgency had gone out of the situation. For one thing, it was a Sunday and the village post office would be open only in the late afternoon. No matter how quickly she recruited Major Bob's help, they could do nothing about a telegram until then.

'You swim. Never mind the – the spearguns. I will watch.' Tembo gave her a bleak smile.

'All right.' There was no point in pressing him. She changed into a frayed swimsuit rescued from one of the storage lockers and led him to the cliff's edge.

The sea stretched smooth and calm to the distant reef. The boom of the surf came in slow rhythmic waves. From where they stood it was possible to look straight down into clear water where coral niggerheads filled the lagoon. Here the water was patched in blues and blacks and bright greens with an occasional splash of bright yellow where the sand had drifted into small pockets.

A small white boat was barely visible on the reef. There was no other sign of life. Jackie ran along the cliff until she found a pockmarked ledge of black coral. From here, iron bars had been driven into the cliff face to provide a way down to the small cove of blinding white sand. To reach the sea they had to cross a short plateau of wet rock, slippery with seaweed and pitted with small pools of water.

'Be careful of sea urchins,' said Jackie as her companion took his first tentative steps into the water.

He drew back alarmed. 'What are they?'

'Look.' She poked around the edges of a pool. Clinging to the rock were delicately marked creatures like mushrooms covered in long spikes that waved menacingly when touched. 'When we get clear of the rocks, we will lose the sea urchins.' She took two pairs of weathered goggles that were looped around her arm. 'Then you should put on these goggles and duck your head under the water, and you will see the fish.'

'Perhaps,' he said cautiously. He followed her through the shallows, stepping awkwardly, his large feet slapping against the water. He had stripped to his khaki shorts and his black skin shone with perspiration.

Jackie examined the wall of water on the horizon. It looked like a tidal wave that never moved, a permanent line of foam curling along the reef. The boat was strangely still.

'I'm going to swim out there.' She pointed to the boat, and slipped the goggles down over her eyes.

Tembo took the extra pair and followed her example, but refused to advance any further into the sea.

'Won't be long.' She dived and was gone.

Tembo gingerly lowered himself into the water. When he was sure the girl had gone and could no longer see him he took a breath and ducked. He found himself staring in stupefaction at a petrified forest of coral antlers reaching up from the first of the niggerheads. The antlers were coloured pink and cobalt, heliotrope and mustard yellow, and between them flashed the tiny darting shapes of fish. In his astonishment he tried to shout aloud and swallowed a lungful of water. He rose coughing and spluttering and fell backwards, landing hard on a jagged piece of rock. This time he roared with pain and completely lost balance, falling like a log into the sea again.

By the time he had floundered to safer ground the girl had

swum from sight. He sat down gratefully in a sandy-bottomed pool and hoped he would recover his dignity before the girl's return.

She swam with slow leisurely strokes, breathing steadily through a bent rubber tube, her eyes big behind the goggles. Almost since she could walk the sea had been her element. Now and again she dived, kicking her heels so that bubbles streamed behind her to meet the silvered mirror of the sea's surface. She was aware of the larger fish hovering secretively on the edge of her vision. These were the mournful parrot fish, moving quietly in the middle depths, not ready yet to begin feeding on the live coral. When they did feed, moving along the coral like herds of sea cattle, you could hear their fused teeth crunch and crackle on coral delicacies. Smaller fish, sparkling like diamonds and flashing their brilliant colours, swarmed around her.

It was strange how she remembered this tortured landscape below the waves. Little had changed. Here were the same magic pools enclosed in swaying forests of weed like secret grottoes bathed in a sacred green light, enclosed in fissured rocks, and inhabited by gay little fish dancing and twisting to an unknown rhythm. She swam over them, and sometimes she jack-knifed down between mountains of coral or volplaned to the beds of shadow-dappled sand. She felt bird-like. She could spread her arms and dive and loop, chasing the little fish to sow panic among them.

In these waters her father had taken her by the hand to point out the deadly scorpion fish, whose pink-laced spikes could kill. He had shown her the boxfish with a tail that whirred like a toy propeller. Her father had taught her confidence in this element. Here her gawkiness vanished.

She arrived at the reef in this state of exultation. The tide had receded. Much of the reef was now above water, its colour a drab oyster-grey instead of the dazzling pastels below. Frowning, she saw that the boat was wedged into a cleft in the rock. She clambered up beside it.

The boat was empty. Oars, rowlocks, even the rudder

were gone. She pulled herself over the side and looked under the boards. The whole boat was stripped bare.

Her first thought was that Major Bob had fallen overboard. But it seemed that the boat had not been used at all. She clambered about the reef, hopping between the spiky urchins. Far away on the smoky-blue horizon hovered a dagger-sailed dhow. Nothing else moved.

She swam back to the beach with a sense of foreboding. She noticed now that the fish were not feeding. The sea felt muggy. These, she knew, were signs of an impending storm.

She waded up the beach to where Tembo waited. Overhead a skein of seabirds streamed inland.

'Major Bob's not there!' she called.

Tembo shrugged. He was so impressed by the girl's ability to swim like a fish that he felt there was nothing she could not do. He grinned and helped her across the sand. 'How did the boat get there?' he asked, as if he addressed an oracle.

'I expect it got swept up. It's usually left on the beach and it might have drifted after an unusually high tide.' She stopped, her brow furrowed. 'Look at the crabs.' Hundreds of ghost-grey fiddler crabs were scurrying towards the high-tide line of sea-weed.

'I wish we could have some thunder,' she said. The sea was flat, and hazed over slightly as if someone had breathed on a mirror.

Tembo looked at the sky. 'The rain will not come yet,' he said with finality.

He followed her back up the cliff. At the top they stood together for a moment, watching the crabs advancing inland with pincer-claws upraised.

Major Bob's farmhouse was bolted and shuttered. Jackie knew without having to peer through the dusty windows that nobody was inside.

She stopped when she saw the old palm tree that sloped over the rust-coloured iron roof. It was a tree the Rhodes' children used to climb in the holidays, rattling banyan seeds on the roof to annoy the occupants.

Jackie remembered something else. There was a rain-water tank up there. She scrambled along the tree. The corrugated roof was so hot that it burned her hands and bare feet. She skipped across it and hastily pushed aside the wooden cover to the tank. There was a short piece of rope inside and an empty paraffin tin tied to the end. Shading her eyes, she peered down the rope. The can floated in a few inches of water.

'I've found water!' She cupped her hands and projected her voice up the crumbling slopes of the ravine. There was an answering shout and she shinned back down the tree.

The place seemed derelict. It had been a good many years since anyone had actually farmed here. Major Bob had retired to the old house, content to let neighbouring Africans cultivate what little soil there was. There were more weeds than grass pushing up between the slabs of coral.

She saw a torn bit of notepaper pinned to the door facing the sea. The paper was curled at the edges and brown from the sun and weather.

TO ANYONE CONCERNED, *it said*. GONE TO NAIROBI FOR A FEW WEEKS UNTIL THE RAINS. It was signed by Major Bob.

Now that she realized how much she had counted on finding Major Bob, tears rushed to her eyes. She brushed them away hastily at the sound of someone running along the path of crushed coral.

Tembo stood in the sunlight, chest heaving. The girl had retreated into the shadow cast by the overhanging roof. In this land of fierce colours, where the sun climbed vertically overhead and eyes were permanently screwed against the blinding light, there were no shades and gradations. Shadows were solid blocks of profound darkness. Every landscape was a quilt of black squares with intervening chunks of brilliant greens and blues, splashes of yellow against the earth's background of glowing red.

At first the man was conscious only of Jackie standing there. It was several seconds before he was able to distinguish her face.

'What is it, Baba?'

'Major Bob has gone.' The words came with a rush. Suddenly she was holding tight against Tembo's chest, trying to control her sobs.

'It is no use to cry, little one.' He stroked her head and gently pushed her away.

'I know. I'm sorry.' She flopped into a worm-eaten garden seat. 'I did want to see him. He would have known exactly how to send the telegram to the ship, and what we should do next.'

Tembo ran his hand over his crinkly black hair. 'You have shown me the sea and the fish in the sea. You will show me how to catch the fish, and how to cook it. There is my chakula ready for you now. Later I will show you how to travel safely through the bush. There is nothing of which to be afraid.'

She sat hugging her knees.

'You said there was water,' said Tembo. 'Tell me where the water is, and I will fetch it.'

She looked up. 'The water is on the roof, in the tank.'

A kind of lethargy seemed to envelop her. The shock of knowing that Major Bob could not help her, and the tension of the few few hours, left her suddenly tired and dispirited. For Tembo's sake she put on a brave front, even making herself eat the meal he had prepared. Afterwards, with tea boiling in the billy, Tembo tapped his harmonica against the ground and began to play a Kamba war-song.

Jackie lay in a favourite position on her stomach, under a wild fig tree whose radish-like roots drooped to the ground. Her legs were crooked, ankles interlocked, as she gently rocked them in the air. She found herself gazing at a tiny volcano of red earth. A small black ant had walked on to the soft shoulders and immediately began to slip down the hole in the centre of the cone. The more the ant struggled, the deeper it fell.

Jackie peered down the hole, surprised and curious. Right at the bottom, partly buried in soil, two pincers appeared. Before she could intervene, the little ant fell between the claws of the creature concealed below and disappeared. She dug her finger into the ground and excavated a tiny sand-coloured insect in the process of consuming the ant.

'What is it?' she asked Tembo who had stopped playing.

He squinted down. 'We call it ant-lion. It digs a trap and lies in wait. Once the ant walks on to the newly dug soil nothing can save it. It is a trick used by poachers.'

'Did they learn it from the ant-lion?'

'It is possible.' He stirred the ashes of the fire with a stick. 'In Africa everything is done by imitation. We are simple people. We learn from the life around us. That is why small children are told stories that contain a lesson.'

'Is there a story about the ant-lion?'

'Yes.' Tembo squatted on his haunches and let his arms dangle between his knees. 'We call it Do-you-remember. The gods were angry with the ants, and so they made the ant-lions. They were angry because the ants showed no gratitude to the gods who put them on earth to rule above all other creatures. The ants were the most numerous creatures in the world, and as you know they have always been able to work together like armies. But they became too proud and forgot that everything was due to the generosity of the gods.

'So the gods made the ant-lion. They gave him the secret of the trap from which no ant can escape. But in the last few seconds, as the ant feels the earth crumble beneath him, and he knows he is about to die, in those few seconds he is given time for remorse. And as the ant-lion's pincers take him the ant-lion whispers: "Do-you-remember?" And if the ant is wise, he will answer: "Yes, I remember all the good things in my life." And he quickly recounts them. And if he shows a proper gratitude his death is mercifully swift.' He reached over and removed the billy from the hot stones. 'Chai, baba?'

'Yes.' She sat up. 'That is a good story, old friend.'

'It is a good story,' he agreed, pouring tea into a mug. 'When everything goes wrong, remember the good things.'

'Do you remember . . .?' she began, and laughed.

'Yes, baba?'

'Do you remember the baby rhinoceros my father brought home? It was lost and we fed it on gallons and gallons of milk.'

'And it got bigger and bigger,' Tembo added. 'So big that it got in everybody's way.'

'It used to run up to be scratched and stand on your toes and nearly break them. And when you did scratch the back of its neck your fingers were caught suddenly in neck muscles like nutcrackers.'

They were both laughing now. Suddenly the girl stopped. 'What time is it?'

Tembo glanced at the sky. 'Perhaps three o'clock by your time.'

'Why do you calculate time differently?' she asked.

'The Arabs taught us to count the hours from sunrise to sunset.' His face became sullen. He had an inherited dislike of Arabs.

The girl put down her steaming mug. 'It is late and I must send the telegram. The Indian at the post office will show me how.' She had some money in a pocket of her jodhpurs – enough, she hoped, to pay the cost.

'Finish your tea first.' Tembo was polite but firm. 'Nothing is so important that you must suddenly start to run.'

'You are right.' They had fallen into elaborate Swahili again. She sipped the rest of the hot sweet tea.

'Tembo.' She peered at him over the rim of the mug. 'This message by radio I am sending to my father on the ship . . . While I do this you must search the cottage – '

He began to protest and she adopted an even more forthright style of address. 'I do not know yet what we must do after I send this telegram. In the cottage there is enough food in tins for many days. Put them aside, and also equipment for safari . . .'

She spoke firmly, knowing his reluctance. Her voice unconsciously imitated that of her father when he was making plans for a safari. She had no intention of sounding bossy. It was a tone of voice used between equals. Her father would have been just as precise, in order to avoid misunderstanding. Tembo recognized this. He was glad to jog her out of the earlier mood of despair. Later he would persuade her to return to Mombasa. Now that Major Bob was away, it would be best if she went to the port authorities for help. But he judged it better to wait a while. Jackie was obstinate, like her father, and he must catch her in the right mood.

She had gone into the cottage to check Kamau. The bushbaby was still asleep. She lifted him out of the basket and he bit her gently in protest. 'I want you sleeping at night!' she said, and tugged a green leather harness from her shirt pocket. It was always a struggle to strap the harness on Kamau. It fitted around his waist and over his arms, and she could hook a nylon lead to it. The harness also served as a jerkin and it was useful when she had to travel any distance with the bushbaby, but she used it sparingly.

He continued to mutter angrily. She was about to clip the lead to the harness, but hesitated. 'Perhaps I won't take you to Vipingo. But try not to go to sleep again.'

His tail was uncoiled, a sure sign that he was waking up. She decided to leave him in the larder, hoping he would find enough to distract him.

She ran like the wind down the coastal road, then paused for breath before turning inland towards the village.

## 5. 'Arrest this man'

MacRae, captain of the United States motor vessel *Thoreau*, looked suspiciously at the slow oily swell. The Indian Ocean was otherwise flat and eerie in its stillness, tinted orange in the early mist. He felt a dull throb behind his eyes and as he climbed to the bridge he nodded to the Third, who gave him a brisk greeting.

'Barometer's low. Still slipping.'

MacRae checked the log and heading, then moved to the starboard side of the bridge. 'Ask Sparks for all the weather he can get.'

He looked at the new day with frank dislike. The mist was lifting. High sheets of cirrus cloud shone like mares' tails in the ice-blue sky.

'Mozambique has issued a storm warning,' said the Third,

back from the radio-room. 'The Portuguese want all shipping to report local conditions.'

MacRae sighed. In twenty years on the African coast he had never known weather information to be so scanty.

'The passengers?'

'Still sleeping. Tired out, I guess. Nice kids but they looked real tuckered out when they came aboard yesterday.'

MacRae grunted. 'Any pets?'

The Third shot him a quizzical glance, and let the question go.

'They had a calm sea for their first night.'

'Too calm.' MacRae ambled distractedly on to the port wing. His head ached atrociously. He was not prone to this kind of thing. When MacRae got headaches it generally meant troubled weather. He leaned his bare arms on the moist rail, watching the flying fish skitter ahead of the bows and sink in a spatter of spray. Under his feet the deck throbbed.

*A mature cyclone is preceded by a distinct ocean swell with frequency two to four times less than that of normal waves.* He knew the manual by heart.

His immediate goal was Mozambique, four hundred miles south, and not quite five degrees below the Equator. A tropical storm was unusual between latitudes five degrees north or south. Whatever you called such a storm – cyclone, hurricane, typhoon – it began in the most deceptive way. Nothing appeared to happen. There was a flat sea whose temperature had been heightened during the long summer months. At some point the heat of the sun and the growing warmth of the sea created a disturbance in the air. The lower levels of air began to rise with critical rapidity. An area of low pressure was created and more air moved in from further afield to replace the spiralling thermals. The most violent upheavals would begin in this innocent way.

He took out the big gold watch that always nestled in his

shirt pocket, and timed the swells. They were coming every
twelve seconds. The average was normally eight.

*The presence of a cyclone may be suspected if the swells
arrive every twelve to fifteen seconds.* But there had to be
other indications MacRae told himself, amending the manual. A cyclone cut down the frequency of the swells and sent
them moving outwards from the centre. He made a mental
note of their direction.

The things that made a cyclone – hot rising air and flat
sea – still required the friction of the spinning earth. *The
component of this rotation is zero at the Equator,* said the
manual. *Thus cyclones cannot develop in the Equator's immediate vicinity.*

But *Thoreau* was sailing south away from the Equator,
towards one of the world's five main regions of tropical
storms. MacRae decided to duck his head into the radio-
room. He found Sparks scribbling on his pad. 'Mozambique
reports a tropical disturbance. The Portuguese are treating it
as an area of suspicion.'

MacRae massaged his temples. It felt as if an iron band
had been tightened around his head. The Portuguese could
call it what they liked. He knew now that a bad storm was
certainly shaping up.

It was Sunday morning, 25 October, and below decks
Trapper Rhodes stirred and looked at his watch. Like the
rest of the family, he had overslept.

It was Sally who actually raised the alarm.

'Jackie's gone!' She came rushing into her parents'
cabin.

There was no panic at first. Everyone assumed that Jackie
was exploring the ship. They looked for her in a leisurely
way until Andrew pointed out that her bunk had not been
slept in.

'Yet her clothes have gone, so she must have got up this
morning to dress,' said Penny. An awful fear clutched her
heart. 'She couldn't have – ' Penny stopped dead. Even to

utter the dreadful words '*gone overboard*' seemed to give them reality. They brought the news to Captain MacRae. 'You *must* turn back!' said Penny.

MacRae mopped his brow. 'I'm stopping engines, Ma'am. I'm having the ship searched from stem to stern. But I can't turn back until the true state of affairs is known.'

'It's funny the bushbaby's gone too,' said Andrew, opening a new avenue of speculation.

Trapper Rhodes said quietly: 'I think we should radio Mombasa, Captain. I have a hunch that child has done something quite drastic.'

By noon the *Thoreau* had reported Jackie's disappearance to the port authorities at Mombasa. Two hours later the cabin steward decided to risk MacRae's wrath. He repeated Jackie's conversation about the captain's hostility to pets.

'D'you think she left the ship before we sailed?' Penny asked. Even this, suddenly, seemed a straw to clutch.

There was a long silence. 'It's probable,' said her husband. He looked grey and his big hands opened and closed at his sides. He was a man of action. He had been with the look-outs as *Thoreau* circled the area, his heart jumping each time he saw – or fancied he saw – a floating object. It had been difficult standing there powerless to intervene, knowing that the captain's decisions were binding.

Late in the afternoon a seaman who had slept through the hours of chaos and anxiety came back on watch.

'The missing girl,' he said. 'She was hanging around the gangway just before we sailed. She had a basket.'

'That seems to clinch it,' said MacRae. He turned to Trapper Rhodes. 'My guess, sir, is that your daughter jumped ship.'

'Thank goodness,' Penny Rhodes said unexpectedly. She closed her eyes, swaying, and seemed about to faint.

Her husband grabbed her quickly by the shoulders. 'Hold on!' He turned to MacRae. 'Is there a chance we can put back to Mombasa?'

'Ay, there is.' MacRae lifted his peaked cap and scratched the grey thatch underneath. 'I'll have to get permission from the owners. *If* we get the okay we could catch the forenoon tide tomorrow.'

Back on the bridge, later, he shook his head. 'I'll never understand children,' he muttered.

There was a patter of rain on the glass. A gust of wind struck the *Thoreau* broadside. MacRae judged the direction of the rising wind. *As a result of the earth's rotation, the rotation of the vortex of the storm will be clockwise in the southern hemisphere and counter-clockwise in the northern.* The manual only put into technical jargon what every seaman had known since Hippalus the Roman sailed down this coast two thousand years ago. If you faced the wind, south of the Equator, your left hand pointed at the storm centre. His rule-of-thumb check confirmed what MacRae had learned from the sea swell.

He sniffed the wind. 'The owners may have cause to bless that child,' he told Number One. 'By turning back, we may escape the storm I think is blowing up.'

All over this part of the ocean, and on the long coastal beaches the flat-topped islands, fishermen would be preparing against the fury to come. The warning was in the winds that span around the centre of the developing storm, spinning slowly near the rim but with increasing velocity at the hub.

The storm was like a great top that still lacked the speed to spin on its own axis. But it would gain strength from its own velocity, turning faster and faster until it began to move slowly along the predictable curve. The axis of the storm was still far from the *Thoreau* and it would be a long time before it achieved enough ferocity to move. When it did, as MacRae knew too well, its exact path would be forecast to give ships time to get out of its way, but vessels like his might get the warning too late. The storm would come spinning inshore until it struck the African coast. There it would swirl into the hills and die swiftly as a result of the braking effect of dry land. But in its brief lifetime it would leave a trail of havoc.

So MacRae was secretly pleased when Mombasa radioed that night: RETURN MOMBASA. The rest of the message was less reassuring. MISSING CHILD OBSERVED LEAVING DOCKS WITH AFRICAN. GENERAL ALARM ISSUED ALL POLICE POSTS.

Vipingo was no great distance from the cottage but the air was heavy and still and Jackie arrived in a sweat. She felt untidy and unwashed, and this was something she could not bear at any time. She had no desire to appear before the villagers until she had time to rinse her face.

The village straggled on either side of a dirt road. Africans dozed in the shade of tin-topped shanties or squatted on the lumpy, hard-pounded ground. Radios screeched in the tumbledown Indian dukahs where you could buy coca-cola and gasolene, corned beef and biscuits, and the all-purpose paraffin tins called *debes*. These four-gallon tins were used as measuring cans, water-vessels, and for roofing material, and they seemed to be everywhere. In any African village you were sure to see bare-bottomed children banging happily on a debe, while the flies crawled on their dirt-streaked faces.

Jackie knew that if she dodged through the coconut trees to the south of the village she could approach the bunker-like post office unseen. She told herself that she wanted to avoid being seen because she felt so grubby. Yet some sixth sense also impelled her to choose this indirect path.

She heard voices long before she saw the crowd outside the post office. Above the black heads of the villagers she spied the red-tasselled turban of an Indian police inspector. He was gesticulating with his malacca cane. His voice was raised and he sounded angry.

Jackie ducked behind the bole of a palm tree. Beside the Indian policeman stood Vipingo's chief merchant. He was an orange-bearded Hadj who stained his beard in henna because he had made the pilgrimage to Mecca and kissed the sacred Kaaba stone. She could hear his voice above all the others, now that the inspector fell silent.

'It is said by the Bwana Kubwa that this bad fellow may have come this way with the white girl.' She heard every word clearly. 'A big search is taking place. If it is found that anyone has been hiding this man and the girl there will be big trouble.' The Hadj held up a sheet of paper. 'This is the order for the arrest of the man who has kidnapped the white girl, Rhodes.'

There was a rustle of gossip through the crowd. Heads bobbed. Her name was on all lips.

Jackie huddled closer behind the tree, holding her breath, unable to believe this fresh disaster. Her legs had gone limp with fear for Tembo. Unwittingly she had cast her old friend in the role of a wanted criminal.

She remained in hiding for what seemed a long time, until at last the crowd began to disperse. The Indian police inspector strode importantly to his parked Land-Rover. The shopkeepers returned to the bazaar. Small groups of Africans began strolling down the baked mud street, chattering and speculating about the day's strange news. All knew the Rhodes family, and especially Jackie, whose golden hair and friendly freckled face had been a familiar sight in the holidays.

Fearful of recognition, she waited until the last of the crowd had gone, and then slipped back through the coconut grove to the lonely cottage where she must tell Tembo that he had become a hunted man. As she ran she tried to imagine how this had all happened and guessed that her father, waking aboard ship that morning and finding she had slipped ashore before they sailed, had radioed Mombasa.

Once a search began, the police would find plenty of dockers who had seen the man and girl. It was only a matter of time before the police encountered a passenger on the Vipingo bus who would remember the runaways. Then the search would focus on the village. Discovery would be certain. Nobody would believe in Tembo's innocence.

Jackie walked through the thorn-trees to the cottage. A thin column of smoke twisted skywards. She felt a surge of affection for the slender figure tending the fire. He looked up and grinned when he saw her. Before he could speak she called: 'Has anyone passed by, old friend?'

'No. It has been silent as the nest of an owl before the dawn.'

'You are sure? No fisherman? Nobody?'

He looked at her in puzzlement and scratched his head. 'No, baba. Nobody.'

'Good.' She sank beside him. 'You must put this fire out at once. Then we must pack all we can and leave tonight.'

The man tried to keep astonishment from his voice. 'Tonight? For where?'

'Ndi. Near the Place of the Hippopotamus. We will travel up-country as fast as we can. At Ndi there are friends of my father, and your friends too, who will help us.'

'It is far.' He watched her, trying to fathom the cause of her obvious distress.

'We must.' Quickly, she described the scene at the post office.

'Wa!' Tembo sprang to his feet and drops of sweat appeared on his forehead. 'The police – it is bad to be in trouble with them. They will throw me in prison and beat me.'

'Even African police?'

'Especially Africans, if they are not of my tribe.'

He fetched the debe and hastily doused the fire. A cloud of smoke rose on the still air and slowly dispersed in the branches of the fig tree. He kicked the cooking stones apart and then, unaccountably, he laughed. The girl stood in the doorway of the cottage and caught his eye. Her answering smile was uncertain.

'Baba, do you really want to walk through the bush to Ndi?'

'Of course. There I will return Kamau among the bushbabies and explain everything to Bwana Gauntlet, the district commissioner.'

'Gauntlet. Yes, he is my friend too. But you are sure you want to make this journey?'

'Yes.'

He laughed again. 'It will be hard, little one. If you do not mind it being hard, you will be very happy.'

'Why do you laugh?'

He straightened up. 'Until now I did not know what we should do. Now there is no choice. It is possible to walk to Ndi without being seen and along the way there will be much I can teach you.'

'How long will it take us?'

'For you . . .' He made a quick calculation. 'Perhaps five or six days.'

'I am strong and can walk as quickly as you. We must try to take less time. I cannot send the telegram now and my parents will be worried. We *must* travel quickly.'

Tembo picked up a stick and began drawing lines in the sandy soil at his feet. 'There is the river . . .'

'Of course.' The girl clapped her hands. 'We will borrow a fisherman's canoe and go upriver as far as possible.'

'It is very low, the river. Without rain it will be dry up-country.' Tembo continued to sketch in the sand. 'We can go perhaps this far. It will shorten the journey by a day or more.'

He threw away the stick in a decisive gesture. 'Tonight we must sleep here.'

'But suppose the police come?'

'It is a risk,' he admitted. 'Did the inspector say why he was in Vipingo especially?'

She shook her head. 'No. I think it was a general alarm.'

'Then it is better to leave tomorrow. You must have one good night's rest and a big meal. We will leave very early, before sunup.' He smiled apologetically. 'I have been in the cottage. There are many things we shall need. You do not mind?'

'That's what I wanted.' She took his arm. 'Old friend, we are in this together. You are not my servant and you must do what is best. I do not care to stay here much longer but it will be dark soon.'

She looked up. She was standing near the gauze-covered ventilator to the larder where she had left Kamau, and could hear a light irregular tapping noise.

'Kamau's still awake,' she said. 'I'll see if he's hungry.'

It sounded as if the bushbaby was hopping with impatience. She knew that soft thudding noise only too well. At such times Kamau leapt like a rubber ball, perching briefly on unlikely foot-holds, now clinging to a piece of plumbing, next bouncing off a ledge.

She tugged open the door of the larder. There was no sign of Kamau. Instead, an iron bolt on the end of a rope swayed in the draft from the ventilator, banging against the wooden partition.

Jackie told herself not to panic. A narrow gap existed between the top of the partition and the makeshift hardboard ceiling that her father had put over the larder to keep out the bats. She examined it carefully. The bushbaby had left droppings on top. Somehow he must have squeezed through.

'Tembo!' She ran into the garden. 'The bushbaby has gone.'

The man lifted his hands in a gesture of surprise. 'Gone?'

'He must be in the roof somewhere.'

'He will not have gone far.'

Together they walked through the cottage, searching the forest of mangrove poles supporting the thatch. The girl clucked her tongue and Tembo rattled a broomstick against the cross-beams. Finally he said: 'We must put out food. I am sure he will come back.'

'If he doesn't get caught by hawks or a python or something.' Jackie walked out to the avocado tree. 'What a mess I'm making of everything.'

A movement in the tree caught her eye and she looked up eagerly. It was only an emerald-spotted woodpecker. As she watched, the bird began his well-known dirge:

> My mother is dead.
> My father is dead.
> All my relations are dead.
> And my heart goes
>
> > dum
> > dum
> > dum.

## 6. Kamau gets a ducking

Tembo clasped and unclasped his hands. They were strong hands, knuckled like the gnarled roots of a tree. He looked down at the golden head of the girl, wishing desperately to rescue her from her mood of black despair caused by the loss of her bushbaby.

He would fight a lion to save her from such grief. He would risk his life, everything, to protect her. Her courage in swimming to the reef had dispelled all his doubts; he believed implicitly in her physical stamina, and in her ability to face the long overland journey that she had proposed in the face of his original misgivings. He was angry that he knew only one way to defend the things he loved and admired – by fighting. What he needed now was to find the right words, to talk to her as he knew her father sometimes talked.

'Baba?' He hesitated.

'What is it?'

He rubbed his chin. 'In my tribe, as you surely know, we have many proverbs. There is a proverb for almost everything that can happen to a man. Or,' he added, 'to young girls.'

She looked up, cheeks smudged.

'One of these proverbs is: "When the cheetah is lost and afraid, he sings." '

Jackie nodded. 'Yes. It is true. I have seen a cheetah looking for his mate, and sort of whistling.'

She recalled the incident vividly. She had come upon the cheetah in the long grass of the plains. Its coat of matching gold made it difficult to see. The cheetah had turned its squat head and looked directly at the girl.

The cheetah had a royal arrogance. His forelegs were inflexible and he thus seemed to look down on the rest of the animal kingdom. His face was a wrinkled mask of yellow fur and black lines drawn back in a snarl. The golden eyes blazed. He lifted each paw with delicacy, neck arched, a king in spotted robes. Then he uttered the most beautiful cry she had ever heard. It was pitched high enough to sound like a two-note whistle. He seemed to make it by pulling back his mouth and blowing out his cheeks. He had stared right through Jackie, intent upon finding his lost mate. He had called four or five times in this way, taking a step forward at each interval. Finally, a long way off, came an answering cry. She had seen the muscles tighten under the cheetah's coat. Suddenly he exploded into action, lunging past her in that terrible ten-second, seventy-mile-an-hour sprint for which the animal was famous.

Tembo groped in his trouser pocket and found the mouth-organ. 'When the Saints go marching in' had been known to cheer the most depressed of armies and he played it with all the gusto of a former King's African Rifleman.

He stopped for breath and the notes lingered in the still-ness of the bush. For a moment neither of them heard the soft rustle in the eaves of the cottage. There was a gentle *plop* on the ground beside Jackie. She turned, unbelieving. It was Kamau.

He squatted at her feet, head cocked. Jackie scooped him up with such speed that her hand dislodged a large stone balanced against the doorstep. The stone rolled over, un-covering a metal object.

'Kamau!' The girl held the bushbaby tight against her cheek. 'You devil. You scared us out of our minds. Where have you been?' The words tumbled out. As Jackie whirled into the cottage, the bushbaby clinging to her neck, Tembo tapped his mouth-organ against the firestones. His eye caught the glint of metal and he retrieved the round object which he recognized vaguely as something he had seen in army days.

'With this it is possible to walk through the bush,' he said later to Jackie as they sat over a supper of mashed bananas and maize. 'I cannot find the proper name for it, but it may be useful.'

'It's called a compass,' said Jackie. 'I had one in the Girl Guides. I bet this is it, because it got lost when we were here last summer. See. If you hold it like this the black point of the needle turns to the north.'

'North?'

'Yes. North is always over there.' She pointed. 'Now I shall be able to tell what direction to take when we leave the river.'

Kamau, nestling inside her shirt, stirred. Jackie addressed herself to the small head that popped out. 'We start our journey tomorrow. And you' – she tapped him gently – 'you must always sleep at nights now.' She withdrew the bush-baby. He was still wearing his soft leather jerkin, to which Jackie clipped the nylon lead.

'There. You can play now without running away. Tonight I'll keep you with me, and perhaps you'll sleep.' She had tried the technique before. After watching her sleep Kamau would also curl up.

'He has been awake a long time,' said the man. He had found Kamau's droppings some distance from the cottage, and he guessed the bushbaby had been missing longer than Jackie suspected. 'He should sleep tonight.'

'Here's a mint to put you in a good mood.' Jackie fished out one of the dwindling number of candies. 'It's also a reward for finding the compass.'

'I am sorry I do not know how to use it,' said Tembo, examining the compass. 'I am a very simple man, as you will find out, baba. It is a big responsibility to take you all the way to Ndi.' He slapped his forehead with the palm of his hand. 'I wish I had something more here besides rocks.'

Jackie laughed. 'Rocks? In *your* head. You speak foolishness. If you had not played our song just now Kamau might never have come back.'

Tembo's face brightened. 'Do you think he returned because of my song?'

'Our song,' said the girl firmly. 'From now on we should make it the song of all of us, and the story of Do-you-remember should be our game. These will link us together, like the song of the cheetah.'

Kamau curled up inside Jackie's arms and slept right through their last night under a roof. He woke up once, heard the man moving about in the darkness outside, and pricked up his ears a moment later at the barking of a dog baboon. He awoke the second time to the bubbling notes of the water-bottle bird which sounded exactly like water being poured into a long-necked bottle.

This refreshing sound was to be Kamau's alarm clock from now onwards. He flicked out his long rough tongue and washed himself from nose to tail, rubbing his hands together and then smoothing out his ears.

He hopped out of the blankets as far as he could go to the

end of the lead attached to Jackie's wrist. She lay with her
arms flung back, heedless of the pale light creeping through
the cottage. The bushbaby squatted on his long legs, head
twisted on one side, and watched her. Finally he hopped
back and licked her eyelids.

She opened her eyes at once. 'Dear Kamau, you really did
sleep through the night.' She lifted him in her two hands.
'Thank you for calling me. We ought to be on our way.'

Kamau blew out his cheeks and made a non-committal
chuckling sound.

The girl stretched, sat up, and massaged her right foot.
There was an irritation in the big toe as if a splinter festered
there. Her bed was surrounded by the debris of the previous
night's preparations. Trapper Rhodes had spent many years
in the bush, and he had provisioned the cottage as if he were
leaving an emergency store-room for successive explorers.
Bits of equipment, still unsorted, lay under the refectory
table where Jackie had pushed them.

Now she turned over the old canvas buckets, the coils of
rope, and rusted tools. There was a small battery-powered
transistor, a bit mildewed, under some fishing tackle. She
pulled it out and twiddled a knob. For a time music filled the
cottage. She was outside when a man began to speak and she
returned only in time to hear the last words of a news bulletin.

'. . . and the search continues.' The voice of the Nairobi
announcer surprised her by its clarity. 'That is the end of the
news from the Voice of Kenya. Please stand by for a special
statement.'

There was a pause. Then another voice said in Swahili:
'Here is the special notice released from the office of the
Prime Minister at midnight last night. An English trans-
lation will follow. "A severe tropical storm reported in a wide
area south of Zanzibar is expected to be the prelude to a
break in the drought that has caused devastation on a bigger
scale in East Africa than at any other period of recorded
history. Special precautions are being taken, based upon the

experience of 1961, when similar drought conditions were
followed by floods causing widespread havoc".'

Jackie switched off. She had a sudden fear that if Tembo
heard the news he might also recall the 1961 floods and try to
dissuade her from continuing their journey. She stepped outside the cottage and saw him walking up from the cliff's edge.

'Jambo! Habari?' he called.

'Jambo! M'zuri.'

'I did not wake you,' he said, stepping on to the porch.
'You will need the rest. We shall have another hot day, and
no rain.'

They both looked at the pearl-grey sky veiled with thin
clouds.

'Do you wish a fire?'

'No,' said the girl. 'It will draw attention. We can make a
cold breakfast and leave at once.' For a moment she was
tempted to mention the possibility of a break in the drought,
but only added: 'I have found my father's old radio. It will
be useful.'

'We must travel light,' he warned her.

'I have been thinking.' She drew him into the cottage and
displayed two crude home-made spearguns. 'We should
catch and dry some fish. They will sustain us. Also, here are
two knapsacks. We can fill them with just enough canned
food for emergency. And matches in candlewax' – she
paused and blushed slightly – 'in case it rains. And we should
each take a knife . . .'

She rattled on while Tembo assembled the items. An hour
later they were ready to move. The discarded articles had
been neatly put back in place. Tembo's city clothes were
buried. The cottage looked much as it had before.

Before she closed up the cottage again Jackie displayed a
copy of an old map left hanging in a back room. Her father
had kept the original, drawn by a young British naval
lieutenant and still bearing his faded signature. It was dated
1882 and it recorded the known trails followed by the Arab
slaving caravans.

'This man hunted the Arab slavers.'

Tembo's face lit up. 'Who was this man?'

Proudly she pronounced the name. 'John Flaxman.' She knew exactly what kind of man he was. There was a very dog-eared photograph of him in later life among her mother's mementoes. John Flaxman had been her grandfather.

'Wa!' said Tembo. 'He must have killed many slavers.'

'His job was chasing them into the mangrove swamps in the mouths of the rivers. Sometimes the Arabs laid traps and jumped on the naval boats.'

Flaxman had recorded some of these adventures on the back of the chart. The photo-copy faithfully reproduced the ink, faded to a faint brown wriggle, and the way the paper had been creased and fly-brown. The map still showed in useful detail the lower reaches of the river on which they planned to sail.

'We can – borrow – a canoe here,' she said, 'and catch some fish before going upriver.' She salved her conscience with the reflection that John Flaxman would not have scrupled to steal a canoe in a good cause.

She drew great comfort from the chart. She remembered her mother's stories of how Flaxman had risked an early death from malaria or an Arab muzzle-loader, and it seemed almost as if he were marching right beside her.

They struck out first towards the north-east; the man, in his fibre cloak and battered askari's kepi, his big feet bare, and the girl in jodhpurs and whipcord jacket and the boots made from the ear of an elephant. Their path lay through a sprawling plantation of sisal. They walked in single file between the rows of grey-green spears. Here and there the sisal plants had been allowed to 'pole'. Instead of a bunch of stiff needle-pointed clustered-like cacti, there soared tall knotted stems with puffs of seed-pods at the top.

Few people were abroad. Near the estate's water-tower, marking the manager's house, voices could be heard. A few sisal workers clustered around a truck on the Mombasa road.

Wisely Tembo gave them all a wide berth, and shortly they came to the mouth of the river.

A big old baobab sheltered them from view. The tree was fat and grey, with huge warts and goitres, and its branches were like the roots of an upturned carrot. The man and the girl rested their loads against this venerable tree and took stock.

In normal times the river was a good half-mile wide. The drought had reduced it considerably. Midstream floated several *ngalawas*, the outrigger canoes used by fishermen. They were equipped with large white dagger sails, borrowed from the Arabs whose dhows came down this coast before the November monsoon. For centuries past the crescent sails were to be seen poised on the horizon like a flock of birds; in the holds of the dhows came dried fish and Mangalore tiles, carpets, and camphorwood chests.

Jackie studied the little canoes, a crude blend of Arab and African tradition. Not long ago, as she knew from the notes on John Flaxman's map, this place had been the base of an Arab slave route. *The caravans march inland,* Flaxman had written in his tiny copperplate hand. *Each is made up of hundreds of white-clad Arabs under the red flag of the Sultan.... The captured slaves are roped together in single file, each slave's neck in a forked stick about six feet long supported on the shoulders of the slave in front – flogged along the forest paths with rawhide whips.*

The girl shivered. In the early-morning light it was easy to imagine the ghosts of slaves passing through the shafts of green that penetrated the forest beside the river.

'We must steal one of the canoes,' she said, interrupting her own thoughts. 'Later we can arrange for its return.'

'Yes,' said Tembo. His mind must have been pursuing a similar course. He added: 'It is always possible to trace the Arab slave routes by following the line of the old mango trees.'

She gave him a startled look. It had never occurred to her that a Kamba warrior would have such a strong memory of slaving days.

'Why?'

Tembo shrugged and held out the palms of his hands. 'Perhaps the Arabs brought the mango here in the first place. Perhaps they took mangoes on the long marches inland, and scattered the seeds. It is the saying of many Africans here. The mango tree is the footprint of the slaver.'

Struck by an idea, Jackie fished out the old map. Sure enough, Flaxman had marked a slave route starting at this very point. It ran alongside the river to just about where Jackie and Tembo had agreed they would have to turn inland and travel on foot.

'Look,' she said excitedly. 'There was a slave route from here' – she spread the map on the baked earth – 'to here.' Her finger found the intersection of the Mombasa railroad and the dirt highway to Nairobi. It was less than a couple of miles from Ndi, their destination.

'Which means,' she said slowly, 'when we leave the river we can check our direction by the mango trees. If,' she added, 'they're still there.'

Tembo pointed a few yards up the river, where the bank sloped steeply to the sluggish waters. A dark mango tree towered above the bananas whose huge torn leaves drooped like tattered wings.

'I think the mangoes will be always with us,' he said sadly.

The girl thought it strange and terrible that the mango should represent, for Africans like Tembo, the years when thousands were torn from their native villages to be sold into slavery.

And yet it was natural for Africans to view the alien tree with suspicion. For the mango was not native to Africa. Its tiny pink and fragrant flowers were more familiar to Buddha and the people of Asia, from where they came. The mango flowers were like a trail of blood. The Arabs who dropped the seeds had unwittingly left a permanent record of their raids.

'I must stop dreaming,' said Jackie aloud.

The man smiled. 'It is better sometimes to stand and dream than to engage in futile action.' He pointed downstream where the white roots of the mangrove trees stretched like spider's legs into the estuary. Around the western cape, advancing towards them, chugged a coastguard launch.

'Gosh!' Instinctively Jackie picked up Kamau's basket. 'They might have caught us in the act of stealing . . .'

The launch moved slowly upstream. When it was almost abreast Jackie saw a uniformed figure on the bows studying both banks through binoculars. It occurred to her that the object of this search might be Tembo, but she kept this disquieting thought to herself. Instead, she flattened herself against the trunk of the baobab tree and waited for the launch to vanish from sight. The river was so quiet that long after the launch had gone they could hear its wake ripple against the banks.

'We must take the canoe now,' said Tembo, 'before fishermen begin to stir.'

'Suppose the launch returns?'

'You must keep out of sight. Let us hope nobody looks too closely.'

Each canoe was tied to a mangrove pole. Warped planks of wood were lashed to the poles, forming a rough kind of jetty. Tembo inched gingerly along the planks above the shallow muddy water until he found a canoe to his taste. He returned with it, manoeuvring with a paddle shaped at the bottom like a water-lily leaf.

He steered the canoe under the vegetation that spilled over the bank at Jackie's feet. She lowered their packs first, hugging Kamau's basket before jumping down last of all.

The hull of the canoe was deep and narrow, carved from the trunk of a single tree. It would have overbalanced except for the outriggers, two pairs of horizontal poles lashed to bow and stern at right angles to the hull. A crudely carved plank ran lengthwise at the extremity of each pair of outriggers, so that when the canoe rolled there was always a stabilizing counter-action from one of the planks.

'Where did you learn to canoe?'

'I was an askari on an expedition to Lake Rudolf. We were many weeks on the water in dugouts.' He used the Swahili word ngalawa. The girl liked the word. She liked speaking Swahili. It was a simple language but in the man's mouth it had a considerable dignity.

They paddled first beyond the river's mouth, turning eastwards along the coast a short way. Tembo had lost some of his inherent dislike of the sea itself and watched eagerly as the girl manoeuvred them above the coral. There was a rope, weighted with a rock, that served as an anchor. This she lowered until it lodged in the niggerhead.

'We must not stay long,' he warned.

'Ten minutes,' she promised, snapping on the goggles and taking a speargun. 'There are many fish here and easy to catch.'

'Perhaps I could try?'

'Of course!' Her eyes lit up. 'You can hang on to the canoe's side and rest your feet on the coral.'

She picked up a speargun and showed him how to use it. As so often happened, she found Swahili a limiting language in which to explain technicalities. And yet it forced a simplicity of phrase that made her think more clearly.

The speargun was a two-foot stick bleached white by the sun and sea. Near the thick butt was a second piece of wood, secured like a peg by stout rubber bands. A piece of straight thick wire, fashioned into a crude arrow, lay in a groove along the top of the speargun. A notch had been cut in the back of this rough harpoon.

'You load it this way,' said Jackie, putting the butt of the gun against her chest and pulling back a hunk of powerful elastic. Where the rubber looped, wire had been twisted protectively around it and was now engaged in the notch of the harpoon.

'You clip it like this.' She adjusted the wooden peg so it gripped the end of the harpoon.

It was a simple device. Tembo saw that if you depressed the peg the wire harpoon would be flung a short distance. There was a light piece of nylon fishing line that secured the harpoon to the swimmer to prevent the escape of an injured fish. His love of the hunt was aroused and he fingered the gun with lively curiosity.

'Let's go!' Jackie picked up the second harpoon and lowered herself over the side of the canoe. Tembo followed her, and found that he could balance on the niggerhead by leaning against one of the canoe's outriggers.

'What about Kamau?' he shouted, catching sight of the bushbaby creeping out of the basket.

But Jackie was already stalking a flat, diamond-shaped creature moving slowly across a bed of sand. It was a sand-grey plaice, propelling itself with the graceful undulations of a large bird. She sighted along the speargun and fired. Her eyes, magnified by the goggles, gleamed triumphantly. The little harpoon, still attached to her wrist by the line, had pinned the fish to the sea-bed.

She surfaced, took a deep breath, and dived to retrieve the

speared fish. On her way down she had unhitched the knife
at her waist and she hacked through the foremost point of
the fish where two closely placed eyes peered helplessly up at
her. Then she grabbed the harpoon with her free hand and
shot back to the surface, the dying fish flapping on the harpoon's barb.

'It is small but good to eat,' she said, swimming back to
the canoe and tossing the fish into the bottom.

She caught sight of Kamau, who was squatting on the
prow. His ears were pinned back and he regarded the fish
with evident distaste, uttering a cry of distress that sounded
like the twanging of a guitar string.

'Will he be safe?' asked Tembo.

'Yes.' The girl spoke with conviction. 'He fears water.'

She dived back under the sea.

Tembo frowned. The bushbaby seemed to be frozen to his
perch, and it was unlikely that he would move. The man
smiled to himself at the way in which Jackie had become
immersed in the excitement of pursuing her prey. It was
something Tembo understood very well.

Holding the outrigger with one hand, he sank below the
sea's surface, peering through the goggles Jackie had given
him. Almost at once a large sea bass, a grouper, swam lazily
into his vision, its huge mouth agape.

Tembo lifted his head and gulped a great lungful of air.
When he ducked under again the grouper had swum so close
that it seemed enormous. Shakily he aimed the speargun and
fired.

To his surprise and delight the harpoon struck the grouper in one of its unblinking eyes. The fish seemed to become
fiery red and turned tail in a flash, almost jerking the harpoon line from Tembo's hand. He staggered back, astonished by the weight of its pull. The grouper threshed back
and forth on the end of the line and then dived for a hole in
another arched cathedral of coral.

The man's excited shouts now brought Jackie splashing to
his side. She yelled instructions to keep the line taut, and

dived for the hole. He saw her sink slowly down the side of the niggerhead, saw the grouper peer at her from the darkness of the hole, and then watched in horror as an unspeakably grotesque creature like a fat and wart-ridden snake reared up from an adjoining cavity.

Tembo tried to cry a warning but water clogged his throat. He vomited, caught his breath, and ducked once more under water. His hand gripping the outrigger shook violently.

The girl had thrust her hand into the grouper's retreat. Gripping it by the gills, she hauled the struggling fish into open water. Behind her the creature resembling a snake emerged clear from its hole. It was a good five feet in length, with a crinkly green head and gaping jaws sewn with teeth. The body was smooth and scaleless, and it moved in a series of convulsive jerks through the profound silence of the sea's depths.

Tembo forgot his fear and prepared to plunge from his position on the niggerhead. He had pushed away from the outrigger and with his head once again under water he glanced back at the bubble-sheathed hull of the canoe.

He was horrified to see Kamau struggling beside it. The bushbaby was paddling with hands and feet, but each time he kicked against the canoe's hull he floated away from it. Already the weight of water in his fur was dragging him inexorably below the surface.

Tembo glanced from the bushbaby to the girl. She had turned to face her attacker and seemed to be parrying it with her speargun. He turned back to Kamau, whose struggles were getting visibly weaker.

The choice was an impossible one. If he tried to help the girl Tembo would have to leave the bushbaby to drown. If he saved the bushbaby he would lose crucial seconds in which the girl could lose her battle.

She had lunged the speargun into the snapping jaws that seemed to be striking for her legs. She was a few feet below water, swimming on her back, her fingers still heroically fastened into the grouper's outspread gills.

Tembo launched himself awkwardly towards the canoe and made a wild grab for the bushbaby. He was unprepared for the awful sensation of having no firm support beneath his feet. With his free hand he somehow discovered the canoe's gun'l and using this as a lever he scooped Kamau out of the water and tossed the semi-conscious bushbaby into the boat.

When he turned back to Jackie he saw that she had poked the speargun straight down her attacker's gullet. The jaws snapped tight on the wooden shaft. At once the rest of the body coiled like a spring. The girl heaved away the speargun and its loathsome victim and kicked frantically for the surface.

She was still gasping as she swam backstroke alongside Tembo.

'I hate those things,' she said, coming to rest on the niggerhead. Seeing Tembo's expression, and interpreting this wrongly, she said: 'It's all right. It was a moray eel. They don't often attack or bite like that.' She spat. The salt water in her mouth reminded her of the eel.

Tembo said: 'The bushbaby –'

She let go the grouper. 'What's happened?' The fish slapped the water with its tail and sank from sight, trailing the harpoon line.

'He's in the boat, baba. He fell in –'

She pulled one of the outrigger poles, and swung the canoe until she could scramble into it. The bushbaby lay sprawled in the bottom, eyes closed, in a pool of water.

She fell on hands and knees beside him. 'Kamau!' Her voice was almost a shriek. She lifted the tiny body and saw water dribble from the half-closed mouth. He seemed lifeless.

The girl raised him to her lips. His fur had turned into stiff little spikes, revealing an alarmingly small body with a rat's tail. She pouted her lips and applied her mouth to his, blowing gently between the bared teeth. She breathed carefully into Kamau's mouth, inflating the waterlogged lungs, and then she pressed gently with hands cupped around his tiny chest and listened to the gentle bubbling hiss of air that emerged. She did this several times, holding him nearly upside down.

Slowly he began to breathe again. A few seconds passed and his eyelids fluttered.

'He lives,' said Tembo.

The girl was shivering. Kamau was retching now, his body convulsed. She placed him on the hot planks of the canoe and ran worried fingers through his matted fur.

'How did this happen?'

Tembo was shocked by the fury in her eyes. 'I don't know, baba.'

'You must have rocked the canoe!' she accused him. She was shaking with rage.

Tembo clamped his mouth shut. He had seen mothers react this way after their babies had given them a bad fright.

'I should never have trusted you alone with him!' Jackie said, and she began to cry.

The man moved slowly to the prow of the canoe and hauled in the stone-weighted rope. 'We must go quickly,' he said quietly. 'Forget the fish.'

The sun was already high. He began paddling back to the river-mouth, his face expressionless, eyes narrowed to slits as he watched for other fishermen. The girl lay sprawled in the bottom of the boat, still stroking the reviving bushbaby.

They moved into the river, the canoe shrouded in silence. Sometimes the girl glanced back at the man in the stern, paddling with a smooth steady rhythm. He avoided her eyes.

The river had lost its usual pace, denied the vital run-off of rain-water from the highlands. They had negotiated the tethered canoes safely, and now the water turned a chocolate-brown full of little swirls and eddies.

Kamau stirred and sat up weakly. He blinked owlishly at the girl, and examined his arms and legs. He looked like a toothbrush, his fur still spiky, his tail bedraggled. He began cautiously to groom himself, combing the fur with the long currying-nail on each of his little fingers. He chuckled as he did this, now and again glancing up at the girl.

She said, her face turned away from Tembo: 'He seems fully recovered.'

'I am glad,' said the man.

'Perhaps I spoke too hastily,' said the girl. 'Forgive me.'

'Of course, baba.' But Tembo's voice was still non-committal.

'I lost my head,' said the girl.

'It is understandable.'

'I was very upset. It was no reason to be rude.' Suddenly she turned and stretched out her hand, resting it lightly on the man's bared knee. 'To rescue the bushbaby you must have had to swim?'

A great smile split his face from ear to ear, and around his eyes appeared a thousand small wrinkles of laughter. His teeth flashed in the sun and he said, choking: 'Swim! Like a camel!'

She giggled. 'Tembo, I'm truly sorry for what I said. Was it awful – *swimming*?'

She started to laugh too. Between them the tension dissolved and left a new sense of comradeship. 'It was terrible,' he told her, and described the incident with many embellishments.

He stopped and his face became grave again. 'It would be better if you put the galago on a lead now.' He looked on either side at the slow-twisting banks of chocolate mud. Sometimes a river was drift-logged with crocodiles. He felt no particular affection for Kamau, but he also had a vision of Jackie's hysteria if the bushbaby vanished down a croc's gullet.

'You are right, old friend.' Her voice was full of humility. She knew how quickly a seeming log was transformed into a racing crocodile, lifting itself like a battering ram on crooked legs, clear out of the mud and into the water without a ripple.

Kamau had finished his toilet. Experimentally, she handed him the last mint. He took it with such alacrity that she nursed no more doubts about his recovery. He held it between sticky fingers, curling his tongue lovingly around it, eyes rolling with ecstasy. Now was the time to slip his harness into place. She was appalled, however, by his appearance. The salt had dried in his fur. He was spiked like a porcupine.

'If only it would rain and wash him out,' she thought. She searched the surrounding landscape. It was a patchwork of rural greens; bright yellow marked the young sugar-cane; dark olive marked the bush; the farming shambas were a dancing green, and the exhausted banana fronds were dipped in a green of melancholy hue.

The land tilted like an easel. Soon it would be hard to navigate the river as it wound upwards through the blue foothills that guarded the long approach to the Rift. Without rain it was likely that the river would soon dry up altogether.

She began to untangle Kamau's lead. The bushbaby paused in his otherwise engrossing task of licking the mint.

He twisted his head to one side, and the muscles in his legs stiffened. Jackie unbuckled the small harness. The bushbaby clucked his tongue softly, crouched on hands and knees, and scuttled away on all fours with the mint still enclosed in one hand. He paused at the feet of the man, and leapt flat on to the exposed knee.

Tembo was visibly shocked. The bushbaby had never shown him the slightest attention. Now he scuttled up the man's arm and squatted on his shoulder, once again sucking his mint.

Tembo stopped paddling and stared straight ahead, afraid to move his head.

'Baba,' he whispered.

'What . . . ?' Jackie looked up from her task. She was astonished to see the bushbaby abandon the mint and begin to lick Tembo's face. The man sat stiff as a poker while the bushbaby explored his ear, pushing tiny fingers into the lobes.

'He's trying to thank you for saving his life,' said the girl. 'He's decided he likes you.'

'He really likes me?'

'Of course.'

'But I cannot paddle while he sits here.'

'You can try.'

The man reached carefully for his paddle. He got a curious sense of pleasure from this sudden display of friendship. For most Africans the bushbaby was in every sense a jungle sprite, a creature with human-like characteristics that sometimes filled them with superstitious awe. Even Tembo shared this innate respect for bushbabies, knowing from observation that their family organization was quite complicated and sensing their intelligence. His smile broadened.

The girl was overwhelmed with laughter at Tembo's mixed reaction of surprise and delight. She leaned backwards on her heels, supporting herself with hands pressed against the bare planks behind her.

'Paddle,' she said.

'I dare not. Suppose he should fall again.'

'He won't!' Her voice was emphatic. 'You never need to teach Kamau a lesson twice. Isn't it strange how quickly he learns?' She became conversational, relishing the man's poker-backed immobility. 'By the end of this journey we shall have Kamau trained to run wild and free.'

'You will miss him.' The man spoke without turning his head, eyes swivelling to follow the bushbaby as it groped beyond his ear.

'Yes.' She dropped her head and became busy again with the harness and lead. 'It will be like losing a baby.'

Meanwhile the canoe had been drifting towards the left bank. One of the outriggers caught in a trailing vine. Before the man could interfere the canoe swung close against the twisting vegetation under wind-creaking palms. The canoe hit the bank and they were suddenly engulfed by a thick web of undergrowth.

Everything seemed to happen at once. The bushbaby hopped into the bottom of the boat where half a coconut husk floated in a few inches of water. A sunbird exploded from the bush, startling Tembo so that he dropped the paddle. While he fished for it and Jackie dived to rescue Kamau from his uneasy perch on the coconut shell, a thunderous roar burst upon them.

The noise was terrifying. It seemed like an endless roll of thunder, of rushing winds overlaid by a jet's high-pitched whine. The surface of the river boiled into chocolate eddies.

Jackie held the bushbaby with one hand and craned her head back. Between the gale-bent palm leaves she saw an Alouette jet helicopter. It hung over them, only partly visible through the wind-divided branches. Then it tipped sideways and shot crab-wise across the river. At once the wind fell and the canoe floated serenely under its forest camouflage.

They saw the helicopter creep along the opposite shore. A

man in sky-blue dungarees stood on one of the helicopter skids, directing the pilot inside the perspex bubble. The man on the skid turned his binoculars downstream. The helicopter lifted its tail, span round, and whipped away. Almost at once the noise subsided, the river returned to its normal placid self, and the only sound was the cry of the white-bellied go-away bird. Its call was loud and rude: 'Go-away! Go-away!'

Cautiously, Jackie raised herself from the bottom of the canoe. 'They didn't see us.' Her voice was triumphant. 'They didn't see us.'

She swooped on Kamau, who had escaped again to curl up into a shivering bundle under one of the thwarts.

Tembo said shakily: 'The galago saved us.'

'Did you hear, Kamau?' The girl lifted the bushbaby into her lap. 'If you hadn't played games with Tembo we would have been out in the middle of the river.'

The man resumed his seat in the stern and dipped his paddle again in the water. 'Twice this morning we have been saved from discovery.' He thrust the canoe out from the overgrown bank. 'It is a lucky sign.'

Jackie looked grave. 'But you know what this means,' she said. 'That was an army helicopter. I'm sure they were searching for us. Tembo, we must be careful.'

He nodded. 'It is better if we travel early in the morning and early night.' He squinted at the river ahead, blinding in its magnification of the sun. He wondered if he should tell the girl of the chief reasons why they must try to travel in the cool hours of morning and evening.

They were entering a region of many wild animals and of very few humans. They were moving into the Tsavo game reserve. It covered both sides of the main road and railway from Mombasa to the capital of Nairobi, an enormous chunk of south-east Kenya that was virtually uninhabited except by one of the biggest collections of wildlife anywhere in the world.

Again Tembo studied the sky. If the drought continued,

the carnivores – the lions and leopards especially – would become easily irritable as they followed the big migrations of elephants searching and digging for water. If the rains came, this part of Tsavo reserve woud be so badly flooded that thousands of animals must die from drowning.

On the whole it seemed to Tembo advisable to say nothing. But his shrouded eyes were watchful as the canoe nosed towards the region known as the Kenya Badlands.

# 7. *The old elephant*

The canoe leaked a little. Jackie, baling out with the coconut husk, was diverted by a water-bug. It was a devil's coach horse. She recalled learning at school how it moved forward by lowering the surface tension of water in its wake.

The chemical warfare of the water-bugs had always fascinated the girl. She crouched over the stagnant water in the bottom of the boat, leaning her elbows on the gun'ls, chin resting on her interlocked hands. The sun beat down upon her back. From either side of the narrow river came an endless chorus of scissor-grinder cicadas.

The devil's coach horse was being pursued by two spidery bugs, and it had started to shoot forward at a startling rate. The two hunter-bugs found themselves in a wake of tension-lowered water and suddenly sank.

She chuckled and scooped the victor into the coconut husk. As she tipped it overboard she glanced at the nearest river-bank. It was flat here, and open, with several tapering

anthills like ruined castles whose red spires poked above the
burned grass. She knew that if you dug you would find a fat
sluggish termite queen like a grotesque white sausage at the
heart of each anthill. What interested her more was that the
canoe had been more or less stationary near these anthills for
some time.

'We're almost going backwards,' she called to Tembo.

'It is the current,' he explained. The banks on either side
were much closer together and the water ran more swiftly to
the sea. Jackie felt a small breeze at her back.

'Let's hoist the sail.'

The man eyed the furled sail doubtfully. 'I do not know
about sails,' he confessed.

'I do.' Jackie spoke with more confidence than she felt.
She could see how the sail boom was attached to a rope that
ran to the top of the stubby mast, passed through a simple
pulley, and returned to a rough wooden cleat at the base.
She had a vague idea that the ropes on a sailing craft were
called 'sheets' and in her mind's eye there sprang the series of
diagrams that illustrated her brother's handbook on din-
ghies. When she had sorted out in her mind the purpose of
the remaining ropes coiled under the sail she went to
work.

It proved astonishingly easy to rig the big triangular sail.
The bamboo had to be hoisted half-way up the mast.
Then it assumed a sharp angle so that the sail shook itself
out, the uppermost corner being fastened to that end of the
boom projecting towards the sky. Another corner was held
by the lower tip of the boom close to the hull; and the third
corner bellied out before the wind. The free part of the sail
was brought under Jackie's control by means of a rope that,
when tightened, gave a pleasurable sense of capturing the
wind.

By letting the sail out to form a broad angle to the hull,
Jackie found she could skim the canoe over the sludge-
brown waters while Tembo steered with his paddle. Soon he
discovered a way to hook his leg over the paddle, steering

with one hand, while the other was free to manipulate the harmonica.

The river here seemed deserted. Throwing caution aside, he began to play their adopted song. The girl sang, making up the words as she went along.

'O won't they cheer
When they all hear
That wee Kamau's marching in!
There will be such cheers among the trees
That hide the world of bushbabies.'

The chorus of this singular song was rather more simple. It went:

'O biff biff bang!
O bang bang biff!
Tarrump terreee ti-tiddledee.
Biff! Bang! Biff! Bang! Biff! Bang! Biff! Biff!
To all the baby bushbabies . . .'

They proceeded in this somewhat noisy manner for a considerable distance until, when they rounded a big loop in the river, the wind dropped. Tembo paddled the canoe from side to side in a vain search for even the slightest breeze, but the air had become still and stifling.

Jackie dropped the sail again. Here at least the river ran less urgently. It turned and twisted, so narrow at some points that it was almost overhung by trees.

The bushbaby had perched himself in the blunt bow of the canoe, spoon ears extended. Suddenly his body stiffened. His tail, curled in repose, stretched out. His sensitive ears had caught some sound indistinguishable to his fellow passengers. He turned and jumped to the safety of Jackie's arms. Tembo stopped paddling and grabbed a passing vine. The canoe swung across the river.

There was dense jungle on either side. A family of red and yellow barbets skimmed along one bank, keeping up a steady chorus that sounded like Bow Bells, their tails wagging. A long way off, some unknown animal snorted. But none of these sounds warranted Kamau's alarm.

'What – ?' Jackie stopped herself as the man raised a warning hand.

There was a muffled sound of snapping wood. It was such a low-pitched and stealthy noise that at first it appeared to be part of the river's own mutter. Somewhere close at hand a log snapped with a soft explosion.

'Elephant!' Tembo took his paddle again and began stroking the canoe vigorously upstream. 'They are moving parallel to the river. We must try to keep out of their way.'

Jackie tucked the bushbaby inside her shirt. Her heart beat faster and she saw that the man dug his paddle into the water with quick, nervous strokes. She was not afraid of elephants but she did not relish alarming an entire herd. She knew also that enormous migrating herds had been reported during the past weeks of drought, moving downcountry in search of water.

The canoe shot round the bend in the river. Confronting them was an island matted with vegetation. They chose the wider branch of the river and Jackie saw how the water-level fell, so that here and there large boulders of rock protruded. They negotiated the island and came upon a wide stretch of stagnant water. Each dip of the paddle produced a trail of stinking weeds.

A grey heron flapped lazily ahead of the canoe. Jackie's eyes, following it, took in a landscape whose implications only slowly penetrated her mind. Another half-mile and the river became a millpond. Here, in normal weather, streams fell from steep cliffs to feed the river. Now the land was dry. Their canoe voyage was almost ended.

The noises made by the moving herd were far more distinct in this boulder-rimmed basin. Tembo directed the canoe to a stony beach. They grounded on shingle. The girl and the man, wading through shallow water, hauled the canoe on to a ledge of cracked earth. They could hear the alarming noise of tearing branches and crackling underbrush, and then the shrill scream of an elephant.

'Leave everything!' Tembo gripped the girl's hand and

hauled her to the top of the bank. Quickly she buttoned the jacket pocket where Kamau lay asleep. They moved cautiously forward, through a screen of treacherous 'wait-a-bit' thorn and came to a *luga*, the dry bed of the river's western tributary. The luga was hillocked with elephant dung and flanked by brittle-looking trees.

It was a little time before they saw the elephants. By then they had walked some distance inland, Tembo heading for a dark mango tree. Suddenly he stopped.

There is something uncanny about the way elephants can be noisy and stealthy at one and the same time. They encircle the unwary traveller within seconds. First one appears, and then another. Their thick hides are impregnated with the soil of the country, providing an extraordinary camouflage that effectively conceals the huge beasts.

Now along the sides of the luga, came the bigger members of the herd, browsing among the few bushes and trees that still boasted some foliage, and occasionally lifting their great trunks to blow dust over their backs.

Between the massive legs of the cows scampered the calves. They hid between their mothers' legs and it seemed a miracle to Jackie that none was trampled under foot. Each time the cows moved forward the calves broke into nervous little trots, and some curled their trunks to hang on to the big ones' tails. The calves were doing all the screeching and their cries of caution had not yet alarmed the bulk of the herd.

The crashing of trees and branches continued, away to the left, downriver where more elephants had evidently lumbered ahead. Jackie could hear their belly-rumbling talk. What held her startled attention was the big old bull swaying in the middle of the luga. He faced the man and the girl, his sail-like ears flapping at flies with the sound of hand-claps.

'Don't move,' whispered the man, gripping Jackie's shoulder. His eyes swivelled to the mango tree and he measured the distance.

The bull seemed to rear above them, lonely and vast, seven plastic tons of ochre monster, tiny eyes inflamed in a high-domed skull. His ridged trunk snaked out and up, the weaving tip testing the wind.

Jackie told herself that few animals will charge without provocation. But she also knew that elephants sometimes ran amok, irritated beyond endurance by ants crawling up their trunks, or perhaps from the pain of old spear wounds. Sometimes a lonely bull, shunned by the herd, went madly rogue.

This one rocked to and fro, and she saw the inward-curving tusks that must have weighed a hundred pounds each. He had lifted his head, ears forward, and now he blew through his trunk a trumpet-blasting screech that shook the ground. He turned his head aside and his forelegs swung far in the opposite direction so that he seemed about to topple over. Then he swayed back as if to gather momentum and lurched forward, trunk raised and 'S'-curved, dirt squirting under platter-shaped feet.

Tembo stood firm, the girl squeezing against him. The old bull pounded forward a few yards and slithered to a stop. Behind him pandemonium broke out. The browsing herd wheeled like an armada, with a speed that belied their clumsy bulk. Panic spread among mothers and calves, but from the confusion emerged a pattern of movement. The cow elephants moved ponderously out to form an encircling shield. The terrified calves stumbled blindly within the circle, trunks groping in the dust-clouded air.

'Now!' Tembo pushed the girl. 'Run for the tree!'

Already the bull was retreating, shoving his rump into the solid ranks of mothers. The earth quivered from the pounding of many leaden feet. The air trembled with trumpetings.

Scarcely aware of Tembo's hands in her back, the girl scooted across the open ground with both hands clutched to her breast where Kamau had taken refuge. Reluctantly she let go, reaching for the lowest branches of the mango tree, praying the bushbaby would have sense enough to hang on.

She swung up like an acrobat, hooking her legs over the smooth-barked branches and bit by bit working her way into the tree. She could hear Tembo behind her. Together they climbed higher, never daring to look back.

A great sense of elation erupted inside Jackie as she wedged herself into the sheltering branches. She had heard of bull elephants who made a mock charge. It was vital to stand your ground, and it took great courage. She looked down to where Tembo perched immediately beneath her, his club dangling from his wrist. He had kept beside her when it would have been easy for him to sprint to the tree.

'Thanks,' she said, and touched his dust-grizzled head.

He glanced up and grinned. 'We are safe now. But make no sound.'

There were several dozen elephants still milling around. Carefully parting the leaves, the girl watched in awe. Inside her jacket Kamau chittered, and finally stuck out his head with an expression of fierce annoyance. His *kek-kek-kek* sounded unnaturally loud. She giggled a bit hysterically at the incongruity of a bushbaby squeaking defiance at the mammoths.

They continued to shuffle in a frightened circle. The calves had curled back their trunks, straining for the wind. The cow elephants bellowed in a matronly way, ears pinned back, trunks restless. Gradually their fear subsided. One or two of the mothers called to each other. A baby whimpered. The clouds of dust began to disperse. Slowly the herd re-formed ranks.

The old bull moved ponderously to the further bank. His dignity recovered, he mounted a ridge and looked down upon the herd.

Some of the mothers came plodding along the luga, heading for the river-basin abandoned by Jackie and her companion. The girl was surprised by the amount of ground they covered when their movements seemed so slow. She counted more than a score before she gave up.

They shuffled past the tree, all their screams and bellowing forgotten. They kept their heads down like cowled monks deep in thought. Their manners now seemed gentle. They nudged each other with tusks that were short and yellow, and the only sounds were again the distant crackle of dry wood and a soft stirring of feet.

The last baby passed under the mango tree, trunk hooked around his mother's tail. Tembo eased his legs and whispered: 'We may be here a long time. They've gone to bathe.'

From the basin of the river came the new sounds of elephant at play: of water squirting through trunks and vast balloon-like carcasses slapping on mud.

'What was wrong with the old bull?' asked Jackie.

'Age.' The man lifted himself into a crouching position, his face close to Jackie's. Tension gone, he was tempted to talk, but his voice was low. 'It is possible that the big bull who pretended to charge was very old. No elephant can live more than seventy years. After that he must die of starvation. He must die this way because an elephant only grows a certain number of teeth. The last ones appear when the elephant is sixty years old and there are none to replace them when these fall out.'

Jackie looked at him with new respect. She had assumed that, like many Africans, Tembo seldom thought in terms of years but rather in a seasonal way about 'short' and 'long' rains. She imagined his life to be ruled by nothing more than sun and rain, wet and dry, cold and heat.

'Seventy years is very old,' she said.

He shook his head. 'But it is a terrible way to die, unable to eat. A big elephant needs five hundredweight of food a day.'

'How do you know all this?' Jackie questioned him, frankly astonished.

'I worked among elephants in the game parks. With your father.'

'Will you go back there?'

'I do not know, baba.'

'What *will* you do, now my father has gone?' The question had been in the back of her mind. She realized with a pang that she had been too selfishly absorbed in her own misfortunes to voice it sooner.

Tembo shrugged. 'I feel like an old elephant myself.'

The girl forced a laugh. 'You? You are still young and strong.'

Tembo tugged the tuft of black whiskers on his chin. 'In Africa you can be old at twenty.'

A ground hornbill, black and dirty grey, rocketed into the sandy soil under the tree. He looked top-heavy, a relic like the dodo.

'The bird there, he lives against all the natural laws,' said the man. 'But he lives in the bush where it is possible to stay alive. I am an African who has lived his life outdoors. I cannot fit into the new world of Africa where a man must have gone to many schools.'

'You know so much about the bush, can't you use this knowledge?'

'Perhaps.' The man closed his mouth suddenly, locking his hands around his ankles and lowering his head. He had almost added: 'If I don't go to jail.' An awkward silence fell between them.

The old bull still kept guard. Jackie rummaged inside her jacket and withdrew John Flaxman's chart. The bushbaby was asleep in her breast pocket. She balanced herself more comfortably and unfolded the old map.

'If it were not for the drought,' she said, half to herself, 'we might have sailed all the way up here as far as Voi.' She traced the path of the sand-river.

It was a river in name. For most of the year it was a dry sun-baked bed of sand. But when the heavy rains fell on the western hills, it would become a torrent and bring destruction down through the desolate stretches of the Tsavo game reserve, an area bigger than Wales.

Now the watercourse was a gleaming expanse of sand through which water filtered at a depth of several feet. Along its length for a hundred miles herds of elephant had been gathering as the dry spell continued. They were there for a specific purpose. They alone, with their trunks like powerful hosepipes, could dig deep enough to reach the hidden water reserves. They followed a simple ritual. The big experienced elephants dug the holes and then stood back waiting for water to accumulate. Sometimes an eager baby elephant would have to be whacked on the rear end. Sometimes an impatient rhinoceros had to be driven away. But when the elephants had finished they stood aside for the other animals to follow.

Thus the wild life for many hundreds of square miles followed the elephants in time of drought. Small antelopes and zebras, buffalos and eland, giraffes and kudu, and even the proud lions, were obliged to take their turn at the elephant wells. Last of all came the baboons and butterflies, bees and birds and bugs, gathering in the first grey streaks of each dawn.

The sand-river drew every wild creature like an enormous piece of bait. It was for this reason that Tembo had brooded over the elephants. They were a guarantee of water, and also of violence. Through no fault of their own they were responsible for the old name given to the region: The Badlands.

Tembo raised his head. 'The gods must be displeased to stop the rain for so long.'

'Not the gods. It's been a bad summer, that's all.'

'There are good gods and bad gods,' he corrected her. 'There is the white man's God who is great and powerful. There are also the bad tribal gods who sent you, your brothers and sister, your mother and your father, away from this land. It is a wicked thing and more wickedness will follow.'

Jackie crinkled the map to disguise her irritation with this superstitious view. 'Look, old friend, I've just realized. This tree. It's a mango. And the map shows Arab slavers came this way.'

Tembo perked up. '*Follow the mangoes,*' he quoted. 'How far, then, to Ndi?'

'The slave route turned north a few miles from here.' She touched the trunk of the tree in wonder. 'Just think. Arabs dropped the seeds that made this tree. And these trees will help us. If we follow the slave route the journey will be cut by many miles.'

It was strange to think that the mangoes would help them, and stranger to see them as footprints left by Arab slavers. She measured off the distance and said: 'It is perhaps forty miles to Ndi.'

'We can walk there in two days.'

'And then Kamau will be home.' She pushed aside the thought that it would be time to say good-bye. She felt depressed and tired, and curled into a framework of branches where she could relax safely.

'If I go to sleep will you watch I don't fall?'

She hardly heard his reply. Legs and arms dangling in a net of vines, she closed her eyes and drifted into light sleep.

A red-cheeked cuckoo startled her with his raw, persistent call. The sun had dropped far down the sky. Tembo saw her eyes open and said quietly: 'The elephants have gone. We can get on our way.'

There was no sign of the great herd, except for countless footprints in the luga. They climbed stiff-jointedly out of the tree. Jackie felt the pain in her foot again as they returned to the canoe to collect their belongings. Nothing had been touched, although the surrounding soil was pitted with small craters. The water was littered with broken branches and the opposite bank had collapsed under the trampling feet of giants.

'We must move quickly,' said Tembo, checking the knapsacks. 'I would like to make camp a good distance from here.'

'What's that?' asked the girl. 'Over there.' She pointed to a bush.

The man strolled over and lifted up a black animal-bladder. 'A water-bag.' He bent down. 'And another.'

He came back lugging the bloated skins.

'Isn't that odd?' asked Jackie. 'I never saw them before.'

'I think,' Tembo said hesitantly, 'they belong to the *Waliangulu*. The elephant hunters.'

'Then they passed us in the tree?' Jackie shivered. She knew about the little men of the forest. Years ago they were great hunters. Later they were branded as poachers because they refused to observe white laws for the killing of wild animals in East Africa. They hunted with bow and arrow and used a devastating poison. There was no antidote for this poison made from *acokanthera*, a tall and easily identified tree. The brewing of it was accompanied by queer tribal rites, conducted by men of great skill. They added their own specialities to the brew – the gall-bladder of a crocodile, a live rat, or the stomach of a puff-adder.

Jackie had never seen the Waliangulu. Some people said they were not to blame if white men's laws forced them to poach. They were elephant eaters and could not live long on anything else.

'We would do well to keep the water-bags,' she said.

The man looked down at the bulging bladders. 'It is true. We shall need much water.' Then he braced himself, gripping his club, and examined the surrounding trees.

'The hunters have gone in pursuit of the elephants. They will not come back for many days.' He shared the girl's distaste for anyone who would bring harm to the mammoth beasts. 'Let us keep the water and be thankful.'

They hoisted their knapsacks over their shoulders, took a water-bag each, and began to trudge along the sandy riverbed. 'It is good that I have brought my panga with me,' said Tembo. The panga could be used to chop branches for making a shelter; or it might be employed as a weapon. Jackie did not ask which purpose the man had in mind. She knew only that the Waliangulu were on the prowl. How many had passed unnoticed she could not guess. Perhaps two or three. Perhaps an entire team of hunters.

She remembered a friend of her father, a magistrate. He

had confiscated the poison arrows of a captured poacher and kept one as a souvenir. The tip of the arrow was smeared with a black, tarry substance. 'See this,' the magistrate had told Jackie. 'There's enough poison there to kill two hundred men.'

The Waliangulu were hunters of the elephant, she reminded herself. They did not kill other animals, nor did they kill human beings. All the same she wondered how many were watching her now.

## 8. At the saltlick

They came, at the end of that first long arduous day of foot travel, upon a water-hole. The earth here was dry and cracked and perforated with holes of wart-hogs. It was the man's idea to camp in this arid region. Since their encounter with the water-seeking elephants he had taken command. On the coast and sailing upriver he was out of his element. The girl could teach him, and he was content to fetch and carry and to listen. There was no false pride. The man had survived in the past by knowing when to follow and when to lead.

The girl was aware of this shift in responsibility. It seemed perfectly natural. The man knew the African bush as thoroughly as she knew her schoolbooks.

She remembered her father's words: 'Never despise an African for his lack of book learning. He's gone to a tougher school of the bush where failure to learn a lesson can easily mean death.' So she carefully followed the man. He had dropped his kit beside a eucalyptus tree and examined the adjoining bushes.

'See. The drought will end very soon.' He lifted a with-ered branch. It appeared to be dead. The girl looked closely and saw tiny clusters of buds, so small they easily escaped notice. At the first drop of rain they would burst into flower.

They made a tidy heap of the water-skins and packsacks. 'I will start a fire and prepare a meal while you catch the dudus for Kamau,' said Tembo.

'Golly!' The girl flopped to the bare ground. 'There isn't a blade of grass in sight. What insects would come here?'

'You will find some if you look,' said Tembo.

'Couldn't I just feed Kamau from our own supper?' The bushbaby had gone without his insect diet before, and she was tired.

'I think it is better to feed him insects while you can,' he said gently.

She rose wearily to her feet. 'You are right. Come on, Kamau. Rise and shine!' She prodded the bushbaby out of her shirt. He had snoozed, on and off, since they left the mango tree.

The hunting was not good. By the time Jackie had collected half a dozen undernourished grasshoppers the man had built a fire and cooked a meal of posho and bananas. There was also hot soup from a can. They had agreed to carry a limited number of food tins and to dispose of these first, to lighten the load.

While Kamau licked the plates clean, and the girl and Tembo sipped scalding tea, the moon climbed higher. The sky was filled with stars of brilliance such as you find only in equatorial Africa. Between the sky-glow and the blazing fire it was possible to see a considerable distance.

'I will make you a shelter and a bed,' said the man, picking up his panga. Jackie, dozing over the fire with Kamau's lead on her wrist, made a feeble protest.

'It will not take long.' She heard his feet pad through the sandy soil and closed her eyes gratefully. The heat from the fire, the warm food in her stomach, the peace of the night: these were hard to resist.

She was awoken by the familiar scratching of Kamau's

rough tongue against her cheek. The water-bottle bird was calling, and already the sun's first rays touched the branches fashioned into a crude roof over her head. She turned over and found she was lying on more branches woven to form a bed on which Tembo had carefully placed her.

He was sitting over the fire, intent on boiling water in the billycan.

'Have you slept, old friend?' Jackie looked at him suspiciously.

'Yes,' said Tembo, avoiding her eyes.

'You haven't slept a wink!' She looked swiftly around their improvised camp. 'Look. Your footprints. Why did you not sleep?'

He raised his head slowly. 'I am sorry. I wanted to sleep. But last night there were many animals. It was better that I kept watch.'

'Then you must sleep now.'

He shook his head. 'There are more elephants coming. The animals are moving. It is the drought.'

They both looked at the glazed blue sky. There were mares' tails like braided silk, very high up, but nothing that promised rain. Northwards, where the land began to break into abrupt hills as it mounted plateau by plateau towards the Rift, there were dark patches that might have been distant showers.

'Did you see elephants last night?'

'No,' The man laughed suddenly. 'And you? You heard nothing?'

'I remember going to sleep over the fire and that is all until now.'

He laughed again. 'The night was filled with noises. Hyaenas. Lions.'

'Lions?'

The man rose unsteadily to his feet. 'I am stiff. Let us begin the march.'

'But what about the lions?'

Again he avoided her eye. It had been a mistake, he decided, to mention the lions. Finally: 'A long way off,' he said. 'An old one, and his mate perhaps. Anyway, I am glad you slept well.' He began to collect their kit together. 'From today we must march at sunup until it gets too hot. And again before nightfall. This way we will make good speed.'

Jackie fished the transistor from her knapsack. She extended the aerial and tuned in to the Voice of Kenya. They struck camp while music poured from the set. The news followed just as they were ready to move off. 'Wait!' said Jackie, and the man turned and reluctantly lowered his pack.

There were items of news that meant nothing to the girl. Then: 'The search for Jacqueline Rhodes continues. Police officials in charge of the hunt tonight issued a warning. They said kidnapping was a grave offence. The authorities might be compelled to issue a shoot-on-sight order if the girl's abductor remains at large.'

Shoot on sight! Tembo knew a region of lava beds and scrubby thorn, between Masailand and the Kamba country of his own people, that offered a perfect hideout, but he was instantly ashamed of these cowardly thoughts. 'What day is it?' he asked, to cover his confusion.

She had to work it out. So many things had happened. It was hard to believe this was only Tuesday morning.

'We must reach Ndi quickly,' he said when she told him.

'They won't really *shoot* you?'

'No!' His chuckle was hollow. 'They have not given my name, even. They do not know who this – this kidnapper is.'

'That is true. So we should keep apart.'

'Only if we meet travellers,' he acknowledged. 'There will be few of those where we are going.'

'I am glad I am with you,' the girl said, shouldering her pack again. 'Why do the police think anyone would kidnap me?'

He looked at her strangely and turned abruptly away. 'Do not forget the radio,' he called over his shoulder. She bent to switch it off. The announcer was saying: 'First signs of a reversal in the weather pattern were reported in the lower Tana and Galana river-basins where rain is falling. The Ministry of Agriculture issued a statement this morning that showed an average rainfall over the whole country during the past eight months far below any known previous figure. Ministry officials added, however, there were hopes rain would spread over all Kenya within the next forty-eight hours.'

Jackie switched off. 'I'm frightened for you,' she said.

Without looking round he said gruffly: 'Do not be foolish. It will be all right. Come. We have no time to waste.'

They made fast progress along the river-bed. Nothing disturbed the peace of that long day except an occasional high-flying aircraft, and the flighting of sandgrouse and big blue and green pigeons. The boulder-rimmed sands, blinding in the sun, had been churned up by elephants tusking for water in deep springs. It seemed ironical to Jackie that the threatened rain might prove to be her worst enemy, when the animals needed it so desperately. She hated the idea of animals dying uselessly. Death in a fight, or the hunt, she could accept. Death that struck without warning when the victim was weak and helpless wore the mask of the hyaena. She glanced at Tembo and felt a deep sense of responsibility for exposing him to the risk of being struck down by the police who, with the hyaena, shared her contempt.

He remained very quiet. Early in the afternoon he stopped and pointed ahead, and Jackie saw two immense blobs that slowly materialized into a double-horned rhinoceros circling an elephant. The elephant seemed to be performing a clumsy dance. The rhino pawed the ground and shook his head from side to side, swaying like a clown in clay-coloured baggy pants.

Tembo said: 'The *kifaru* must be very thirsty to challenge an elephant.' He pointed to a spray of acacias: 'Look! Two more rhinos. *And* elephants.' They formed two clusters. Above them, hugely grotesque on top of an acacia, sat a vulture rattling his tattered wings.

The elephant in the river-bed shifted his bulk from side to side. His trunk was hanging in the hole that he made by moving from one leg to another, like kneading dough. Sometimes he raised a foot several inches high, rocking back and forth, and sinking a little deeper in the sand.

The rhino began circling again.

The elephant raised his trunk and squirted wet sand over his back and flanks. The wetness of the sand was clearly visible to the watchers. It stained the surrounding river-bed with its moisture. When the rhinoceros saw this he moved impatiently to the edge of the hole.

The wind was blowing from the animals to the two watchers, and Jackie heard the rhinoceros squeal as his forelegs slipped into the hole. The elephant backed away two paces and faced the newcomer, ears flapping. Before the rhinoceros could recover his wits the elephant knelt forward and eased his tusks under the intruder. Then he coiled his trunk around the struggling rhino and levered him out of the hole.

The silence was rent by the squeals of the rhino and the indignant screech of the elephant. Staggering a pace forward, the elephant hurled his victim sideways. The rhino fell sprawling in the dust, his feet scrabbled wildly until he was up, and then he scuttled away a few yards. There he remained, breathing heavily, apparently on the point of collapse. Normally he must have weighed nearly two tons but the girl could see now that he was badly emaciated. Finally he turned and ran bow-legged for cover.

'We cannot go further,' said Tembo. 'Let us leave the river-bed and make camp on high ground.'

Jackie understood his motives. Along the length of the sand-rivers elephants had been performing this essential role as water-finders, or what the white settlers used to call 'dowsers'. The other animals were forced to depend upon them, for no other beast could dig through the dried surface soil and produce these shallow wells. Therefore it was almost certain that every kind of predatory animal lurked in the vicinity.

'How do these elephants find water, while the others could not?' She spoke without fear of being heard, for their voices and their scent were blown away from the animals.

'The first herd was in a greater hurry,' said the man. 'I do not think these elephants will find much water. Tonight they will all drink and there will be many fights when the hole runs dry.'

The fighting would be among the beasts that followed the elephants. For this reason the man wished to leave the river-bed. By morning, in all likelihood, the animals would have moved on.

As they climbed out of the river-bed Jackie saw that more elephants were at work, treading their way into holes and dowsing themselves with wet sand. The dustbath blew sand into the open sores that afflict elephants and Jackie could imagine the relief they must get from sealing the sores against the flies.

Her own foot was becoming increasingly painful. When Tembo stopped and proposed making camp on a flat-topped kopje she readily agreed and sat down, squeezing the aching foot.

'What hurts you?' The man, kneeling, watched her face.

'I think I've got a jigga. It's been growing under my toe-nail.'

He made her remove her boots and examined the foot. 'Yes.' He began to search his pack. 'It is ready to come out.'

The operation was a simple one. Jiggas burrowed under your toenails and laid an egg that caused a red and tor-menting sore. You waited for the egg to ripen and extracted it by opening the skin.

Tembo heated the thin blade of his knife in a match-flame, watched by the bushbaby who had climbed to his favourite position on the girl's shoulder.

'Hurt?'

'No,' said Jackie.

The man slit open the flesh below the nail and exposed a fat white bug which he flicked out. Kamau made a grab for it but the girl stopped him. 'Ugh!' She squashed it into the ground with the heel of her boot.

'Remember the first time you did that for me?' Jackie asked. 'I was very tiny then.'

Tembo, who had been feeling oppressed all day, brightened. 'Do you remember the noise you made?' They began to play Do-you-remember while they unpacked.

Later the girl made Tembo sleep. He offered no resistance, only insisting that she wake him before sundown. He had slept little during the previous two nights and stretched out gratefully.

'What animal made this?'

'Rhino.' Tembo dropped to his knees beside the kicked-up mound of strawy dung. 'And not far away.'

'How can you tell?' Jackie asked.

He broke the mound open with a stick. 'It is still warm. If it were dry, if there were termites inside, or if the grass had changed colour underneath, then you would know the rhino passed here a day or more ago.'

She had woken Tembo after a couple of hours, having heard noises in the surrounding bush, and knowing there was not much daylight left.

'So you think it was a rhino?'

'Look at the footprints.'

She circled the mound. 'There were *two* rhinos,' she said, rather pleased with herself. 'One was a calf.'

'No.' He grinned. 'One rhino. You see the rhinoceros has very big front feet and puts all his weight on them. He leaves two sets of prints, big and small.'

The tracks were wide as a tank and barged straight through the bush.

'Is tracking difficult to teach?'

They were following the prints, and Tembo paused. 'I cannot tell, baba. It is something you learn from infancy. It is like learning to speak. I talk Swahili because that is the language I have always heard. I understand some English because from a boy I have also heard it spoken.'

He stooped over a print. 'See, the rhino speaks a language too. Here he tells me that he passed about an hour ago. The footprint has a sharp edge. The edge is blown by a small breeze. The dirt crumbles and falls away.

'Here is a stalk of grass pressed under the rhino's foot. It is springing back. Over here is a broken twig and the sap is still sticky but also very nearly dry. These are like words. Strung together, they mean something.'

'Does every animal leave messages that you can read?'

'Every animal leaves its own message. Sometimes I can read them.' He pointed his chin at Kamau, whose sleepy fox-face peered from Jackie's breast pocket. 'The galago leaves his message everywhere by wetting his hands.'

'Why?'

'So his family can follow him.'

'Is that why he urinates sometimes, leaving a trail?'

'Yes. He also talks, as you know. But he needs a silent language that will not attract enemies.'

They were walking as they talked, and came upon a patch of earth worn into deep circles and grooved around the edges. It was a saltlick. Here animals literally licked the dirt in search of minerals, forming deep hollows with their tongues, forefeet, and horns. At the very centre was a small black water-hole.

The wind, blowing from the water-hole towards them, carried a sound like a train puffing uphill.

'*Kwa kifaru!*' The man pointed his panga at the hole.

An old rhino was kicking back the sand, his blunt nose pushing deeper into the hole. The sun was so low that the hole was in shadow and it was hard to distinguish the beast from the surrounding saltlick. He was paddling with his hind legs, pausing at intervals to sniff the air like a steam engine.

Jackie thought he looked pathetic with his long awkward horn, armoured head, and tiny twitching ears. She remembered her father's affection for the rhino, whom he regarded as badly misunderstood. The beast was timid and vulnerable, and had the misfortune to look red-eyed and ill-tempered.

A low growl made her jump.

'Lion?'

Tembo nodded and placed a restraining hand on her shoulder.

The rhino was backing from the hole. Suddenly he whirled and trotted off into the bush. A flock of guineafowl squealed like pigs and again Jackie heard the lion's rumble.

'Into the bushes!' Tembo whispered. They were both lying full-length on their stomachs and he led the way crabwise into a clump of wait-a-bit thorn. The girl closed her eyes and gritted her teeth as she followed him through the ensnaring hook-like thorns. She heard them ripping the back of her jacket, and she kept a protective hand over Kamau. There was space enough for all of them at the centre of the bushes. It was worth the discomfort to acquire an effective shield against any famished man-eater.

Yet the girl was not conscious of fear. She had lived too long in Africa to nurse the usual illusions about voracious beasts who attacked human beings on sight. The truth, as she knew, was that animals lived on the basis of mutual respect. They killed for food and they fought to protect their rights. They seldom attacked a man without provocation.

Two Egyptian geese flew over the saltlick, conducting their habitual quarrel in an exchange of loud honks. The girl watched them flap lazily across the face of a red slow-rising moon. She could see the saltlick from where she crouched, illuminated by the dying green light of sunset and already touched by the silver glow of the moon.

She was filled with a sense of the immensity of Africa. The sky, from horizon to horizon, was barred with melancholy greens and yellows. Away to her left stretched the plains, to the very edge of the world. On her right the pink-crested foothills vanished slowly into black obscurity. The floodlights of day were dimmed. The footlights of night came up, setting a different scene.

Tembo and the girl, now ensnared by the unseen animals, settled comfortably on their heels, prepared to enjoy the drama, resigned to the likelihood that they could not leave their seats until dawn.

The lion had been sprawled over a sun-warmed rock, absorbing the heat. Now he grunted, it seemed, right under their noses. 'Yow ... yow ... yow. Whose land is this? Mine. Mine. Mine.'

A Thomson's gazelle was moving towards the hole, darting her head from side to side, small tail swinging. Jackie wanted to cry a warning. The gazelle craned her neck and drank from the hole, forelegs splayed. Then she sprang to one side and vanished.

The lion emerged from the other side of the saltlick. He walked a few feet, inflated his chest, grunted, and plodded forward again with his black-maned head lowered. He weighed at least four hundred and eighty pounds, but moved lightly, his black-tufted tail curled. Behind him came a lioness and four woolly cubs.

The lion drank first while the cubs rolled in the dirt, fat bellies gleaming white in the growing moonlight. Every few seconds the lion lifted his maned head and listened intently. Once, when a cub pitched against his loose flanks, he clouted the tiny creature so hard that it flew a distance of several feet. Jackie remembered stories of irate lions that sometimes killed their cubs in this off-hand way.

Another lioness had joined the group. The male turned at her approach and grunted. His tail stiffened and he seemed uneasy.

'He smells our man-smell,' whispered Tembo. 'Keep very still.'

Suddenly the lion bounded across the saltlick with long

strides. Behind him the pride closed around the water-hole, dipping their heads.

The lion's growl had deepened into a rumble. It conveyed to Jackie an impression of brutal strength. He stopped near their hideout and began to grunt again like a locomotive climbing a steep incline.

An elephant trumpeted behind them. Without warning, a number of shadows seemed to converge on the saltlick. Once again the elephants had taken the girl by surprise, and she saw now why the lion had been disturbed. He turned and grunted to his pride, a series of short sharp coughs. The first lioness cantered around the bowl of the saltlick, and the cubs followed, still wrestling and tumbling over each other. The second lioness came at a more leisurely pace, as if unwilling to yield to the newcomers.

They came, one elephant after another, in the same uncanny silence that had so impressed Jackie before. Apart from the shrill trumpeting of a leader, and the snapping of a few dry logs, they seemed to tiptoe on stage. In the wings the lion growled defiantly: 'Whose land is this? Mine! Mine! Mine!'

The girl nudged her companion. 'We *shall* be here all night.'

Tembo nodded. He spread his fibre cloak and fitted it around the girl's shoulders. The night was cold now. Even the bushbaby had snuggled up, and lay sleeping inside Jackie's torn jacket.

The eerie wail of the hyaena made her jump. Others joined in. She was conscious of Tembo's body stiffening beside her. Many Africans regarded the hyaena with superstitious awe. Its banshee cry was a long-drawn Ooooo-ah! on an ascending scale.

The girl shivered. She could picture the hyaena leaving his hollow in the rocks and prowling in search of the dead. His big front legs and huge powerful jaws were strong enough to tear apart any carcass, bones and all. Some tribes disposed of their dead by leaving them to be eaten by the hyaenas, and this had given the scavengers an unenviable graveyard reputation.

The moon had quartered the star-chalked sky when Jackie, who had fallen into a light slumber, was disturbed by Kamau's cold fingers plucking gently at her eyebrows. She had slipped sideways, and her head rested against the man's shoulder. When he saw she was awake he said quietly: 'It will be dawn soon and we can go.'

The rusty metallic call of the bubu shrike screeched across the deserted saltlick. Other birds joined in. Soon their calls blended and gave a fresh texture to the background of murmurings and rustlings, squeaks and whispers, that seemed for ever to haunt the African bush. Like an old iron gate creaked the plantain eater, flashing across the tinted eastern sky on crimson-banded wings. The dawn chorus rose in volume.

'You should sleep before we move on,' said Jackie. It seemed to her that Tembo must soon drop from fatigue.

But he shook his head. 'I am worried about the rains.' He thrust his club into the surrounding thorn, preparing to make a path out. A dog yelped in the distance, and then another. Hastily he drew back.

'Wild dogs! We must have a little more patience.'

A pack of wild dogs could be extremely dangerous. They hunted in teams. They were the wolves of Africa. Jackie had no love for them. She could forgive the scavenging hyaena, who, despite his disproportionately big and ugly head, was an oddly likeable beast. She was not even repelled by the hook-nosed vultures who gathered at the smell of approaching death. But she detested the way the dogs worked, in bloodthirsty gangs.

The cries grew louder. Out of a distant bush sprang a water-buck, high in the air, with four or five dogs leaping and snapping at his quarters and flank. The water-buck shot down the slopes of the saltlick and Jackie saw gouts of blood spout from his hindquarters where the dogs took it in turn to tear at the living flesh. The rest of the pack followed, a dozen compact round-eared little brutes bouncing as if on springs.

The buck collapsed into the water-hole and faced his attackers. He had shaken himself free and now turned, lowering his head so that two great curved horns confronted the pack with the danger of death by impalement.

He was a fine young buck. Jackie saw that his reddish-brown coat was gashed with vivid wounds. The buck braced himself on quivering legs. The dogs ran back and forth at the water's edge, cackling to each other. They were cowards in the face of this challenge and two of them worked their way to the buck's rear quarters, hoping to take him by surprise.

But as the two cunning ones leaped forward the buck whirled and lunged with his horns. One dog went flying. The other was pierced through the neck by a rapier-like horn, and a scream came from his torn throat as the buck shook him free. The rest of the pack, driven wild by the sight of flying fur, charged together. The buck seemed to summon up a last reserve of strength. His antlered head swung back and forth. He kept his feet. And one by one the dogs were thrown back.

The water-buck tottered, still flailing blindly with his horns. The rhythmic scythe-like swinging of the head slowed down. The almond eyes lost their look of terror. Then the last of the dogs bellied to the edge of the water-hole and the buck folded his forelegs, presenting his horns for the last time. The dog crouched, looking for an opening, and then

drew back its lips in a disappointed snarl before backing away.

A long slanting ray of the new day's sun sprang across the saltlick and flooded the kneeling buck in gold. The surviving dogs retreated into the shadows. The buck staggered erect again. He was covered in blood that glistened in the golden light, and around him lay the dogs he had killed and injured. The rest loped away, calling softly to each other in the darkness that covered their retreat.

A flock of helmeted guineafowl trotted down the ridges of the saltlick, heads bobbing, legs twinkling, chattering away like children on an outing.

The water-buck waded painfully from the hole, turned, and drank long and deep.

A vulture volplaned from the sky, bumping on extended legs a few feet short of the dead dogs. More vultures circled. Soon the saltlick was astir with the rattle of wings. The buzzards stood in a crook-necked circle, respectful of the shuddering water-buck, waiting to move in with their muscular necks and claw-like beaks.

'Did you see how the buck fought?' asked the girl as they crawled out of the wait-a-bit thorn. 'Did you see? He was almost finished and he turned and beat them back. He was outnumbered twenty to one, and he beat them!'

Down in the saltlick the vultures turned their sexton heads and hopped uneasily on half-spread wings. The waterbuck raised his head and looked at the girl.

'It was a brave fight,' said Tembo.

When they resumed their journey, having recovered their packs, the day seemed brighter and more full of promise. Thousands of butterflies rose and fell in clouds of gorgeous colour above the abandoned water-hole. As the sun sucked the last moisture from the sand, the butterflies departed too, and with them the heavy-bellied vultures. All that remained were the tracks of animals, a few bones in the half-filled hollows, and feathers that drifted on a light morning breeze.

## 9. Poisoned arrows

The girl was worried, and yet in a curious way she was also exhilarated. This was their third day of travel. Her spirits rose like the hawks riding on bubbles of hot rising air. Birds sang. The earth yielded the bitter-sweet pungencies that she would always remember as the smell of Africa. She and the man plodding steadily beside her might have been the first people on earth except that under the thick red dust, covering them from head to foot, it was possible to discern clothing made from modern fabrics. Her new found sense of freedom made despondency difficult.

Yet uneasy thoughts persisted in bubbling to the surface of her mind.

There was the question of Tembo. And the bushbaby was clearly unwell. Instead of sitting jaunty on her shoulder, he clung to her neck and sheltered under her tangled hair. If she fussed about the bushbaby there would be more delays.

Again she counted the days since they had left the cottage. She might have made a mistake. No. It was Wednesday morning all right.

The man, noticing that she was unusually self-absorbed, said: 'You are tired, baba?'

He stopped and faced her, removing his desert kepi and leaving a deep ridge around his damp forehead. He wore his cloak like a toga, revealing the ribbed leopard welts, and a neat scar on either side of one bared shoulder where a greased bullet had once passed clean through.

'No.' She hesitated. 'Kamau is sick.'

'Let me see.' He examined Kamau's lacklustre eyes and felt the warm nose and hands.

'Too much sun, perhaps. He is not accustomed to it.' He squatted on the ground and gently massaged Kamau's ears.

They were on the edge of a *donga,* one of the gullies creasing the surface of the brown-streaked plain. The donga terminated the sand-river, like the crossbar of a 'T'.

'This is a good time to rest,' said Tembo, fanning himself with the kepi. Suddenly the bushbaby sneezed. The man's face folded into a grin. 'The galago has a cold. That is all.'

Kamau sneezed again, and curled up miserably in the man's big horny palms.

'I hope it's nothing worse,' said Jackie with ill-disguised relief.

'No.' He deposited the bushbaby in her lap. 'Stay here and I will take a look beyond those mango trees.'

'So this is where we branch off!' Jackie felt under her shirt for the chart of the Arab slave routes. 'We've picked up the Arab mangoes again.'

She searched among their bags and found a dry biscuit. She held out the broken pieces, but the bushbaby made no response. She tried offering him water. He lapped some, and washed his hands in the remaining drops.

When the man returned from his brief survey Jackie said worriedly: 'He doesn't show much interest in food.'

'He needs plenty of sugar.' Tembo stroked the bushbaby cautiously under the chin. 'I have found honey. It will be good for him.'

'Honey?'

'Yes.' He waved his naked arm in the direction of the mangoes. Beyond them, suspended in a scattering of flat-topped thorn-trees, Jackie saw the hollow logs that Africans hang to attract bees.

'Are there men about?' she asked apprehensively.

'I do not think so,' said Tembo. 'I will be careful, but I think the beekeepers have gone, like the animals, in search of water.'

'And the bees?'

'I will show you how to take the honeycomb without being hurt by the bees.' He searched for the waxed matches in his kit.

He could have made fire by twisting a hard stick in a block of soft wood. There were many things Tembo could do, by means that might have seemed unorthodox to a white man. He knew, for example, how to tap a baobab tree for water; how to cut a creeper and extract life-saving moisture.

He had lived too long, however, to despise the white man's short-cuts. If matches were available he used matches. When gourds of water lay around he did not waste time looking for the bulbous water-plants.

In getting at the honey he knew of no other technique than that of his poaching fathers. So Tembo struck a match and set light to a brittle lump of elephant's dung. It burned quickly and well. Thick smoke belched around him.

Then he covered his head and neck with the fibre cloak. Holding the smoke-plumed dung as a screen, he walked into a swarm of bees that hovered above a fallen honey-barrel.

'Be careful,' called the girl, keeping her distance.

'It is quite safe.' His muffled voice agitated the bees. They rose in a cloud, buzzing angrily.

Jackie watched in admiration. The man knew what he was doing. The vulnerable parts of his body were his face and neck, which he had covered. The thick smoke would confuse the bees and knock some of them out.

He returned, trailing smoke, with broken honeycombs in one hand. The enraged bees made no attempt to follow. He held out the honeycombs. 'The honey will make the galago feel better, and it will give us strength.'

Kamau stretched out his hands and grasped a piece of honeycomb with eager fingers. 'He seems to know it's good medicine,' said the girl gratefully.

'Animals always do.' Tembo shook out his cloak. 'We Africans have learned much from watching them. It is only when we go against the laws of nature that we act like the chicken that loses it head.'

'What do you mean?'

Tembo pointed northwards. 'You see smoke?'

The only smoke Jackie had noticed was the faint smudge still floating above the honey containers. Then her eyes focused on a darker column of smoke rising far beyond the thorn-trees, almost invisible against the purple hills. She stood up.

'What is it?'

'I think the Masai have set fire to the dry grass. They are frightened there will be no grazing.'

'That's dangerous at this time,' said Jackie, alarmed. 'How do you know it is the Masai?'

'I am not sure. But we are near the edge of Masailand. It is their habit to burn the grass at the end of a dry season. When the rains come, new grass will grow quickly to provide food for their cattle. It is a wasteful practice but they refuse to learn.'

'If we are near Masailand we should see Kilimanjaro soon.'

The man grinned suddenly. He had been saving the best news for this moment. 'Come and see.'

With the bushbaby on her shoulder, his sticky hands against her face, she followed the man to the thorn-trees. The ground rose here, and when she reached the top of a small incline her eyes followed the direction of the man's outstretched arm.

She saw what appeared to be a long silver cloud suspended high above an indistinct horizon. She frowned. The sky overhead was burnished by the sun and she shaded her eyes against the glare. Slowly she studied the patch of silver.

'It's the top of Kilimanjaro!' she burst out excitedly.

The Kamba's smile broadened. 'You can see the mountain if you look through your fingers, like this.' He clenched his fist and peered through it, closing one eye. Jackie did the same. Her fist filtered out the brilliant sunlight, and now she saw the stark outline of the great mountain. The highest peak was smothered in snow.

'It is still many miles away,' she said, 'but it will be a good landmark.' She took out John Flaxman's parchment map. 'We should be here.' She spread the map on the ground and set the compass on the spot where they seemed now to stand. 'And that means we have Ndi almost in a direct line between ourselves and the mountain. Yes, look . . .' Her finger followed the line of small crosses drawn by Flaxman to mark the slave route. 'If you are right about the mango trees we *must* be here.'

Tembo wrinkled his eyes. 'I do not understand this at all.'

'It is very simple.' She crouched over the map, her ponytail falling over one shoulder. 'You see, this is the river and over here is the mountain, marked by all these contour lines.'

Tembo bent forward, his hands on his knees, determined to understand. His face was furrowed. He listened carefully and then sighed. 'It is no use. I have rocks in my head.'

'That's nonsense. I keep telling you, Tembo. You belong to a people who read the signs that nature leaves everywhere. I belong to a people who are too stupid to read those signs. You have learned to know the tracks of the lion. I have learned to read a map. You can teach me as I can teach you.'

The man shook his head. 'It is not so simple.'

Their attention was distracted by the squeals of an animal in pain. They came from some distance away, accompanied by bellowings that ended as abruptly as they began. Tembo was instantly alert, slipping the leather thong of the club from his wrist.

A profound silence descended upon the open plains, as if every living thing in that wilderness held its breath.

'Elephant.' Tembo whispered the word.

Jackie twisted on her heels to face the way they had come.

'No. More elephants – over there.' The man pointed across the gully. His arm quivered. Every muscle in his body was taut. He balanced his weight on the balls of his feet and his nostrils flared. He put his free hand on the girl's shoulder. 'It is a strange time of the day – '

He was interrupted by more squeals. This time they continued, one after another, in the most heart-rending way. Jackie thought of a baby crying and said: 'It sounds like a calf.'

'It is.' Tembo glanced down at the girl. 'We must hide. Quickly!'

He took her hand and together they ran back to where they had piled their provisions. There was a large candelabra tree nearby, its grey stalk-like trunk rising from a clump of bushes. Tembo dragged their possessions into the bushes. The girl followed him, asking no questions until they were both safely within the circles of bushes. Overhead the candle-like branches of the tree projected towards the sky.

'The elephants sounded a long way off,' said Jackie. 'Why must we hide?'

The man cautiously raised his head so that he could see over the bushes. 'We are still in the country of the Waliangulu,' he said cryptically. He examined the surrounding countryside with narrowed eyes.

'The elephant hunters,' said Jackie.

'It is better to keep out of their way. They do not like strangers.'

'What makes you think they are here?'

'Those cries. Only the Waliangulu would be hunting at this time of day. They lie in wait wherever there is a promise of water. Some elephants perhaps were digging a well. The first cry we heard. It was the cry of a mother elephant before she dies.'

They could still hear the squeals of the calf, less frequent now, but still as pitiful. The cries were more distant, as if the baby had run away.

'We should rest here,' said Tembo, relaxing a little. 'Go to sleep, and I will keep watch.' He squatted beside the girl. 'How is the galago now?'

She felt under her shirt and withdrew the bushbaby, who regarded them both with sleepy eyes. 'He seems better.' She stopped, struck by a sudden thought. 'The honey. I left the map and the compass near the honeycombs.'

'I will get them. They might attract attention.' Before the girl could protest the man slipped the cloak over his shoulders and darted from the bushes.

The girl watched him move swiftly down the gully, a red and black figure who blended with the stark landscape. Instead of running, he loped along, stopping frequently to listen. It soon became difficult to distinguish him. The cloak provided a natural camouflage and he paused every few feet, motionless like a ground bird.

Jackie lost sight of him and fell into a gentle doze, lulled by the heat of the day. A slight sound caused her eyes to fly open again.

A tiny man, hardly bigger than a dwarf, stood a few feet from the candelabra. His limbs were lightly coloured and he wore a bushbuck cloak, a leather cap, and rings in his ears. He made quick darting movements around a gnarled oak-like tree, and near him on the baked earth lay a longbow and a quiver of vulture-feathered arrows.

The Waliangulu poacher. He looked harmless enough, almost endearing. He was so small and lively and gnome-like. But each of his arrows would be smeared with deadly poison.

The girl was in a dangerous situation. The Waliangulu, meeting her in the open, would be friendly. If she startled him now, however, he might let fly with an arrow and ask questions later.

He was tugging at the branches of the tree, one of the *acokanthera* species. The girl remembered what Tembo had told her. Not every tree was potent. The poacher recognized a really poisonous tree by the dead birds and bugs that fell victim to the pretty cherry-like fruit. Later, when he had boiled the twigs and roots into a sticky liquid, he could measure the strength of the poison by applying it to blood trickling from a fresh cut in the arm. If the poison was effective the blood turned black. Then the poacher quickly plugged the cut in his arm with animal dung, wiped off the poison, and began to treat his arrows with it. The arrowheads were made from flattened nails. The bowstrings came from the sinews of giraffes, plaited. In his own way the poacher was an efficient little fellow who managed to stay alive in the waterless desert, and who kept up with the migrating herds for days on end. He knew all the ways of the elephant, and took tremendous toll.

This one had evidently recognized a potent tree. An alarming possibility flashed across Jackie's mind. Suppose Tembo returned and surprised the poacher?

He was so close now that she detected the fat-smeared rancid smell of his body. She measured the distance between him and the arrows. If Tembo suddenly appeared she might be able to reach the arrows first. And soon, as she searched the edge of the gully, she saw the returning figure of the Kamba. The poacher seemed to see him at the same moment, for he stopped what he was doing and lifted his head like an animal. But what the poacher's alert ears had picked up was the alien sound of an aircraft engine. Jackie heard it a second later. The little man hopped bird-like away from the tree. He collected the bow and the bark-wrapped arrows and vanished into his own secret world, leaving only the rancid body-smell as sole proof that he had ever existed.

Tembo ducked behind a termite hill as the noise of the aircraft spread across the plain. The girl peered through the umbrella spokes of the candelabra tree, searching the sky. Here and there a hawk hung above the earth on invisible wires. One speck, however, moved with unnatural regularity.

It flew low from the direction of the hills and the girl's heart beat faster when she heard the distinctive beat of the motor: *gloop-glub! gloop-glub!* a liquid note like an overworked water-pump.

There was only one aircraft capable of making this singular sound: *Mother Goose*.

The girl moved involuntarily forward. She could see the gull wings, the clumsy flywheel linked to the Volkswagen engine mounted above the centre-section, and the pilot's scarf-wrapped head peering from his open cockpit in the bullet-shaped nose.

The small craft floated through the shimmering waves of heat that rose from the plain, and the engine died. Only one pilot in all Africa would kill his motor in midair like this. It could only be Professor Crankshaw, archaeologist and honorary game warden.

The craft was quite close now, wheeling to stay aloft on the bubbles of hot air.

What was Crankshaw doing here? Jackie frowned and cuddled the bushbaby closer. It was quite possible that he was taking part in the search for her alleged kidnapper. She tried to pick out the termite hill where Tembo was lying concealed.

Crankshaw was a crafty old man. He was skilled in trapping poachers. It was one of his most useful contributions to the work of protecting East African wildlife. Quite a number of white settlers served in their spare time as honorary game wardens. None was so useful as the little archaeologist. In his unique craft he would climb to a good height on the converted auto-engine, switch off, and creep upon his quarry on silent wings. Few law-breakers were aware of this observer who hovered quietly as any bird.

Two things might attract him now. There was a risk that he would spot the cow elephant, who, from the noises she had heard, appeared to lie dying somewhere nearby. And there was the feathery tell-tale trail of smoke that rose from the smouldering dung used by Tembo to drive away the bees.

In her anxiety the girl broke through the cover of bushes, the armed Waliangulu forgotten. She saw the gull-winged machine drift slowly along the horizon in a series of flat turns, the pilot dodging from one thermal to another as if they were stepping-stones across a river. Her movement through the bushes was sudden. Twigs cracked. Her foot struck a pebble. To the poacher she appeared with the stealth of a prowling animal, and his trigger-quick reaction was to shoot.

She never heard the *twang* of the bow. Something struck her bared forearm and ricochetted into the bushes. She felt a tiny sharp pain and saw blood run down the back of her hand.

Her cry was one of alarm more than pain. It was enough to bring Tembo from his hiding place. He came running and tripping across the open ground, waving his knobkerrie, shouting to her to remain still.

Twenty yards away in the opposite direction she saw the alarmed poacher rise from a clump of thorn, hesitating between flight and attack. She saw him draw the string of the bow again, taking aim.

'Look out!' she screamed.

Tembo belly-flopped behind a rock.

The Waliangulu remained motionless for what seemed a long time. Then he lowered the bow, turned and ran. He was not a man-killer and he wanted no trouble now.

The girl sat down heavily and looked at the wound, trying vainly to control the quick pumping of her heart. She was dazed and terrified. Kamau, scrambling down her arm, tried to lick the free flow of blood. She pulled him away and looked up in fear as Tembo loomed above her.

'He nicked my arm.'

'Let me see.' The man fell to his knees. For the first time in her life she saw him tremble. His face had become a mask, deeply grooved, the lips mauve and the eyes reduced to narrow slits. He took her arm and bit deeply into the brown flesh around the wound.

She closed her eyes, fighting down the scream that distended her throat.

The man spat blood and put his mouth back to the enlarged cut. With his left hand he gripped her arm above the elbow, a vice-like grip that seemed to dig deep into the bone.

He held her like this until he had sucked and spat blood several times. Each time he spat he turned and examined her face.

Finally he sat back on his haunches.

'A tourniquet. Make a tourniquet.' She dragged out a handkerchief with her free hand.

The word had no meaning for Tembo, but he knew what to do. He rolled the square of cloth into a tight bandage with one hand, released his grip of her arm, and swiftly knotted the handkerchief close to her armpit. Then he broke off a thick piece of wood from a bush, slipped it under the improvised bandage, and turned it until she felt her arm go numb.

'Don't move, baba.' His voice now was calm. 'Try to remain very still.'

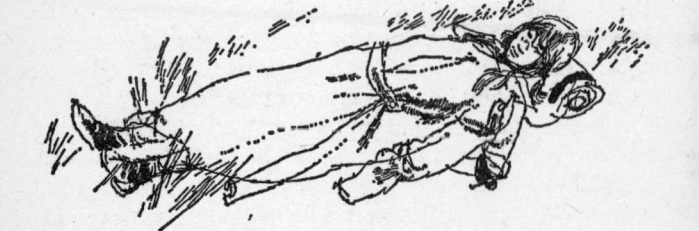

The girl lay with her head on the baked red earth. The bushbaby ran through the tangle of golden hair shrouding her pale cheeks and licked her closed eyelids. The man lifted her limp arm and examined the cut with an experienced eye. Then he began quickly to build a fire.

He was ready to light the dry twigs when again his attention was caught by the sailplane. It had slipped much closer and he could hear the wind whistle through the curved wings. He saw the large striped rudder move in response to the pilot's controls, and he saw how the machine skidded in tight turns to remain balanced in the rising spouts of hot air.

He rose to his full height and cupped his hands. '*Waaa-ba-seee!*' He repeated the war-cry several times, the sound echoing through the plain. The sailplane seemed almost to jerk round. The muffled head in the nose leaned out, and spectacles glinted.

Tembo bent swiftly to the fire and set light to the twigs. A plume of smoke rose lazily into the air. He fanned the flames into a blaze.

The girl stirred and felt Kamau's tongue rasping against her cheek. She felt weak and dizzy. With difficulty she rose on one elbow and saw Tembo running now across the open ground, flapping his cloak and shouting.

The white wings of the sailplane settled on a direct course for the gully, but the strange little machine was no longer suspended on invisible thermals. Like a celluloid ball on a fountain of water, it had slipped out of the sustaining stream and descended rapidly until it sank into the gully. She heard the scrape of skids on sand and rock, the ripping of fabric, and then she fainted again.

## 10. Enter the professor

*Mother Goose* came to a splintering halt under the astonished eye of Tembo, shielded by a thin screen of tinder-dry
thorn. He had not expected the sailplane to drop so rapidly
out of the sky. A padded figure emerged from the crushed
nose, and tore away the muffling scarf to reveal a jungle of
mutton-chop whiskers and grey beard.

Tembo launched himself down the steep gully that led
into the ravine, slipping and sliding over chipped stones,
arms torn by needle-sharp thorns. Far away, the calf elephant squealed.

Professor Crankshaw turned to face the African whose
noisy approach and whirling arms were suggestive of attack.

'Keep your distance!' Crankshaw reached back into the
cockpit and hauled out a light .22 rifle. He levelled it at the
dishevelled Kamba who staggered towards him with the

club at his wrist swinging more by accident than design, although it contributed to the general air of menace.

'The girl.' Tembo slithered to a stop and pointed wildly at the cliff-top.

'What girl?' The wiry little archaeologist watched the African with undisguised suspicion. He had ripped off his weather-worn windbreaker and stood with legs braced, an expanse of tanned flesh stretching between his tattered shorts and his thick beard. He wore an old gardening cap, turned so that the peak protected the back of his neck, and his black-gloved artificial hand balanced the barrel of the rifle with practised ease.

'The white girl,' Tembo amended, breathing heavily. 'She is hurt.'

Behind the steel-rimmed spectacles a pair of faded blue eyes seemed to widen.

'Jackie Rhodes!'

Tembo nodded.

'What happened?' Crankshaw's voice was shrill and sharp. 'Don't move! Drop that club or I'll blast your head off.'

'But . . .' Tembo fell back, and all at once he realized the terrible mistake he had made. This pink-faced, bushy man would never question the judgement behind a police order.

'So *you're* the kidnapper!' The archaeologist craned forward like an ostrich. 'I know you, too. You were Rhodes' headman.' He pushed out the rifle until the barrel pointed at Tembo's chest. 'You're Tembo Murumbi. I might have guessed.'

'B'wana, please. The girl is hurt.'

'You ruddy black heathen. What have you done to her?'

'Not me, B'wana. The poacher. An arrow – '

Crankshaw gasped. 'Poison?'

'Yes, B'wana. Please hurry.'

'Too true I'll hurry!' The archaeologist refused to be influenced by the fact that Tembo had summoned his aid, and stuck to his hasty conclusions. He reached behind him, hooking his gloved hand through the loops of a waterproof bag. 'Lead me to her. This gun is aimed right at the back of your head, so don't try anything.'

They reached the still form of the girl and Crankshaw exploded. 'By the Lord Harry! You'll have a lot to answer for, if she's been harmed.'

He placed the rifle carefully alongside the girl. 'If you try to run I guarantee to drop you within ten yards.'

Tembo was too worried to argue. He squatted on his haunches and watched in silence as the professor went to work. The wound on Jackie's forearm had glazed over in the sun. The blood on her hand was dry. She seemed to be breathing quietly, and the colour had crept back into her cheeks. There was no sign of Kamau.

Crankshaw felt her pulse and lifted one eyelid. 'You sure it was a poison arrow?'

'Yes, B'wana.' Tembo hesitated. 'It did not stick in her arm. Perhaps – '

'Okay. I'll do the guessing.' Crankshaw groped inside the bag and extracted needles and a small phial. 'What were you planning to do with that fire?'

'Make hot the blade of a knife,' Tembo said in Swahili. 'Cut around the wound.'

'Cauterize it, eh?' Crankshaw replied in English. 'You made a good job of the tourniquet,' he added grudgingly.

Jackie stirred, stretched, and opened her eyes.

'Cranky!'

'It's all right, m'dear. Just lie quietly.'

She heaved herself on to her back and stared up at him unbelievingly. 'You've had a bad shock,' the archaeologist told her. 'Don't try to talk.' He began to loosen the tourniquet.

The girl had started to tremble and beads of moisture broke out on her upper lip. She swivelled her eyes to where Tembo squatted in sullen silence a few feet away.

'I think,' said Crankshaw, 'that whatever hit you, it wasn't the poisoned tip of an arrow.'

He saw how she shivered. He brushed back her hair and felt the dampness of her forehead.

She said, directing the question in Swahili to Tembo: 'Why do you sit there, old friend?'

'The B'wana threatens to shoot – '

'You keep quiet!' Crankshaw's harsh silencing of the Kamba only served to make the girl tremble more violently.

'There's no need to be frightened any more,' the archaeologist told her gently. 'This man will never hurt you again.'

'But he didn't – '

Crankshaw laid a finger on her lips. 'I forbid you to speak. This has been a terrible experience for a child your age. The law will take care of this – ' He choked on the next word and finally nodded in Tembo's direction.

His attitude confirmed Jackie's growing suspicion. Her whole body was wet with perspiration. 'Tembo saved me,' she said. 'I ran away from the ship.'

Cranky smiled with an expression of frank disbelief. 'Yes, m'dear.' He emptied out the bag. 'I was going to give you a shot of snake-bite serum, but there's no evidence of poisoning.' He rummaged among the contents. 'If there'd been poison, you'd be dead by this time. All the same, you're clearly suffering from shock.'

'Cranky!' The girl made a final attempt to penetrate the professor's armoury of obstinacy and prejudice. 'You've got to listen.'

She tried to twist on to one arm, but he pushed her gently back with his stiff gloved hand. She thought weakly that it would be easier to talk later. Crankshaw was correct in recognizing the symptoms of shock.

'These are powerful tablets,' he said, shaking two white pills from a bottle. 'They'll make you sleep. Take them with water. What you need more than anything is rest. Just as well I carry an emergency kit. Surprising how few people do.'

Obediently she took the pills, sipped the water, and lay back fighting desperately to focus her mind and return to the subject of Tembo.

'I carry a bit of everything in this old bag.' Crankshaw went on talking. 'If I ever crashed I could always walk out of the bush fit as a fiddle. The rifle fires a forty-grain bullet – effective at five yards against a lion, provided you make it a brain shot. Yes, m'dear, even an old man in his sixties and with only one good hand is still able to handle life in the bush if he keeps his wits . . .'

She struggled against the verbal tide, and found herself drifting into sleep. In the last few seconds she remembered the bushbaby and tried vainly to utter his name. 'Ka – ' She concentrated her mind on him but across her eyes span a dizzy cartwheel of colour. Even his name seemed to escape her, losing itself in the hurrying fiery tail of the cartwheel.

Crankshaw closed his bag. 'Pick this up and take it back to the plane. Keep right beside me.' His manner was more peremptory than ever before. The girl moaned softly as Crankshaw attempted to lift her. He was spry, but the girl was a dead weight.

'I will carry her.' Tembo moved forward.

'Not on your life! You put another finger on her and I'll shoot you on the spot.'

The Kamba retreated, wiping the back of his hand across his tight-lipped mouth. Inside him a great anger was building up and he knew that he must control it or flee.

'Never mind the bag, then.' The little professor shaded the girl's face with his hand. 'We'll camp here a while. You. Go to the sailplane. You'll find a padded raincoat in the cockpit. I'll cover you every inch with this gun, so watch yourself.'

The sun had retreated behind black clouds billowing up in the west. Tembo worked quickly, anxious to ensure the girl's comfort, but he knew that if he did not get away he might be goaded into striking the old man. He pillowed the girl's head on the professor's raincoat and stood back.

Crankshaw gazed for a long time at the girl's face. He saw

her blonde hair knotted like a fish-net, her cheeks grimy with dirt. He saw the rips and tears and stains in her jodhpurs and jacket. 'I'll see you pay for this,' he said finally to Tembo.

The Kamba abandoned any further attempt to explain himself to this stubborn and misguided old man. He stood erect, suppressing his rage. Behind half-closed eyelids the pupils were large and black. His big hands hung loosely at his sides.

There was a nervous squeak from inside Jackie's shirt. Professor Crankshaw saw the bushbaby for the first time as Kamau emerged, rubbing his eyes and blinking.

'So the child still kept you,' muttered the archaeologist. He stopped to pick the animal up, but Kamau evaded him and scuttled to Tembo's feet.

Tembo scooped the bushbaby into his hands and said: 'There is a basket among our possessions. There, in the bushes.'

'Get it.'

Tembo thrust his way into the bushes and brought out their knapsacks and the basket. He removed the bushbaby from his shoulder and pushed the animal, protesting, into the basket. He closed the lid and placed the basket beside the girl. He moved slowly and deliberately, keeping his head down, watching the archaeologist from under his tufted eye-brows.

Crankshaw looked at their assembled gear and, unable to contain his curiosity, he stirred one of the knapsacks with his foot. At once the Kamba dropped to his haunches, seized the foot and swung the professor backwards so that the older man lost balance and fell sprawling in the dust. In the same lithe movement Tembo swung on his heels and grabbed the rifle. It was not in his nature to steal. He knew that it would look bad in the eyes of the law if he kept the rifle. But he feared Crankshaw, and the blind prejudice that the little professor represented. He dared not risk leaving the weapon in the hands of a man who might be tempted, out of ignorance, to use it.

He sprang back, scooped a handful of red dust and flung it in Crankshaw's direction. Then, hooking his fingers into the wide leather brass-buckled belt whose loops contained the archaeologist's ammunition, the African leapt to his feet and was gone.

The baby elephant's cries aroused the girl from her stupor. She gazed for long seconds at the darkening sky, herding her thoughts together like stray sheep. Her arm throbbed. When she bent her head to examine it, a flash of pain in her neck made her wince. The cut was bandaged. She wiggled her fingers. The tips prickled with the returning circulation.

The calf's lament continued. A voice nearby said: 'I'd shoot every poacher if I had my way.'

She turned her head and saw Cranky doubled over the fire and talking to himself. He looked like a bushy-haired gnome.

'Cranky?'

He straightened up. 'Good! You're awake.' He joined her, rubbing his hands.

'Cranky, where's my bushbaby?' She twisted her head feverishly from side to side.

'The bushbaby? In the basket. Quite safe.' He felt her pulse. 'You slept for two good hours.'

'Where's Tembo?'

'He ran away.' The professor's face seemed to inflate with rage. 'Tipped me on m'back, stole the gun, and bolted.'

Jackie groaned.

'How d'you feel?'

'Fine. A bit dizzy.'

Crankshaw emptied one of the pockets in his shorts and held out a handful of cloves. 'Chew one of these. Refresh your mouth.'

She remembered that he ordered cloves by the bushel from Zanzibar, chewing them like gum. 'No thanks.' She pushed the hand away. 'What were you doing?'

'Planning our getaway. Now you're conscious, I'll start work on the motor while we still have some light.' He peered closely into her face. 'Certain you feel well?'

'Yes, but – '

'Now don't excite yourself again.' He cut her sentence short with an impatient gesture. 'That "poison" arrow. Found it. The feathers on the shaft are bound with wire. *That*'s what struck your arm.'

'Thank goodness.' She lay back, relaxed.

'However,' said Professor Crankshaw, and his voice had become pedantic and self-important, 'you have undergone a most terrible and exhausting experience. We must get you away from here as soon as possible. Your family had just arrived in Mombasa when I last heard, this morning. The ship turned back and your father's planning to fly to Nairobi – probably tomorrow.'

Jackie groaned again. Crankshaw said hastily: 'But there, I mustn't tax your strength.'

The girl turned her head and closed her eyes. She needed time to think. Why had Tembo run off? It could only make things look blacker against him. An idea struck her. 'How do you mean – our getaway?'

Crankshaw pulled his bulbous red nose. 'You know *Mother Goose* is built to fly with one person? If I throw out some fuel, and dump the radio and other bits of junk, I can squeeze you into the cockpit too. First light tomorrow morning we'll be off!'

'But what about Tembo?'

'For heaven's sake, girl! He's done you enough harm already – '

'He's done me no harm!' The girl struggled to her knees. 'Don't you understand, Cranky? It's *me* who got *him* into trouble.' A mist closed over her eyes and she fell forward, shaking her head. The after-effects of sedation were still strong, and she felt Crankshaw ease her back to the ground.

'I'm quite safe by the fire, Cranky.'

'Yes. Of course.' He stood irresolutely in front of her. 'You're sure . . .?'

'I'm really quite all right.'

He nodded again and hurried away, a flashlight's beam dancing in front of him. When she could no longer see the light, the girl got unsteadily to her feet and called softly into the surrounding bush. 'Tembo?'

There was no answer. The night was early yet, and the only sounds were the usual background noises of the African bush, an unbroken mutter of nocturnal insects and birds, with the deeper bass notes of frogs who seemed to be still unaffected by the drought.

'Tembo?'

Far away, the orphaned elephant trumpeted. Tears filled the girl's eyes. 'Oh, Tembo, where are you?'

She watched the spreading red stain along the northern horizon. The grass-fire must be approaching, driven by a rising wind.

'Tembo!' She took the risk of raising her voice. When Crankshaw came back she turned swiftly and busied herself with Kamau's basket. 'It's time to feed the bushbaby,' she said with a finality that stopped all further conversation.

When she had fed Kamau and sat playing with him beside the fire, Crankshaw said in his most ingratiating manner: 'Is something on your mind, m'dear?'

'No, Cranky.' She had the bushbaby lying on his back in her lap, excitedly waiting for her to continue tickling his stomach. The yellow belly-fur was still tangled from his un-premeditated dip in the ocean. It seemed long ago now. The girl rubbed the knotted fur and fought down the rising sense of panic that became worse each time she thought of Tembo.

'I've made a sort of bed for you,' said the archaeologist. 'You can bunk down any time.'

'I'm not tired.' She tried to put some gratitude into her voice. She knew he meant well. She only wished she could talk some sense into him.

As if reading her thoughts, he said: 'You haven't told me what happened these last few days.'

'You won't let me.' Head bent, she pretended to be playing with Kamau while furtively she watched the surrounding shadows. Some sixth sense had made her alert.

'I didn't want you to get upset, m'dear. You don't need to talk about this awful experience with that Kamba fellow . . .'

Something had moved near the candelabra tree. She was sure.

She turned hastily back to the professor. 'Why was that baby elephant crying?' she asked, anxious now to make conversation and distract Crankshaw's attention from the dark shape slithering along the perimeter of firelight.

The professor, glad to be on his own ground, visibly brightened. 'Well, you see, I spotted this poor beast – the mother, I mean – this big cow elephant, when I was soaring. That's the advantage of a machine like mine. Doesn't surprise the animals. These poaching chaps – they botched the job. Hit the beast but didn't penetrate. The poison took a long time to work.'

He warmed to the subject. 'The really bad poaching is done by hunters in search of ivory. They kill an elephant just for the tusks. Or they kill a rhino to get the horn. Simply the horn. An entire marvellous beast like a rhino – killed, so greedy men can hack away the horn! Foolish men in the East buy it because they think it has magical properties.'

His voice droned on and on. Jackie squinted sideways into the bush. She was sure now that it was Tembo who waited. But for what? Did he want her to make a run for it? Or was the Kamba waiting to spring upon the garrulous professor?

She decided that she didn't care. What mattered was that Tembo should be safe. As a neighbour, Professor Crankshaw was kindly and considerate. As a human being, he seemed not to have learned one single thing about the Africans among whom he had lived for so many years.

'Why shouldn't Africans kill animals?' she prodded him. 'Who decides if they're poaching or not?'

'It is expected that anyone shooting a wild animal is in possession of a hunting licence,' Crankshaw quoted sonorously.

'That means if you're a white man you can kill them, because you can afford the licence.'

'My dear child, the issue of licences is part of an overall plan to ensure a maintenance in the balance of nature. Indiscriminate killing . . .' He paused, rolling the words on his tongue. '*That* could wipe out some species altogether.'

The girl rolled over on her stomach. 'If I were an African I would hate white men telling me what animals I could or could not kill.'

'What an extraordinary thing to say.' The professor was still ignorant of the man coming up behind him.

Jackie became ever more deliberately provocative. 'Before the white man came these plains were covered in wild animals. The Africans didn't kill them off. *We* did. And now we're going and the Africans are taking over again . . .'

'Good gracious, child. Never let your father hear you say such a thing.' In his agitation the professor had risen from the fire.

'That's what my daddy *does* say.' Jackie's voice rose. If Crankshaw turned he would come face to face with the waiting Kamba. 'Did you – did you see the map we used to get this far?' She searched inside her shirt. 'Look!' She held out John Flaxman's chart.

His curiosity was aroused. 'The old Arab slave routes, eh?' The professor wiped his spectacles and carried the map closer to the fire. 'This *is* interesting.'

Jackie said: 'I'm going into the bushes.'

'Hmm?' Crankshaw glanced up. 'Yes, of course.'

She edged round him and walked towards Tembo, who backed down in the long grass.

'What are you doing?' she hissed, crouching beside the Kamba.

'You must leave that foolish old man. It is impossible for two of you to fly in that machine. It will crash.'

'Why did you run away?'

'He was making me very angry.' Tembo's voice trembled.

'I think you are right,' she said. 'I must get away from him when he sleeps. We should finish this journey together. I am afraid of what the police might do if you run away alone.'

They talked in whispers. Crankshaw was still bent over the chart, deciphering the handwriting on the back.

'Don't think too ill of him,' she said to Tembo.

'The old man – he is not worth worrying about. But he has also caused me to lose my club.'

The words were almost an anticlimax. She suppressed a giggle. Then she remembered that the club was of close-grained smooth Cape walnut, something that had been in Tembo's family for several generations. She had never seen him without the orange-red club with its coloured beads at the neck.

'What happened to it?'

'I don't know. The old man's words were like thorns to a buffalo. I lost my head, and dropped the club somewhere.'

She put her hand on Tembo's bared shoulder. 'Wait. I will find your club.'

Professor Crankshaw, discoverer of the Naivasha Tomb, humanist and explorer, scourge of the ivory poachers, lay spreadeagled on his back gently snoring. His face was covered in a film of fine grey ash. Near his artificial right hand was the black leather bag that carried his emergency kit.

The girl reached across his sleeping body and removed the bad. Inside was a pouch of dried biltong, black meat that you chewed like liquorice; a plastic bag of tea and maize-flour; but no club. She kept the biltong and replaced the bag. Crankshaw stirred, grunted, and turned on his side.

She crawled round him on hands and knees, back to where Tembo had gathered their knapsacks. 'I can't find it.'

'Wa!' The Kamba's distress was plain, but he strove to hide his bitterness. 'We must start moving. The grass-fire has spread.'

They both looked automatically at the sky. The stars were obscured by smoke or cloud, and much of the sky was a sinister crimson.

'I'm sorry about the club,' said the girl, lifting her pack.

The man shrugged. 'My father, as you know, was a chief. He would be angry. It cannot be helped.'

They made a makeshift camp on the far side of the gully, snatching an hour's sleep before dawn. It was late in coming, and Jackie saw the reason when a fiery red sun finally broke through the heavy drifting smoke.

'There is a hill, there. Perhaps three miles.' Tembo pointed. It rose from the plain almost with the abruptness of a sandcastle. Thousands of years ago some volcanic upheaval had jarred the land, throwing up this great outcrop of lava. Now it was coated with a thin layer of poor soil, and fringed with forest. It would make a safe retreat if the fire should sweep down upon them.

The girl wiped flecks of grey ash from her face. 'I feel jittery. Why is it so quiet?'

'The birds and animals have run away. Or else they hide. Because of the fire.'

The unfamiliar silence was eerie. For the first time she realized just how noisy an African dawn could be. She missed the morning birdsong, the twang and chirrup of insects, the distant chorus of animal growls.

She began to prepare Kamau's breakfast. They still had a little condensed milk left. Into this she mashed a banana, using the mug they all shared.

A faint squeal nearby reminded her of the orphaned calf elephant. She glanced round. Tembo was checking the stolen ammunition belt and rifle. The bushbaby was drywashing his hands as a fastidious preliminary to eating breakfast.

She took some bananas from the sack and walked a short way into the bush.

The calf stood under a thorn-tree, an indistinct shadow. He backed away from the girl, waving his tiny trunk in nervous gestures, and flapping his baby ears. The girl advanced at a slightly faster pace than the calf's slow retreat. When she came within arm's reach she held out the bananas.

The little elephant curled his trunk and cautiously explored the contours of the bananas and Jackie's hand. He gave another small squeal of alarm and stepped back again, colliding with a tree. This time, when Jackie caught up, the elephant was bolder. The trunk snaked out, the delicate tip softly caressing the girl's arm. She was surprised by the trunk's flexibility. It was soft and gentle and it curled to take possession of the banana, conveying them to the calf's pointed mouth as if it had a will of its own.

'The calf will follow us,' Tembo warned her, when she told him of the incident. 'Watch that he steals nothing.'

They began the day's march in a sombre silence that was broken by the grating roar of an engine. Chains rattled, gears creaked, and the girl was sure she detected the clank of the heavy flywheel that characterized Crankshaw's unorthodox craft. Moments later, *Mother Goose* rose unsteadily out of the gully behind them.

'The old man has courage,' said Tembo in reluctant admiration.

Jackie kept her eyes on the frail machine as it drifted sideways through veils of smoke. She said: 'He'll want to report to the Nairobi police.'

'And this time they will have my name.'

'All the more reason to hurry,' said Jackie. 'We shall find people at Ndi who *will* believe our story.'

Tembo shifted the rifle under his arm. 'I have a gun,' he said simply. 'It might help them to understand.'

'You would be foolish to use it,' she said sharply.

'I might have no other choice. Many people will think like B'wana Crankshaw.'

'I wish we had never seen him.'

Already his sailplane had been swallowed up in the low-lying banks of smoke. He had gone as quickly as he came, and this worried her. It would have been more normal if he had circled the area. Of course he would have searched the ground for her before taking off, but there was something ominous in the manner of his swift departure, as if he could not wait to summon help.

'He thinks you have kidnapped me again,' she said aloud. Impulsively she took the arm of the man at her side.

Tembo gave her a bleak smile. 'The B'wana is a very clever man. But he is old. And obstinate. And he distrusted me because I am African.'

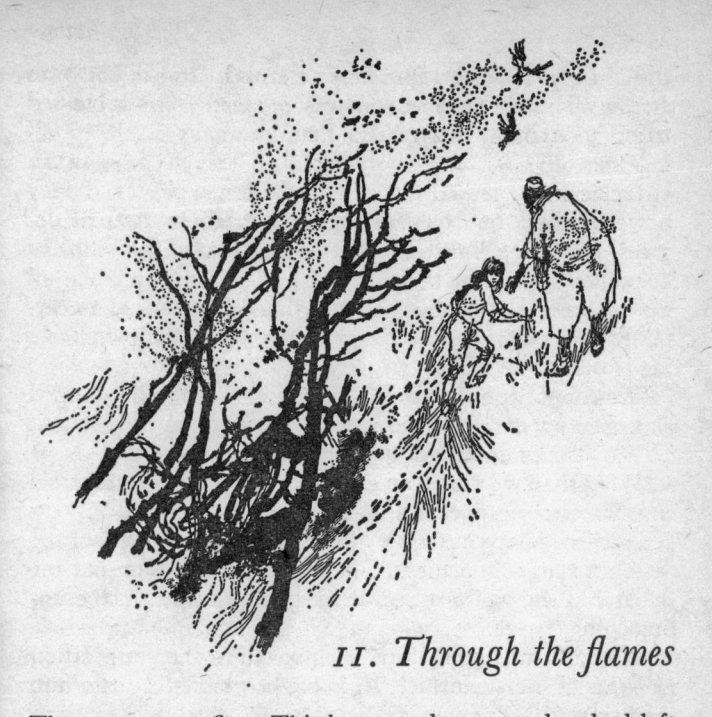

## II. *Through the flames*

There were two fires. This became clear once they had left
the gully far behind. The bigger fire advanced rapidly along
a broad front, consuming the tall plumed grass in flaming
red gulps, and preceded by ribbed curtains of black smoke.
The girl thought this fire resembled a black-robed witch
leaning towards them in skirts edged with scarlet. It burned
remorselessly across the western grasslands. The second fire
was altogether more secretive and sinister. It was sheltered
from the wind and crouched in a shallow valley. Directly the
wind veered, however slightly, this fire would pounce.

Their path to the naked hill lay between these two fires
that formed a wide 'V' of which the point already lay behind
Jackie and the man. The western arm of the 'V' was pivot-
ing inwards and they were forced to move obliquely across
the central plain. They walked through the grass reaching to

the girl's waist. In a short time tendrils of smoke began to weave about them. The sun was reduced from a big red moon to a small orange orb that gradually vanished altogether.

Jackie had checked direction on the compass, and they now marched on roughly three-hundred-and-twenty degrees, which she insisted would bring them to the hill. She knew how easily the senses could lead you astray when all the landmarks were blacked out, and she glanced uncertainly at the wavering needle as the smoke came down like a fog blanket.

'We cannot continue in this direction . . .' Tembo stopped as a gap appeared in the smoke. He pointed in eloquent silence. The grass-fire was almost upon them.

'What shall we do?' The girl felt a panic urge to turn and run. She had wrapped Kamau's old sweater around his basket, where he lay chittering with frustration, unaware of the reason for his confinement. The blanket would filter out the smoke but she was terrified of his being trapped in the approaching flames.

'We must run *into* the fire.' Tembo wiped the perspiration from his dust-creased face. 'It is the best thing. To run into the flames.'

'That's impossible!' She looked at him in astonishment.

'No. The fire moves too quickly. If we run away it will catch us. If we run into it, it will soon be left behind. When it is very close you must take a deep breath and run *into* it. The ground will burn for a little distance and then it will be clear.'

She made no effort to move. 'Trust me,' he said. 'I have seen these fires before.'

Again the smoke came down between them. Jackie loosened the basket and slipped her hand protectively around the bushbaby. Her knapsack still hung by a strap from her other shoulder. She wondered what would happen if it caught fire. She began to cough. There was no further time for hesitation. Around her the ground was alive with the faint squeaks and sudden rustlings of small creatures driven before the blaze like cattle at roundup.

Now the fire was all about her. She sucked in a lungful of acrid smoke and began to run. She had no idea where Tembo had gone. She simply ran. Sparks rose like fireflies around her head. Flames scorched her legs. Hot cinders stung her face and the ground under her feet was like a molten lake. She felt a stabbing pain in her chest and the fire's growl struck her ear-drums, pounding away inside her head. Once she stumbled and almost fell. Her one thought was not to drop the bushbaby.

Her eyes were tight shut when she ran full tilt into Tembo. 'It is all over, baba. All over.' She heard his deep calm voice and slowly opened her eyes.

They were standing in burned stubble. The fire had swept over them and now crackled further and further away under pressure from the wind. She rubbed her watering eyes. The sky had never seemed so blue. Smoke and fire now leaned away from them like a tattered umbrella blown inside out.

A small hawk plummeted into the blackened underbrush and flew up again with something wriggling between her claws. More scavengers circled in search of victims left in the fire's wake. Jackie remembered hearing of a prairie fire so fierce it had sucked buzzards into its red heart.

'We are still in trouble, *mwanangu*.' Tembo's use of this endearment signified his concern. They stood in a triangle of burnt-over land, and they could feel hot air gusting from the smaller fire to their right. The hill was still more than a hundred yards away, separated from them by a ravine and a belt of forest.

'It will be a race,' said Jackie. 'Either we reach the hill first or we'll be caught in the forest like straw-men in a bonfire.'

For a brief moment the fresh clouds of smoke that lay ahead were divided like a curtain by the wind. Now the hill was plain to view.

'Mark the tree!' said Tembo. 'At the very top of the hill.'

'I see it.' It was an old fig tree, surrounded by bare ground.

'We must make it our goal. If we become separated do not stop until you reach the tree. The fire cannot climb so high.'

They began to run again, jog-trotting side by side. Already the hill had become a blur, soon to vanish behind another drifting screen of smoke. The girl found that she could breathe only with difficulty. Her lungs creaked and whistled. Her mouth tasted of dead things, of wet charcoal and cinders. Out of the corner of her eye she thought she saw the lumbering shape of the baby elephant. She could not be sure. She was sure of nothing except the necessity to find the lonely fig tree at the top of the hill. Her eyes began to smart. Tears rolled down her cheeks. Her ears resounded with the roar of her own blood, and her legs seemed to be pounding through quicksands.

Together they stumbled upon the staircase of crumbling sandbanks that descended into the forested ravine. Jackie thought it presented an insurmountable obstacle. The tree on the hill receded in her imagination. She saw in front of her a net of vegetation that sagged from every branch of every tinder-dry tree.

'The fire! Can you hear the fire?' She had stopped, using the question as an excuse.

'Keep running, baba.' The man flung himself ahead of her, slashing with his panga at the entangling brushwood. Sweat dripped along the clean edge of his jaw and he paused at intervals to wipe a glistening forearm across his face.

Jackie let him get ahead. It was quieter here in the forest. She leaned against a tree. She felt less confused, and able to breathe again. Her legs trembled with exhaustion, but there was no longer the double beat of her own blood drumming in her ears.

The smoke writhed through the upper branches of the trees, muffling all sounds and reducing the light once again to an eerie gloom. She sank to the ground, grateful because the smoke stayed way above her, giving her space to breathe and think.

'Baba!' The man shook her angrily. 'You must not stop.' He jerked her upright and took her knapsack. The girl swayed and grabbed his shoulder. 'Please. We must keep going.'

She swallowed. 'I cannot move.'

He stooped and picked up the basket at her feet. She watched him with tired eyes. He lifted the lid and said: 'At least give the galago a chance to escape.'

'No!' She thrust her hand inside, calming the bushbaby.

'Then run. For Kamau's sake, run.'

She snatched the basket from him. 'I will run, old friend. Only you must help me.'

'That is better.' He turned away. 'If you feel faint, hang on to my cloak.'

He moved forward again, burdened with both knapsacks slung together from one shoulder, the rifle resting across his bulging neck muscles, and around his waist the broad leather brass-buckled strap whose loops carried the neat little copper-nosed bullets.

Once more he fixed his mind upon the symbol of their safety – the tree at the top of the hill. The forest was dry as kindling. He knew what to expect once the second fire licked its hem of elephant grass. If only the thickening underbrush would give way just for a moment and allow them to force a less devious path. But the tendrils of vine were tough and tangled like the scrambling nets he had used as a soldier. His panga arm scythed back and forth with the rhythm of a pendulum.

The secret sounds of the forest were interrupted by distant explosions as the fire raced through a clump of bamboo. Nearer to hand, Jackie heard the quick movements of animals alarmed already by whispers of danger.

Something crashed ahead. For some time they had lost contact with the baby elephant. Now he came blundering into their path again. Jackie saw that he dragged one of his hind legs, and she had the impression that from it trailed wire and some object of an orange colour. Then Tembo lurched forward with a shout of triumph and snatched at the calf's retreating tail. He caught it with the hand that held the panga, and the metal blade slapped the baby's hide.

The shock goaded the calf into a sudden rush. He fled through the brushwood that had seemed, a moment before, to be impenetrable. Instinctively he made for the hill, trumpeting with indignation as Tembo twisted the tail to get a firmer grip. It was like driving a bulldozer, thought Jackie, as she clung to the man.

Tembo lost his hold when the young elephant charged blindly through a smouldering windrow of leaves five feet high. But their rescuer had served his purpose. His squeals were now matched by the rumble of flames biting along the forest's edge. A wind, partly the creation of the shimmering heat from the fire, scattered sparks through the tree-tops. Sheets of flame were flung from crown to crown across the roof of the forest. Burning brands toppled into the depths to start smaller fires. The top of the forest became a blowtorch. Its depths expelled a great rush of air like the foul breath of some vast primeval animal.

The man and the girl were vomited out of the forest into a clearing that penetrated the flank of the hill. At the end of this cleft were boulders providing access to a game trail above the doomed forest. Jackie studied the hill through patches of drifting smoke. It was a big square-headed hill with pleated skirts of grey volcanic rock. There was enough shale to form a natural firebreak. Beyond this, the grass was sere and yellow. Patches of thorn-scrub fringed an escarpment. After that the details were blurred.

'We should be safe here.' She was standing where the boulders had piled one upon another to form a barricade across the ascending path.

'Not until we reach the fig tree,' said Tembo. He shifted the load on his back and sheathed the panga. 'We will have to run to keep ahead of the animals.' He lifted his chin and pointed it over the girl's shoulder.

She turned and saw a red forest duiker, the size of a small dog. The little duiker darted between them and began scrabbling wildly over the shale, tiny hooves slipping and sliding, legs splayed.

Blue starlings flighted from the crowns of trees still untouched by fire. Two hornbills looped beneath them. Unseen and muffled, a rhino whuffed.

The calf elephant had been circling them in a frenzy. Now he trotted towards the man and the girl with a demented look.

'Up the hill!' said Tembo, jabbing the girl's thin shoulders with his elbow. 'Quick.'

Together they climbed the boulders, pursued by a growing volume of noise. A bushbuck barked. Above them a thicket of bamboo popped like gunshot. Already the heat from the fire had warmed the gas inside the bamboo, expanding it until the frail wall of the bamboo burst. They slithered across an ascending field of black lava rock and reached the grass-line.

'Phew!' The girl threw herself down, cradling the bushbaby's basket. 'I thought it was the end.'

Tembo flung the packsacks to the ground and rubbed one shoulder where a badly mended bone still sometimes ached from the injury inflicted by the leopard fifteen years ago. 'We were lucky.' His slanted eyes twinkled. 'The little elephant saved us.'

To her surprise, for she had been too busy climbing to notice anything else, Jackie saw the calf above her, standing calm now under a scraggy grey bush of sansevieria. A shadow under the bush moved and betrayed itself as the duiker. It sprang away as the girl got back on her feet. But the baby elephant remained motionless, only flicking his ears with tiny slapping sounds, and watching the girl with melancholy eyes.

'We must climb to the top of the hill,' said Tembo. 'I heard the cough of a leopard.' Absentmindedly he touched the welts beneath his arm.

The ascent took the best part of an hour. They moved steadily towards their final goal. The old fig tree's outline on the hill's summit became clear as the wind shifted again and carried away the smoke. The draft of cooling air that followed also revealed a lemon sky. The sun was down on the horizon, outshone by wavering red flames that stretched in every direction beneath them. They were still accompanied by the calf elephant. He climbed the incline of the hill with grunts and squeals, his hind legs taking the weight so that he moved like a fat old man in baggy trousers. He was careful to keep his distance, but he stayed abreast and ponderously turned his dented head in their direction whenever they paused. Jackie thought there was something pathetic about the ungainly creature's sudden attachment.

She had released Kamau from his basket at the earliest opportunity, and the bushbaby now sat in the cleft of her bush-shirt, chittering to himself. Every now and then she ran her fingers over his erect ears. There was blood on the back of her hand and she felt his tongue rasp over it, savouring the warm salt taste. They reached the wild fig in a state of total exhaustion.

'The tree is a *mugomo*,' said Tembo with pleased relief in his voice. 'A prayer fig.'

Its radish-like roots drooped to the ground, forming a cathedral of many entrances. A fig tree of any kind was lucky. A prayer fig with an abundance of white tortured roots was thrice blessed so far as Tembo was concerned.

He tossed their kit against the twisted trunk. 'We are surrounded by fire.'

The girl gazed down without speaking. Their hill was topped by a broad flat ridge. The steep slopes ended in a ruby-red glow. The glow of the fire grew fiercer as the sunlight faded. Where the sky remained clear of smoke, Jackie saw stiff-winged vultures circling by the dozen.

'Cranky's out there somewhere,' she said, watching the vultures. 'He's a dangerous enemy, Tembo.'

The man shrugged contemptuously. 'Here on the hill, nobody can take me by surprise.'

Crankshaw, manoeuvring *Mother Goose* above the neck-lace of fires, was tortured with self-condemnation. When he had found the girl gone his duty seemed clear. With his limited supply of fuel he decided to fly straight out of the gully and make an aerial search from high altitude. He had to cut the motor at six thousand feet to conserve fuel, only to find that in some mysterious way the prairie fires had de-stroyed all thermal activity.

Gloomily he watched the vertical tube on his instrument panel. In it sagged a bubble. The tube measured 'lift', the soaring effect that resulted from skilful flying in rising hot air. The bubble showed, by its refusal to bob from the lower red section into the upper green half of the tube, that the sailplane was sinking steadily back to earth. Worse, a stiff southerly wind was pushing him slowly back towards the coast, parallel with the Nairobi–Mombasa rail.

None of these handicaps needed to deter him if he could restart the motor. Fate, in the shape of a choked carburettor, decreed that he could not. Short of leaving the cockpit and crawling along the fuselage to attack the engine, Professor Crankshaw had no choice but to waggle his rudder and flap his elevators in the vain search for a thermal. Meanwhile he continued his stately descent.

It was an awkward predicament for a kindly old man who firmly believed that his friend's daughter was in the rapacious grip of an African tribesman. He readjusted his spectacles and studied the terrain wheeling beneath his wings. If only he had shown sense enough to fly straight to Nairobi under power. By now a police search party would have been mobilized. Jackie's father would have been informed. The whole sorry business could have been ended by nightfall, with Tembo Murumbi safely locked away.

He wiggled his feet impatiently, and noticed how sluggishly the rudder responded. He wondered if the tail had been weakened by yesterday's heavy landing. The sailplane creaked in widening circles. Crankshaw watched the birds of prey congregate far to the east, a sure sign of thermals. He was sinking too rapidly now to join them.

His ears caught a discordant sound among the groans and whistles. The sailplane was like a yacht. The wind blew through the rigging, timbers creaked, and the wings were full of the healthy thrumming sounds of a full-bellied sail. Stays slapped against the hull, pulleys squeaked. Crankshaw knew each of these sounds with the familiarity of an orchestra leader, but his baton was the control stick between his knees. Now he waited for a repetition of that one note of discord.

There it was again. The agonized crunch of wood. It came from the tail section. He peered from his podium, seeking the source of disharmony, and crammed another handful of cloves into his mouth when he saw how close he was to the railroad embankment.

The bubble in the tube was far down into the red now. It was far too late to use a parachute, even supposing he had one. He snatched the spectacles from his nose, having no desire to be blinded by broken glass, and at once the scene in front of him was transformed into a pink and not unpleasant blur.

Behind him, a wooden rib snapped. The nose came up with a jerk, and then dipped violently. The rudder pedals banged loosely under his feet. The elevators fell slack.

The sailplane fell in a slow flat turn. One wing-tip brushed a telegraph pole, swinging the machine head-on into the railroad embankment, and Professor Crankshaw discovered once again the miracle of gravity. This, in combination with his own forward velocity, carried him through a long and graceful arc that ended between two parallel lines of steel.

He sat up and his beard parted to eject a black stream of chewed cloves, followed by the single word: 'Blast!'

Two hundred miles up the railroad line, in the capital of Nairobi, were the police reserves and search planes he needed. Less than four hours' train journey away, Jackie's father waited. All Crankshaw lacked was the train to take him there.

At least his spectacles were unbroken. He replaced them, and at once a scene of havoc sprang to view. The sailplane had dissolved into an untidy mess of wood and fabric scattered far along the line. The engine had rolled down the embankment in a tangle of wire.

Crankshaw cursed again. He had cut the telephone line. Worse than that! He examined his watch.

He had missed the Nairobi train by ten minutes.

## 12. The hut of the Masai

The girl sat happily under the prayer tree, using her thumb-nail to crack the fat tick she had prised from her leg. She tried to run her fingers through the hanks of blonde hair hanging in knots from her dusty scalp, and decided that her only hope would be to cut it all off and grow a new lot.

Her face was streaked with ochre dust made muddy with perspiration. The creases in her neck and in the palms of her hands were black. The sharp ridge of her nose and the high curve of her cheekbones were burned and peeling. She had removed her jacket and the dirty yellow sweater underneath was ripped and smudged by the sticky rouge of the Kenya soil.

'I *am* a mess.' She sighed with deep content. Beside her the bushbaby stretched to the full extremity of his long legs as he tapped the bole of the tree. He would tap for several seconds, using the long curved nail of one finger, and then press an ear against the bark, listening.

Jackie watched him, knees pulled up to her chin. Now he had found a hollow part of the tree, and the tapping became more vigorous. He began tearing away the bark. He chattered as he worked, a conversational two-pitch call. He stripped away the bark, layer by layer, until he arrived at a deep cleft. In the bottom was a nest of grubs. The bushbaby gave a triumphant squeal and pushed both arms into the hole, looking back over his shoulder to make sure Jackie had witnessed his cunning. He picked each grub daintily out of its bed, his tiny tongue protruding between parted lips, as excited as an elderly aunt with a forbidden box of chocolates.

Tembo appeared round a shoulder of rock. 'There will be many animals on the hill tonight.' He flung himself down beside her. 'I have looked everywhere and there is no way to leave the hill until the fire burns itself out.'

'That might be sooner than you expect,' said Jackie. 'I heard thunder just now.'

She slapped a mosquito on her cheek. There was a lump on her knee where she had tripped over a log. Her muscles ached. Every bone in her body felt as if it had been separately tapped with a large hammer. Her jodhpurs were singed and still smelled of woodsmoke. There was a welt over one eye where a bug had stabbed her. Her feet felt twice as big as her chukka boots. And yet she was filled with an absurd sense of gaiety and well-being.

She looked at the man stretched full length on the ground beside her and she watched Kamau grubbing around the tree and she thought she would never again be in such good company. She rolled on her back and folded her hands under her head and thought how wonderful it was to be really and truly *dirty*; to feel the soil plastered over your hands and face, your clothes stiff with it, your hair gloriously tangled in it.

Dirt. Good honest dirt.

She sat up. 'Is there no trace of the flying machine?'

The man said gloomily: 'None.'

She looked down the hill. It was strange how unafraid she felt. She had run through the flames. She had faced a great many dangers. And now, she thought, nothing could possibly hurt her or frighten her again.

And then she remembered the bushbaby. Nothing could hurt her directly. But her stomach gave a lurch when she thought of Kamau and the moment when she would have to give him back to his own family.

'Is there anyone on the hill beside ourselves?' she asked abruptly.

'Only an old woman.' Tembo scrambled back to his feet. 'An old woman who looks after her man's shamba.'

He began to take an inventory of their gear. 'It is well that we still have the rifle. I saw lion.' He pointed with his chin to a slope of flattened and tawny grass.

He had come across the male lion in the grass, lying like a huge dog, guarding a pride that included four cubs. They had forced the man to stay upwind, ignoring him, the lionesses on their bellies crouching and waiting to see what the fire drove from the forest.

He decided to keep these details to himself. 'The old woman will let us shelter in her hut. It will be better for us, and she is frightened.'

The prospect of having to cheer up an abandoned woman was not exhilarating. 'Can we not stay here, under the mugomo? If the fig is lucky it will bring protection.'

Tembo grinned. 'No. You do not think the tree is lucky. You are too lazy to move. Come, before it is dark. The shamba is not very comfortable, but it is strong and safe.'

The little farm was enclosed within a *boma*, a wall of euphorbia thorn. Jackie followed the man to where it lay concealed in a dip. Here the smoke from the forest lingered like fog, cutting out what small daylight remained.

'Must we stop here?' She frowned, not liking the atmosphere of neglect.

'Yes,' said Tembo apologetically but firmly. 'There will be much fighting among the animals tonight.'

As if to underline his words, the snarling grunt of a baboon echoed in the luga that divided their side of the hill. A kingfisher screamed. The curtain of smoke was rolling back across the hill-top again, carried by a fresh wind that brushed the stiff torn leaves of a banana tree. It leaned over the poorly thatched roof of the solitary hut inside the boma. The surrounding earth was beaten into hard cracked clay and littered with discarded utensils.

'Look!' Jackie clapped her hands. 'A Somali canary.' She ran to a pile of mealie-cobs where a small donkey cowered with fear-widened eyes. The animal backed away, the big dun-coloured ears twitching.

'There must be Masai here.' The girl held out a coaxing hand, her legs planted wide, body bent at the waist where her yellow shirt was tucked inside the torn trousers. 'Come on, old fellow.' She clucked her tongue. 'I haven't seen a Somali canary since we camped on Kilimanjaro.'

The 'canary' was a donkey no bigger than a large dog, with tiny feet and a stripe running down the back and across the shoulders. The Masai used such animals as beasts of burden.

Jackie looked in puzzlement around the boma. It was unlike the nomadic Masai to build a permanent structure. The hut, or *manyatta*, ran true to form, however. It was built like an American Indian wickiup, of flexible branches, with a covering of mud and cow-dung, and animal skins for extra warmth. When a Masai moved house he had only to pick up the framework, skins and all, and collapse everything on the back of his donkey.

She decided that some wandering Masai family had stumbled upon this abandoned farm, perhaps owned by another tribe, and retreated behind the boma walls on seeing the prairie fire.

'Where is the woman you speak of?' she asked Tembo.

He shrugged. 'She was here. *Sobaj!*' He called the Masai word of greeting. There was no reply.

'Perhaps we frightened her away.'

'No matter.' The man ducked his head inside the man-yatta, allowing time for his eyes to adjust to the darkness. 'The hut is empty. You sleep here and I will keep guard.'

'We should offer to pay rent,' the girl joked, and stopped. 'If the woman is alone she might want food. In any case we cannot take over the hut without her permission.'

Her eyes strayed to the gun. 'There are many animals on the hill. We have not ourselves eaten fresh meat . . .'

Tembo stroked the butt of the gun. 'You think I should hunt? It is a long time since I used a gun.'

'You could kill something for the woman's cooking pot.' She knew how reluctant he was to hunt without a purpose. He had taken Crankshaw's gun in self-defence. She added: 'Now that we have the gun, it would be foolish to go without the fresh meat we have both been missing.'

'If you think so, baba.' His sense of duty battled with his enjoyment of the hunt. Small wrinkles of pleasure formed around the corners of his mouth. 'It would be good to offer something in return for the use of the hut.'

Already he was slipping his hunting knife into the brass-buckled belt. He picked up the rifle and felt the weight of it, running the palm of one hand over its smooth butt, smiling to himself.

'We must keep near the boma.' He turned and moved away, balanced lightly on the balls of his feet.

The hill was one of those knobby upthrusting chunks of granite that dot the African plains: an enormous flat-topped hill with a thin layer of soil and a great many rocky outcrops of peculiar purplish hue. It rose eight or nine hundred feet above the burning plain, and its isolation had attracted the frightened herds of wild game.

From the knoll outside the shamba Jackie could see an astonishing variety of animals. On a steep bank opposite, baby Thomson's gazelles – known as Tommies – sprang together on stiff legs as if pulled by a string. Behind them came the larger Grant's gazelles, white and top-heavy with big horns. Deeper in the gully, a herd of plump-bellied zebras raced in a dust-laden circle.

Two female ostriches ran through the plumed grass beyond the fig prayer-tree, with high kicking steps, feathers tucked up like skirts, heads back and swaying on stalky necks. They saw Jackie and veered away, grey feathers drooping in their wake.

The girl stood entranced. She loved these moments late in the day when a strange kind of tameness came over so many animals. This evening the herds were more nervous, forced by the fire to abandon their normal grazing. She spotted a black rhino, far away near a group of fever trees, weaving his armoured head in a short-sighted attempt to inspect this island in the sea of flame. There were tick-birds on the rhino and one stood upended to pick inside an ear. Closer to hand, a family of warthogs trotted secretively through the grass, antenna tails waving. One of the warthogs stopped suddenly and manoeuvred to face Jackie, his long sloping face hideous with black lumps and yellow tusks. She turned, looking for Tembo. The warthog squinted up at her through tiny malevolent eyes, then scrambled backwards into his hole. He reminded her of a deformed dwarf. She shuddered and clutched at the African's arm, overwhelmed by the ugliness of the small beast for whom she had a paradoxical affection. She had always felt this softness for warthogs, even when they repelled her the most.

Tembo gently freed his arm. Another small herd of impala had broken cover directly ahead. They were the colour of golden sovereigns and they seemed to drift through veils of firesmoke. The African watched them disappear ghostlike into the fever trees and he began to lope in pursuit.

The girl had never understood the mystery of tracking, despite Tembo's recent attempts to teach her. He tracked with his head erect, eyes level 'to bring the ground up', as he called it. It was said of Tembo that he could stalk the mere whisper of a spoor. 'It is simple,' he had once told her. 'You must imagine you are the animal, and you must follow the direction you would take if you were the animal.'

She had never mastered it, though she tried hard enough. Now she followed him obediently, stepping lightly in his footsteps.

Again the impala crossed their path. Hardly breaking stride, Tembo brought the gun swiftly and easily to his shoulder. She heard the sharp explosion and heard the *gerplunk* of metal shattering bone. She winced, not because of these deadly sounds but at the sight of the male leader jerking back his head in mid-flight. The rest of the herd scattered in graceful ballerina leaps. The ram broke into a death gallop, heart already smashed by the tiny unseen bullet.

Tembo paused to re-load. The girl watched his actions with frank admiration. A thick coil of smoke twisted up the gully, and above it she saw the assembling birds of prey and the scavengers. They circled lazily. They could afford to wait. Once an impatient serpent-eagle spiralled down to scoop up an escaping snake, and soared away with the victim squirming rope-like between his extended claws.

A small female impala exploded out of the long grass immediately in front. This time when Tembo fired the animal fell in its tracks.

He ran to the writhing body, seized the impala by the ears, and cut the vertebra with a swift stab of his hunting knife into the base of the brain. He wiped his hands on the warm throbbing carcass, replaced the knife, and stood up to greet the girl.

'We shall have to track the other one.' He shouldered the rifle again. 'It is *kufa*, dead. But it may have covered much ground in the death run.'

They picked up a trail of pink frothing lung blood. Jackie was self-controlled after her first nausea at the spectacle of the African killing the wounded female. All her life had been spent close to the daily fact of death. She could almost treat it with African indifference; almost, but not quite. And yet she shared Tembo's excitement. When he hunted it was as if he donned his tribal war-bonnet; his mind and body were fused into a single instrument and it was dangerous to get in his way. She had seen this remarkable transformation before; the concentration of energy, directed to a single purpose; the hand quivering, the nostrils distended.

There were rosy splashes of yellowish stomach blood now and Tembo gave a shout of triumph as he fell upon the dead male where it had collapsed in a small thicket.

They brought the two trophies back to the boma, the girl pleased by the twisting pointed horns of the young proud male. She squatted in silence while Tembo skinned them. She was absorbed in watching his skill with a knife. There were few things in life so splendid as this awareness of self-sufficiency. To go forth to kill for the pot; to know that you could survive in this wilderness; to feel truly independent of anyone. She sighed, deeply satisfied.

They had a fire lit before Jackie noticed the disappearance of the donkey. 'First the old woman – and I never saw her. Now the donkey gone. It seems very strange.'

Tembo straightened up. The small flames from the cooking fire were reflected in his eyes, still red-rimmed from smoke, or from the hut.

'The donkey – gone?' He had been so intent on cutting the meat into long strips, preparing the other small details of their first good meal, that his attention had strayed. He stepped back from the circle of firelight. With darkness had come the familiar cosy shrinking of their world, now contained within the four walls of the boma. There was an eerie red glow in the sky, and the night was full of sound, of crackling timber and muffled animal cries.

The man took up his panga and stood where the wall of euphorbia ended. 'Yes, it is strange. First the old woman and then the donkey.'

'Did you speak to the woman?'

'I spoke a few words. I said a white girl was coming for shelter. That I was her protector.'

'Perhaps she heard of the police search and ran in fear?'

'Then who has taken the donkey?'

'Perhaps the donkey ran off by itself?'

She reached for the bushbaby's basket. She had tried to make Kamau sleep, but the lid was jogging up and down. 'Don't *you* run away, *toto*.' She lifted him out, and saw his nose wrinkle at the unaccustomed smell of roasting meat.

The bushbaby seemed restless. Usually, when she talked to him, he would curl up into a contented ball, only his ears and white-striped snout showing. Now he was like a nervous cat sensing a storm. He kept rubbing his hands, his ears twitched, and his tail coiled and uncoiled.

'I think he hears thunder,' said Jackie.

'It is possible. Animals know when bad weather is approaching.'

'Do you remember . . . ?'

'What should I remember?' he asked, gladly taking up the ritual.

'– how we canoed on Lake Baringo – '

'– and the crocodiles were nervous and wouldn't let us get near them – '

'– and you jumped on an island.'

'Only the island was made of floating papyrus and I nearly fell through it.'

'And then a crocodile got between you and the canoe and my brother swam out and everyone said he'd be eaten.'

'But he wasn't. The crocodiles behaved in a very strange way that day. And later there was a bad storm.'

'My brother said crocodiles get pernickety before a storm.' She stopped. 'I miss my family.'

'We all have families whom we miss,' said the man, falling quickly into the new mood of gravity.

'I worry about mine,' she said frankly. 'I keep thinking of all the things that might happen to them. And now this big fire . . .'

Her mood of elation had vanished. If she had been older she would have understood that such an exalted mood followed naturally upon their recent escape from the fire.

And it was just as natural that she should later feel a sudden let-down.

She studied the red glare in the sky. 'Tembo, is everything going wrong?' Her voice trembled. 'It was going to be so easy, walking upcountry. Why is it all becoming so difficult now?'

The man crouched over the cooking fire. 'Things happen to us, and we cannot always understand their purpose. And yet afterwards we may be thankful for those obstacles . . .'

He picked up a stick and drew pictures in the earth. 'A man lived in this house, in a boma, with a pointed bit of garden in the front. There was a pond nearby, with fish. The man got out of bed one night to find the cause of a terrible noise. He took the road to the pond, but he was very confused and at first he ran south. He very soon fell over a stone in the road and then he fell into a ditch and got up. He fell into another ditch and got out of that one, and went in and out of a third ditch. He saw he was going in the wrong direction and he ran back to the north. From here the noise seemed again to be from the south and again he ran back. And all the obstacles got in the way again; the stone, and the three ditches, and he was very discouraged. It seemed that everything conspired to divert him from his action. But he did finally see that the noise was coming from the end of the pond. He rushed there and saw a big leak in the dam. The water was rushing out with all the fishes in it. He stopped the leak in the pond and then he went to bed, very tired. And in the morning he woke up and looked from his window and saw – a stork!'

Tembo finished drawing in the dirt with a flourish.

'What a spiffing story!' said Jackie. 'If the man had given up he would never have finished the stork. And he never knew until the very end that it would all make sense!'

Tembo stroked the tuft of black whiskers on his chin. 'It is an old story told by the fathers of the village where I come from. It is good to remember when you are lost and things seem to go wrong.' He thrust the stick into the blaze and began to sharpen a wooden spit. 'Time to eat, baba. You will sleep soundly tonight.'

Incredibly she did. The last thing she remembered was the sly knowing cough of a passing hyaena.

She awoke reluctantly. Something had disturbed her. She had the vague memory of a distant explosion. She drifted between sleep and wakefulness, glorying in the luxury of a roof again, and then she lay for a long time staring up into the thatch full of rustling fronds.

She was lying on a bed made of sticks lashed together with sisal rope, with posts high enough for goats to sleep underneath. In the middle of the hut were stones for a fire, but she could see no place in the conical roof for the smoke to escape. Small shafts of light pierced the thatch. Lizards clung to the cross-beams, spreadeagled there, scaly fingers twitching nervously.

She sat up, aware now of the significance of the sunlight. The fire-smoke must have cleared. She slid into her jodhpurs and boots and was pulling her jacket over her shoulders when somebody moved outside.

She walked to the doorway, screwing her eyes against the fierceness of the day. A man, much taller than Tembo, stood on the threshold. She sucked in her breath and retreated into the shadows of the hut, stifling a scream.

She saw a Masai *moran*, a warrior, standing stork-like on one leg; grease-smeared and leaning on his shining metal spear. His other leg was hooked behind the unbent knee. The sun glittered on the long deep-grooved blade of his spear. He must have been at least six feet tall.

He watched her through narrow unwinking eyes, a red cloak thrown over one shoulder with all the careless dignity of a Roman bodyguard.

'What do you want?' The girl spoke rapidly in Swahili. She wondered wildly where Tembo had gone, and as she walked backwards she felt behind her for the panga he had left for her protection.

The moran's eyes flickered briefly in the direction of the banana tree where Tembo had kept guard. There were bright splashes of blood on the end of his spear. Jackie found herself gazing at them in horror.

Still the man remained motionless. Under the cloak his naked body had a bronze glow, as if he were a statue cast in metal. This impression was sharpened by the sculpted appearance of his shoulder-length hair which had been plaited and plastered with red clay until it resembled the fleece of a long-haired sheep. The top of the hair was braided and ribbed; a thick forelock hung over his forehead, wired at the end. His face was painted with white lime and grease, and with blodges of red clay. His ears were stretched by copper wire in circlets as big as plates, and by plugs of polished bone. There were blue tattoo welts over his bared shoulder and chest. Around his neck were strings of blue and red beads. He wore bracelets of wire around wrists and ankles so that he seemed to glitter with metal. His thin haughty features completed the effect of savage grandeur.

Jackie knew the meaning of the spear. It was a symbol of rank, given after hand-to-hand combat with a full-grown lion.

Slowly the warrior unhooked his leg.

The girl's groping hand found the panga. She swung it back over her shoulder, and this time she screamed.

### 13. 'Shoot on sight'

The Masai tilted his body slightly forward, raised his free arm, and caught the girl by the wrist as she swung wildly at him with the panga. She struggled to escape, twisting and kicking in a frenzy of fright and fury. He held her away and smiled faintly.

'There is nothing to fear, toto.' He spoke quietly in Swahili, shifting his grip on the spear, grasping it lower down where the shaft widened. Jackie stopped struggling, but her eyes would not leave the blood still wet on the blade of the spear.

'Where is Tembo?'

'Your man is over there.' The moran nodded to his right.

'He disturbed a leopard, a big one. The *chui* was after my cattle.'

For the first time Jackie was aware of the *clank-tonk* of wooden cowbells. Through the gap in the thorn hedge, near the main entrance to the boma, moved the Masai's ribbed cattle. An old woman who stood over them with a switch gave the girl a resentful glance. The cattle were old and so skinny that their red and piebald hides were like dirty sheets thrown over racks. They had Brahmin humps that wobbled to one side and their horns had been broken in odd ways to identify the owner.

'The leopard was after my cattle and your man tried to shoot the leopard,' the Masai was saying.

'Tried to shoot . . .? He's hurt?'

'The leopard is hurt.' The Masai shifted balance to his other leg. 'Also your man has twisted his foot. He is waiting with the gun for the leopard.'

'Where?' The girl wriggled free.

'You are not to go there.' The Masai repeated Tembo's message but his manner was indifferent. Already he was watching the last of his cattle enter the boma.

'But tell me where?'

The Masai lifted his spear and jabbed his arm casually. 'In the defile. In the trees.'

The girl hesitated. She guessed what had happened. There had been a disturbance. Tembo had gone to investigate and stumbled upon the Masai driving their cattle to the boma, unable to graze them on the fire-razed plains. He would have shot and injured the leopard. There had been a chase, perhaps, and Tembo had fallen, twisting his ankle.

'An injured leopard is dangerous,' said the girl, half appealingly.

'Yes, toto. That is why you must remain here.'

'Will you help kill the leopard?'

'Your man is doing that. I have work here.'

She turned her back, meaning to enter the hut, surprised that a Masai moran would show such indifference. She had

heard that many of the Masai had become small farmers and
had lost their warrior instincts but still she was puzzled.

She felt the Masai's hand on her shoulder. 'Your man is
waiting to kill the leopard alone.'

She pulled away and continued into the hut. She found
the bushbaby curled up in his basket and coaxed him out.

'You are not a true moran,' she said, just loud enough.

The Masai remained outside the hut, silently counting his
cattle.

'You are frightened of the chui!' She raised her voice. The
Masai shifted his spear to the other hand and adjusted a
piece of thatching on the roof.

'No true moran would leave a Kamba to fight a leopard
alone.' The girl thrust the bushbaby into her jacket pocket
and emerged again from the hut. The Masai was watching
her through slit eyes. Behind him the old woman rummaged
in the squalor of the maize-cobs.

'You think I am a coward?' He gave an angry toss of the
arrogant head.

'I do not think you are a coward,' said Jackie, working her
way past him. 'I think you are a tiller of soil.' She used an
expression offensive to traditional warriors who looked
down in contempt upon the peasantry. 'You think more of
your cows. You forget that all this was once Masailand.' She
swept an arm in a vague circle. 'My grandfather remembers,
though. My grandfather remembers that the Masai were the
greatest warriors from Kilimanjaro to the coast and
throughout the Great Rift. When my grandfather was a
young man –'

'May every devil take your grandfather,' said the Masai,
stung at last. He thumped the hard-pressed earth with the
end of his spear. 'If your man wants to kill the leopard let
him kill it. He does not want me.'

'First show me where the leopard is.'

The Masai shrugged. 'I am not afraid of a leopard. But
my cattle – I do not like to leave the cattle. It took the old
woman and myself all yesterday to catch them and bring

them here because of the fire. Now at any moment the rains
will begin.'

'Your cattle are safe here in the boma. You speak like an
old man who is afraid of everything.'

'This is not my shamba. The old woman found it before
the fire began. The cattle will stray . . .'

Jackie began to lose patience. 'We will talk like this for
ever. I am going to find the leopard.'

'And I will come but only to show you the way. I have
man's work to do. Man's work is not killing sick animals.
Come, toto.'

He called something to the old woman as they left the
circle of thorn and euphorbia. The girl saw how the fires had
dampened during the night, leaving the hill untouched. The
hill was so green, in contrast with the black smouldering
plains and burning skeletons of trees in the surrounding
woods, that she realized for the first time the meaning of the
phrase 'green hills of Africa'.

She realized too that the hill looked even more green and
pleasant because it outshone the sky. There were still
patches of blue, and the smoke had mostly gone, but now
there were big black clouds piling up to the north-east. Some
of the clouds had drifted southward across the face of the
sun, whose beams fell in perpendicular columns upon the
marble mountains.

She scrambled after the Masai, who was too proud to look
back or help her, moving down into the gentle ravine with
its copse of yellow mottled fever trees and thick underbrush.
The mixed light of a rain-threatening day cast upon the
ravine a grey and sinister gloom. Before she plunged into it
Jackie took a last swift look around her. The scene was to
imprint itself upon her memory.

Thin spirals of smoke rose like signals across the plain. A
pair of fish-eagles, far from their usual haunts, glided up and
down the escarpment on bronze wings, their bodies convulsed at intervals to bring forth the shrill and lonely whistle
that always made the girl's spine tingle. Beneath them the

air was acrid with the stench of smouldering wet wood. A dove cried *oohoo-oohoo-oohoo-o!* Far away to the north, lightning flashed inside an enormous thunderhead whose anvil-shaped crown reached far out over the plains. The lightning revealed an infinite variety of cloud formations within the purple plumpness of the thunderhead, each flash affording a glimpse of smaller clouds that waited to dump millions of gallons of rain upon the burnt plain.

'The leopard is down there,' said the Masai, without looking at the girl. He rested his spear beside a giant pug-mark. She could imagine the pads, big as plates and rough as sharkskin.

'I tried to kill it first with the spear,' said the Masai, unbending a little. The blood was dry now on the blade. 'Then your man shot.' He twirled the spear in the diffused sunlight. 'He shot the leopard in the white belly-fur.'

'Where is he?'

'Also down there. The leopard is lying in wait somewhere, and your man lies waiting too. They are both dangerous. The leopard will kill because it is hurt and will never run away. And your man will kill the leopard if he can.'

Jackie tried to see into the depths of the ravine. The flat-topped trees made a roof of mildewed yellow, hung with thick lianas. A few more steps and they would be swallowed up by the crouching forest.

'Wait here,' the Masai said. 'I will help your man.'

'I will come too.'

He scarcely heard the words. He knew roughly where Tembo had vanished in limping pursuit of the leopard. The girl's taunts still rang in his ears, but only as echoes of his own conscience. His initiation as a warrior had been a violent one and he had been in danger of forgetting what it had cost him, and what it should mean to him now.

A narrow game trail slid like a snake's hole through the tight-packed brush. Crouching, his spear horizontal, the Masai disappeared into the tunnel of leaves and thorned branches. The girl followed, reassured by the chattering of monkeys and the shrill calls of the wood-birds. Within the tunnel was a powerful stench of baboons and wet leaves. Almost at once she lost sight of the Masai.

She waited, wondering if she should call for Tembo. He might be lying hurt, and would be glad to see her. But if he were stalking the wounded leopard he would be angered to find her here. She decided to continue into the copse.

She remembered all the warnings since infancy. Nothing was more dangerous than a wounded leopard. Yet she kept going, torn by the thorn underbrush, bitten by tiny ants, and forced at times to crawl on hands and knees. The clump of trees was squeezed into the ravine a few hundred feet above the plain, and it was untouched by fire. The trees grew down to the edge of a fast gurgling stream where the trout-brown waters rushed over the white ghost-like boulders. The stream gushed out of some hidden spring and it was her first sight of running water since they had abandoned the canoe. She came to the stream without warning, almost toppling through the thick underbrush where it hung above the foaming waters.

There was a sudden heart-stopping explosion of noise downstream. She fell quickly to her knees, head twisted to watch the tops of the trees sway under the swift movement of bodies. A troop of monkeys flew wraith-like through the uppermost branches. Baboons coughed like bronchial old men. Birds of dazzling plumage skated along the stream, bursting out of the foliage with sharp twitterings. Monkeys screamed as if their tails were being pulled. The trees were filled with the alarm signals of birds and chipmunks, of tiny greenish monkeys and flying squirrels. A baboon screamed, not with alarm this time but in bubbling pain.

Then the girl felt fear lay an icy paw between her shoulder blades. She twined her fingers in the bushbaby's tail, where it lay in her pocket, and she felt the tiny body tremble in sleep.

Behind and above her the sound of the leopard rasped through the dense foliage: *hurrh-hurrh-hurrh*, as clear and

nerve-racking as the grate of a wooden rattle. Again the
trees shook with tiny detonations of fleeing birds and chattering monkeys. The leopard seemed to leave a trail of fire-
crackers as he moved, making the bush loud with the
explosion of small creatures.

She remembered that injured leopards often turned man-
eater. 'They are clever and full of venom when hurt,' a Turkana game scout had once told her. 'They go in a big circle
and creep up behind you, to spring on your back after you
pass . . .'

She had wondered how this trick was accomplished when
it was well known that a leopard could be extremely noisy.
Now she understood. The leopard's dry rattle quickened
until it sounded like a rapidly beaten kettledrum. The noise
was all around her. There was no way of telling where the
leopard lay hidden. The Masai had said the beast was *kali*,
ill-tempered and savage with pain. She was surrounded by
the noisy evidence of the leopard's rage.

There was no other sound but his harsh respiration, and
she realized now the purpose of the animal's echoing grunts.
They were intended to confuse and terrify.

Then she saw the leopard. He materialized in the fork of
the tree directly across the stream, a few feet away. She was
staring at nothing but blurred foliage and then he appeared,
a veil of yellow smoke caught in the branches. He lay there
along a branch, a wisp of yellow smoke mottled and spat-

tered with black outline-breaking spots, like a figure hidden
in a child's puzzle picture.

She saw the tail flick, the black-tipped tail that hung
straight from the branch and almost dipped into the rushing
waters of the stream. She saw the ears flattened against the
snake-like head, and flies that danced around the ears. She
saw the head turn, the mottled head that swivelled between
hunched shoulders. She saw the eyes.

The eyes were liquid gold and they filled her world. They
were calm eyes that said as clearly as if the leopard had
spoken to her: 'You're mine, mine, mine.'

The leopard vanished. It went like a drifting cloud of
yellow butterflies that dissolves and disappears. Not a leaf
stirred with its passing. But the girl made no move. She lay
as if transfixed by the memory of the golden eyes with their
savage message, underlined now by the leopard's fading
grunts: 'You're mine, mine, mine.'

Now she had seen the leopard, the girl was filled with a
strange exultation. She had looked deeply into those splendid eyes and seen beauty and freedom and fearlessness. She
had known these things deep inside herself, without feeling
the necessity of words.

Reason alone told her not to stir. Reason said the leopard
had taken her scent, and would lure her into the open.

She turned, making a nest for herself in the slippery leaves
beneath her warm body. She turned soundlessly, as light-
footed and furtive as a field-mouse.

Then to her quick dismay the bushbaby began to chitter.
He had woken instinctively in the presence of the leopard.
Feeling the girl's hand around him, he had started to talk.
When she tightened her grip he became angry and began to
sound his shrill alarm note. She put the palm of her hand
across his mouth, and he dug his sharp little teeth into the
flesh. She withdrew her hand and tried stroking his ears. His
cries increased.

Thoroughly alarmed, she took her hand away altogether
and crouched forward on hands and knees. She had heard

somewhere that leopards disliked water. The stream that flowed beneath her was not wide, nor was it deep but the current ran fast. She put out one hand and grasped a piece of matted undergrowth. Kamau seemed now to be making enough noise to provoke a dozen hungry beasts. He chose this moment to slip out of her pocket and to run up her arm into her hair.

Her hands flew up to catch him and she felt herself sliding into the stream. She fell sideways, striking a boulder, and the pressure of water tugged her downstream. Her hands clutching Kamau, her feet kicking to get a foothold on the rocky bottom of the stream, she was carried several feet before she stumbled against a leaf-plastered rock.

She eased herself upright against the slimy stone and listened to the expanding circle of explosions set off by her mishap. The copse seemed to be one large whispering gallery. It was buried in appalling darkness now, and she saw enormous raindrops dimple the surface of the stream.

Again she heared the rasping asthmatic cough of the leopard. She faced the weather-pressed brown bank of damp vegetation only inches away and smelled the maggoty-meat breath of her tormentor.

The leopard erupted from the bushes above her head, fangs smeared in filthy green slime, claws spread, forelegs stiff as spears. He boiled up out of the mess of leaves and twigs like a gigantic bat, a hundred and fifty pounds of bone and hard muscle, soaring against the black sky with blood dripping from the gleaming white belly.

The roar in his red throat ended in a gurgle. The girl heard the sound of metal dividing flesh from bone. At the same moment a gun blasted the air. The leopard faltered, and the hind legs folded lazily away from the hidden branch that provided a springboard. Jackie looking upward saw him spread-eagled against the weeping sky for long seconds. Then he fell, loosely, like a sack of old bones, splash into the stream.

The thick-muscled hide went limp. The claws, ingrained

with poisonous filth, relaxed. The needle teeth vanished under the rubbery lips, and the long whiskers drooped. The eyes gazed up into the girl's, stricken.

There was a spear driven through the apex of the triangle formed between the flattened ears and the nape of the neck, and the lovely head gaped wide where the rifle had slashed an oblique hole.

She looked down on this creature so abruptly lifeless in the gushing stream. It was not the release from tension that made her cry, nor yet the memory of those bared teeth and scything claws. As she stood in the cold black waters she cried because the leopard lay dead at her feet. The golden leopard, rolling helplessly behind the endless streamers of red blood that danced gaily upon the ripple of dimpled black waters.

The Masai got to her first. He came leaping and laughing down the stream, exultant at the sight of the dead leopard, admiring the girl now for having faced the charge. He lifted her from the water with a sweep of one arm, dumped her on the bank, and returned to retrieve the spear.

'Tembo. Where is Tembo?'

'I am here, baba.' The weak voice alarmed her. She searched the brush.

'Are you hurt, *mzee*?' She used the honorific term of endearment.

'It is nothing. I have twisted my leg.'

He was lying in a tangle of bush and lianas some distance upstream. She saw only the barrel of the gun protruding from the bank, and she waded along the bank, getting her balance from overhanging creepers, one hand still shielding the bushbaby in her pocket.

Tembo was stretched full length on one side of the bank, buried in damp leaves, his grizzled head a few inches from the water.

'I am sorry to be like this, little one.' He pulled himself up on dirt-grimed elbows. 'I will need help to get back to the

shamba.' He jack-knifed his body, and swung his legs out
into the stream.

'What happened?' The girl bent over him, examining the
torn flesh and the purple puffy swelling at his right ankle.

'During the night . . .' He paused. 'You remember how the
donkey was in the boma, and then suddenly it had gone?
After you went to sleep I heard it crying in the bush. It was
frightened and escaped. A donkey is a valuable animal. We
were sleeping in the Masai's shamba and we were responsible for the donkey. So I went to look for it. The leopard
must have taken the donkey. I heard it cry out, and the
leopard grunt.'

He grimaced as Jackie tried to wipe away the dirt around
the tear in his leg. She saw that the ankle was badly
sprained.

'Then the old woman and the moran appeared. They had
been out collecting their cattle, and I told them what happened. They were not pleased. Perhaps they thought it was
our fault for losing the donkey. Anyway, we went to hunt
the leopard. I was alone when I slipped and fell. So I waited,
knowing the leopard must pass this way.' He shook his head
in remorse. 'It was very wrong of me, baba, leaving you like
this.'

'What else could you do?' Jackie understood too well the
quandary Tembo had been placed in. He lived, after all, in
two worlds. In the one she occupied there were certain rules,
but in his own tribal world there were also obligations that
must be met. In tribal law she and Tembo were trespassing.
It was natural that he should want to mollify the occupiers
of the shamba.

The Masai started to speak rapidly in Swahili.

'He wants the leopard's pelt,' Tembo explained.

Jackie thought quickly. 'He can have it. But first he must
help us return to the shamba.'

Tembo smiled. 'Do not worry. He will do whatever he can
for us. He is pleased about the leopard and you have become
somebody in his eyes for not running away when the leopard

attacked.' He paused and then coughed. 'He also says you are very foolish to have come unarmed into the copse.'

The Masai grinned at the girl's expression, and now she grinned back, glad to know they had won an ally.

The trio returned through the copse, Tembo leaning on the moran's arm. The girl had tied her wetted scarf around the swollen ankle. She was dismayed to see how badly he limped. It meant further delay. She had hoped they might leave the hill by noon.

'I think you will have to rest the ankle for some time,' she said when they reached the boma.

Tembo tested the injured foot on the hard ground. He winced, and said apologetically: 'Perhaps if I lie down for an hour . . .'

'No, it will take longer.' She spoke firmly, disguising her anxiety. He knew what was on her mind.

'We must get to the railroad before the rain.' He was leaning against the thorn hedge, and his eyes wandered to the plains below.

She followed his gaze. At this distance the railroad was visible as a winding embankment. While the fires still raged it had been hidden by smoke. She tried to measure how far they were from the nearest section of the track, where it crossed a small bridge over a dried creek.

'We should stay here until tomorrow.' The girl moved in the direction of the hut. 'It will take no more than a few hours to reach the railroad, but it would be foolishness to walk on a sprained ankle.'

'Foolishness?' The Kamba stroked his chin. 'And who was foolish just now, entering the ravine to find me, risking the leopard?' He put his foot down again, and managed this time to hobble behind her.

The Masai's woman had started a fire. There was an appetizing smell of burnt cobs. Her mood had softened. She helped Jackie to rebandage Tembo's ankle, and made him rest on a pile of branches.

The old woman was surprised when Jackie explained the reason for their journey. 'For the sake of a galago?' Her wrinkled face puckered into a toothless grin. 'Truly, my son is right. You are crazy, toto.'

There was a touch of the old impatience in the way Jackie tossed her head. She retreated to the hut and brought out the transistor. She switched on the KBS breakfast programme and rejoiced to see wonder reflected in the faces of the old woman and her son. The radio seemed to them a luxury of great extravagance. Almost at once she felt ashamed of this childish display.

When she opened their last tin of corned beef and offered some to the Masai, they showed no enthusiasm, regarding it as a cold colourless substance. Instead, the moran strode to where the cattle huddled together and selected a brindled bull.

He led the bull to his mother who seized it by the head which she twisted over her skinny thigh. Then she took a firm grip of the bull's neck, so that the jugular vein swelled like damp rope.

The moran picked up a bow and arrow. The head of the arrow was encircled by a block of wood about half an inch from the point. The moran fired the arrow into the throbbing blue vein. The bull stirred, one moist eye bulging upwards. The moran yanked the arrow free and blood spurted from the wound. His mother scooped up a calabash with one hand and caught the jets of blood. When the calabash was full she closed the wound with finger and thumb while her son carried the vessel away. The flow of blood stopped, the bull strolled off as if nothing had happened, and the old woman moved on to jerk milk from one of the cows. Later they would curdle the blood and milk with a little urine, producing a kind of cheese.

In this fashion the Masai lived. Their stomachs were small hard rocks that required little sustenance. Their larder walked on four legs and provided all their needs. They had achieved a communion with the wilderness around them, a

simple link between man and beast, the nature of which the
girl had briefly glimpsed when she looked into the eyes of
the leopard.

But she realized quickly enough how irretrievably she was
part of a different and more complicated world. The radio
was crackling and squawking still, and at first she thought
the batteries were flat. The nine o'clock bulletin of news was
interrupted by screeches that coincided, however, with the
lightning that flashed over Kilimanjaro.

'Instead of our regular transmission of the BBC programme *The World Today* following the news, there will be
a recorded talk . . .' The radio shrieked again, and she waited
patiently.

'. . . and here is Professor – *sqquawwk* – of Makerere Col-
lege to report on parallel conditions.'

A new voice said: 'Weather conditions throughout Kenya
in 1961 were the most severe and extreme to have occurred
since Europeans first set foot in this part of Africa . . . never
since records began had drought and prolonged intensive
rain combined in one year to create such widespread havoc
. . . pattern of events this year has been surprisingly similar . . .'

Jackie settled back on her heels, clasping her ankles, her
head on one side so that the yellow hair fell over one shoulder.

'So far, this year, famine has again engaged all the resources of the armed forces . . . food distributed over wide
area . . . Now comes news of torrential rain on the eastern
slopes of Mount Kenya, and a forecast of general storm conditions . . . It will be recalled that the 1961 floods, because
they struck at a time when the countryside was suffering the
terrible effects of drought, resulted in many communities
being isolated. Bridges were washed away, trains derailed.
As a precaution against a repetition of the tragedy, a Flood
Operational Headquarters is being established . . .'

A fresh fall of light rain crept over the plateau like a grey
veil.

Tembo said quietly: 'What does this mean?' He had caught the urgency in the speaker's voice, but his English was inadequate for the gunfire rattle of words.

'It means,' said Jackie slowly, 'we should get off this hill before the rains.'

Another radio voice was speaking in Swahili. The girl saw the Masai woman look up, her attention suddenly caught. There was something ominous and strange about the way the old woman remained quite still, holding the same bent position, head twisted on scrawny neck, listening to the radio and watching Tembo.

The announcer said: 'The police statement made it clear that no further doubts exist about the identity of the kidnapper. The name was released a few minutes ago. I repeat: the name of the wanted man is Tembo Murumbi . . .'

Tembo pulled himself upright on the pile of branches.

'. . . and a warrant for his arrest has been issued. Police have been authorized if necessary to shoot on sight. Fears for the girl's safety deepened this morning with the arrival in Nairobi of Dr Angus Crankshaw, the well-know archaeologist – '

Jackie turned the radio off with a snap. 'Quick! The moran!'

Too late, she saw the tall Masai vanish through the hedge.

'Never mind.' Tembo rolled on his elbow, smiling weakly. 'If *he* does not tell the police, others will see us.' He fumbled among his possessions and withdrew the purse that he always carried. He emptied the silver Maria Thérèsa dollars upon the ground, picked one up and tossed it to the old woman.

'Tell your son there is another if he comes back.'

The old woman picked up the coin and gave them a toothless smile. She rubbed the coin slowly between her palms. '*Asante sane.* Thank you.' She turned and hobbled away.

'Now we must wait,' said Tembo.

'Wait?' The girl knelt beside his injured ankle. 'This is the time to run.'

'With a leg like a hamstrung cow! I would be caught in the middle of the plains by the rains, like a rat in a sewer. No, we must learn patience, as we have learned so many things on this journey.'

She tossed her head. 'What have we learned?' Her voice was jeering. 'Not to trust men like the professor? You called him – B'wana. You were patient and meek with him.' She was on the point of tears. 'What have we learned? That animals suffer? That the leopard kills the baboon, and the hyaena eats the dying leopard . . .?'

'It is not all cruelty and wickedness,' he interrupted her. 'You have seen that the water-buck lived because it had the courage to endure. The lion respects the elephant, and the elephant respects the lion, because each is strong and brave. You have seen that it is better to run directly into a grass-fire rather than run away from such dangers.'

He stopped to wipe a sprinkle of rain from his face. 'However, there is a proper time for running away. You cannot, for instance, win against the rain. So come, baba, help me to the hut. Let us accept the Masai's invitation, and shelter before we are altogether washed away.'

It was 9.30 on the morning of Friday, 30 October. They were not to know that this date would mark the beginning of what men later called The Hundred Days, more than three months of storm and flood. To Tembo, happily ignorant of the date's significance, the day was ill-favoured for other reasons. It was the first day since his initiation ceremonies that he had been without the smooth-grained club handed down to him by innumerable forefathers.

The loss of a Maria Thérèsa dollar was nothing by comparison. The club was sacred within his family. Without it, he felt naked and deserted by his tribal gods.

## *14. The elephant's parting gift*

A gust of wind struck the side of the hut, lifting the roof and dropping it again. Tembo grunted and shifted his position on the floor, his leg dragging. The girl stood in the doorway. She had braced her hands against the knotted frame, and the knuckles were white with tension.

She could smell the quick bitter tang of refreshed earth: a damp smell, mouldy and acid. It was like opening the door of a cool deep cellar that dripped with moisture. It was like stepping down into the darkness of a tomb, out of the desert heat, down cold stone steps into the grave.

This was not the smell of death, however. It carried a promise of rebirth that brought a grin to the face of the nomads driving their gaunt cattle between the termite hills. It sent the African farmer running to make sure his drainage ditches were unclogged.

Jackie knew and loved this unique smell. It was long over-

due. It would never again tickle the nostrils of the cattle that
had died in their thousands throughout Masailand, some of
whose skeletons gleamed white in the adjoining bush. It was
a good smell, though, for those who were still alive. She
sniffed it appreciatively.

'The safari ants are coming in,' she said.

Behind her the man stirred. 'Hot ashes. Sprinkle ashes
from the fire, around the hut.' He handed her a piece of
flattened tin as she returned to the smoking fire at the centre
of the hut. 'I'm sorry I cannot. . . .' He indicated the bandaged ankle.

'The injury worries me,' she said carefully. 'It has an ugly
look.'

She carried a scoop of hot ashes to the edge of the hut. She
was glad of the diversion. A plan was forming in her mind
and she feared it would meet with Tembo's opposition.

Under the eaves, along the mud walls of the hut, gathered
the ants. Once they began to march, nothing would turn
aside these small black soldiers. Baneful juices circulated
within their armour-plated bodies. Their massive jaws
awaited the hidden command that triggered this army.
They scuttled to and fro, increasingly restless under the
influence of the approaching storm.

The girl finished spreading the ashes.

'I think I shall try to reach the railroad,' she said abruptly.
'The rain is light. It may be another hour before the big
storm breaks.'

'You must not!' The man staggered to one knee. 'It is
dangerous!'

'I can do it. Otherwise we might be here for many days.
And your ankle needs proper care.'

'I will leave here,' he warned her. To prove his words,
he rose unsteadily to his feet and stumbled towards the
door.

She had anticipated the threat. 'I am putting Kamau in
your charge.'

He sat down again heavily and stared up at her with eyes

that reflected an utter astonishment. 'You would leave the galago?'

'Yes.' She spoke brusquely. 'It is the only way I can be sure you will stay.'

'You would do this for me?'

'I am leaving you here with Kamau,' she repeated in a calm voice. 'And I expect you to be here when I return with help.'

She threw the windbreaker over her shoulders, tucked the transistor under her arm, and ran to the door. 'It will take perhaps an hour to reach the railroad,' she called out. 'Do not worry.'

She left the hut without giving a second glance to the basket where Kamau slept. Never in her life had she made such a difficult decision.

Great splashes of rain were falling now upon the hill. Clouds that had built up during the early part of the morning rose in cathedral-like columns above the open country that stretched ahead. The air was black, the light a leaden colour. Sheets of lightning sprang across the horizon as if escaping from the swinging door of an underground cavern. Thunder rolled.

The girl was half-way down the hill when she became aware of the baby elephant. He seemed to be waiting for her at the edge of the ravaged forest. Then a flurry of rain obscured her view.

She had a rough idea of her position. Ever since they had left the coast she and the man had followed the Voi river-bed as it curved into the vast emptiness of the Tsavo game reserve. They had left the river-bed not far from the hamlet also called Voi, a railroad junction from which a spur projected westwards into the foothills of Mount Kilimanjaro.

She knew that once the rains fell in earnest, sand-rivers that had seen no rain for months would become boiling torrents. The most perilous part of her journey would be the few miles from the hill to the railroad embankment. Here the floodwaters would come tumbling through the funnel created between the Teita Hills and the desert uplands to the east.

Every year she had seen the swift change brought by the rains. There were few settlers in Kenya who had not lost relatives or friends in the flash floods that turned the main highway between Nairobi and Mombasa into a muddy waterfall.

She slithered to the bottom of the hill and tried to get her bearings. The rain was falling vertically now. All along the highway that paralleled the railroad she knew that motorists would be pulling into the bulldozed laybys, switching on headlights, winding up windows, and hauling out their emergency safari kits. Bridges would be swept away, cattle drowned, culverts washed from sight. Drivers would bunch together, knee-deep in mud, fighting to reach the nearest railroad station. Some would load their cars on freight wagons, completing their journey by rail. Others would prefer to inch forward between bouts of rain, knowing there was always danger of wash-outs.

Three miles to the embankment, and to the road. It seemed a terrifying distance now that she stood on the brink.

The dark bulk of the baby elephant moved across her vision. She looked at him blankly. He stood a yard or two from her, eyes mournful, trunk swaying. He snorted, and shifted his feet in an awkward attempt to come closer. She saw a piece of wire tangled around his limping hind-leg. She had noticed it before, in the forest, when there was little time to pay attention to such matters. Now, because she felt sorry for the calf (but also because she still hesitated about plunging ahead) she tried to coax him near enough to catch hold of the wire.

His small red eyes winked cautiously from the high-domed head. He squealed and swung his trunk out until the tip touched her face. But he stood firm. By kneeling, she got a grip on the wire and pulled.

The sudden pressure on his leg frightened the calf and he

jerked back so that the wire slowly unlooped. She held tight
to it, letting it unravel, and saw something else: a piece of
smooth grained wood, stained a reddish orange and decorated with beads.

'Tembo's club!' At the sound of her voice the calf broke
free and galloped off, leaving her with the wire in one
hand.

She picked up the club. The leather thong, with its
close-bound spiral of copper, was ensnared in the wire
that she now recognized as coming from Crankshaw's sailplane.

'So that's what happened.' She disentangled the club. On
the night of Tembo's escape from the professor the young
elephant must have trampled around the sailplane and his
foot become entangled in the wire.

She knew how badly Tembo was missing his own club. It
was absurd, of course, but she must go back to the hut.

'This is the Kenya Broadcasting Service transmitting on
reserve power. We shall be broadcasting an emergency
schedule throughout the day. District commissioners are re-
quested to monitor their sets at all times for instructions that
may affect their regions . . .'

Jackie wedged the transistor into the roof of the hut.

The man said: 'You would have drowned.' He raised his
eyes to the doorway where a solid wall of rain cascaded from
the roof. He ran his hands over the club again, shaking his
head in disbelief.

The radio continued: 'Torrential rain began to fall over
most parts of Kenya soon after noon. A force of helicopters
from 824 Squadron has been transferred to Mombasa from
Her Majesty's aircraft carrier *Victorious* and the Royal
Navy announced their crews would be placed at the disposal
of flood-control headquarters.

'East Africa Army Command has issued details of military
units earmarked for flood control and damage repair. These
include Alouette jet helicopters of the 8th Independent Re-

connaissance Flight, and mobile detachments of the 1st Signal Squadron, King's African Rifles.'

At the mention of his old regiment Tembo sat up. Jackie continued drying her hair on the sweater from her knapsack. There was another crackle of thunder outside.

'The Royal Air Force has just announced the deployment of transport and reconnaissance aircraft from 47 Squadron, Transport Command, Abingdon in Great Britain, and from 225 Sycamore Helicopter Squadron at Odiham, also in Great Britain.' The announcer listed the names of more military units: 24 Infantry Group; 36 Corps Engineer Regiment; 24 Field Squadron, Royal Engineers; 2nd Battalion, Coldstream Guards; 1st Battalion, Queen's Own Buffs . . .'

'It sounds like a war,' said the girl, tossing aside the sweater. She laughed. 'At least you've got your war-club ready.'

The man tilted his head. 'My club, yes. I feel a fool, though, unable to walk.' He wiggled his foot. 'Perhaps by tonight – '

'We shall be cut off by tonight.'

'I am glad you turned back, baba.'

'I'm glad I found the club.'

Already they could hear the torrents of rainwater pouring down the hill outside. The girl stirred the smoking fire, seeking warmth from glowing embers that hissed each time the rain penetrated the roof above them. The hut was stuffy and choked with smoke, but she felt the icicles prick her veins each time she thought of what might have happened. She could see herself now, bogged down in thick mud, perhaps half-way to the embankment, while around her the rivulets began to swell and combine to form a muddy lake.

She reached for Kamau's basket, and knew at once that it must be empty.

'Where . . .?'

The man grinned and opened the cloak he had drawn over his shoulders. The bushbaby hung from his shoulder, twitching his nostrils. He looked at the girl with sad accusing eyes.

'I feel – as if I betrayed him,' Jackie said, lifting the bush-baby between her mud-caked hands.

The man watched her, reclining on his makeshift bed, his damaged ankle resting on his pack. 'When you entrusted the galago to me,' he said quietly, 'it was not a betrayal of our friendship. Was it?'

'No.'

He nodded, fingering the bracelet of lion's hair at his wrist. 'In my tribe such a gesture is never forgotten. If a man gives another man something that is precious to himself they are blood brothers. When a woman does this – '

'We are brother and sister, Tembo!' The girl spoke quickly, breathing fast.

'Yes, baba. Sister – and brother.'

Another peal of thunder shook the hut. Rain drummed upon the roof, drowning further conversation.

The girl found a few more damp sticks of wood and threw them on the smouldering fire. She stood at the doorway for a long time, fascinated by the way that huge raindrops danced like ping-pong balls on the beaten earth outside.

When she returned to the centre of the hut Tembo was massaging his ankle again. The rain had subsided.

'I've been thinking,' she said. 'What future is there for you here in Kenya?'

He grinned, showing his filed teeth. 'I am still enough of a savage to live by the spear.'

'But that is not what you wish?'

'No. It is not what I wish.'

An awkward silence fell between them.

'I get angry inside every time you call yourself a savage,' she said finally.

'That is what I have been taught to call myself.'

'By white men?'

'Perhaps.'

'Tembo, do you suppose you could come to my country

some day? You would learn such things as the – the science of animals. With this knowledge, and the understanding that was handed down to you from your father and his father, it would be possible to make Kenya a great country.'

She stroked the bushbaby as she talked, rubbing her finger across his snout, enjoying the way he nibbled the hard skin.

'I would be afraid to come with you.' The Kamba looked directly at her. 'I have known others who went to the big cities of the west. They lost one education. They never got another.'

The day dragged into night, the hours passed slowly, and the girl felt lethargic. The rain never stopped and it was already dark by late afternoon. She boiled water and dressed Tembo's ankle, using what materials lay to hand. She cooked. She made vain efforts to tidy the hut, but this was one task that proved to be beyond her resources. She left the hut several times, defying the rain, to see if there were any signs of life beyond the shamba. Her ear was cocked for the sound of searching aircraft. They seemed to be alone in a world of rising floods, and she likened the hill to a new Noah's Ark, recalling how many animals had taken refuge there.

She went to sleep that night cheered by Tembo's harmonica. He played it softly, his eyes dark and thoughtful. His ankle was much better and he sat late over the fire, planning their escape from the hill.

It was clear by morning that this would be no easy task. There was a respite from the storm and a watery sun had broken through the angry clouds to reveal an expanse of floodwaters that completely enclosed the hill. They could see the railroad embankment very clearly in the rain-soft air, but now it was separated from them by a broad brown river. There were dark patches like islands in the river and the girl saw that these were the tops of trees. Floating in the branches were the bloated carcasses of animals, legs stiff and pointing to the sky, lifeless as upturned sofas.

'Could we make a raft and float ourselves across?'

'I thought we should try.' The man took a swipe at the thorn hedge with his panga. 'There is a great deal of driftwood.'

They paddled through mud to the hut and the girl switched the transistor on. The batteries were running low now, and she preferred to restrict its use to the news bulletins.

There was a brief burst of music. And then: ' "What the Papers Say". We bring you this daily summary of newspaper editorials in East Africa. Referring to the hunt for Tembo Murumbi, the *Daily Nation* said this morning that in effect this means armed police now feel free to shoot the wanted man. The newspaper said this might not be in accordance with British ideas of justice, but Kenya was now a free and independent country, and in Africa it was sometimes necessary to resort to more straightforward measures. The paper pointed out police are satisfied, on the basis of evidence in their possession, that Jacqueline Rhodes was kidnapped. It said no newly independent country in Africa could afford to have its good name besmirched by lawlessness of this kind, especially when a white girl was involved. The newspaper called upon the police authorities to cast aside all false sentiment in hunting down the kidnapper.'

She snapped the radio off.

'We could take a raft across the flood all the way to Ndi,' she said after a pause. 'At Ndi they will listen to me. You will be safe there.'

The man coughed. 'Have you looked at the chart?'

'Yes.' She brought it to him. The map had been carefully wrapped against the damp. She talked as she unfolded it. 'This hill is really *north* of Ndi. It is closer to the Rift.'

'So the floodwaters will be moving towards Ndi from here?'

'That is so.' She spread the map over his knees, explaining its features, aware that he found difficulty in understanding the symbols.

'Even if the rain stopped all day, the floods would continue to rise,' he said.

She knew this to be true. The plain was like a big tilted disc, with the upper western edge capped by the forested Chyulu range of mountains. Their seven-thousand-foot peaks would hose water into the lowlands for a long time to come.

There was a sound of squelching feet outside the hut. Tembo hoisted himself to his full length and hobbled to the door, the rifle under his arm.

It was the Masai warrior who greeted him. 'You have more money?'

The girl heard the rifle click. 'Yes.' Tembo's voice was cold. 'What of it?'

'That is what the old woman said.' The Masai ducked his head inside the hut and pointed the butt of the spear at the girl. 'She is yours?' he asked in his rapid and heavily accented Swahili.

'She travels with me,' Tembo said guardedly.

'And the police are hunting you.' It was a statement of fact.

'Where have you come from?' the Kamba interrupted. 'You ran away. Where did you go?'

'To a place of the wagon-that-makes-smoke.'

The girl looked at him sharply. If he had gone to one of the railroad stations he must have come back across the floodwater.

'Did you speak to anyone?' she asked.

'To the B'wana Kubwa,' the moran said after a pause. He stared down at her, not sure that he was hurting his own dignity to speak with her.

'What did you tell him?' Tembo asked roughly.

'That you were here on the hill.'

Tembo made a threatening move.

'Do not worry,' he said. 'Nobody believed me. And then I thought of the old woman and the money you gave her. So I came back.' He held out his hand.

'Why should I give you money?'

'Because I have a boat!'

Tembo lowered the rifle. 'A boat?' He swallowed.

'Well, a log cut like a canoe,' the Masai amended anxiously. 'It will take you and the girl.' He looked at them both in triumph.

'It is worth one of these dollars,' Tembo said. 'When we see the canoe.'

'Three dollars.'

'I have not three,' Tembo lied.

'The old woman said you had many.'

'The old woman sees things.'

The girl left the men to their haggling. She felt an immense relief. She had been frightened that searchers might locate their hideout on the hill, and hunt down Tembo with guns before she had a chance to talk with someone who was both sensible and in authority. Her failure to convince Professor Crankshaw had been a disturbing lesson.

A pair of dragonflies zigzagged across the open space outside the hut.

'The water-devils are out,' said Tembo, joining her. 'There will be a big storm later.'

'Then we must go at once. What did you pay the Masai?'

Tembo laughed. 'One of these.' He held his palm out. revealing a pile of the heavy silver Maria Thérèsa dollars. 'These people are not very clever,' he said contemptuously.

They gathered their belongings and once more the girl made the treacherous descent. The hill was like a chocolate pudding swamped in sauce, slow-moving and sticky. The sun was out, steaming the soil. All around them sprang new freshets that gurgled out of the earth and tinkled among the bared rocks.

The Masai led the way, keeping as much as possible to the patches of slippery grass. Small knots of zebra had gathered like pretty pebbles in the lee of crumbling cliffs. The rain had swept down the hillside, gouging its way through the insecure red soil that supported the meagre vegetation, washing it ruthlessly away. Much of the region was poor in land. Nomads like the Masai had burned away much of the grass. Elephants trampled down trees. What was left could be washed away in a single cloudburst. Year after year the rich red soil crumbled to dust and was blown into the ocean, or turned to mud and trickled down the sloping plains into the great river estuaries.

The Masai brought them to a wind-ruffled lagoon. 'There!' He pointed with his spear at a slimy log rolling in the shallows.

'That's a canoe?' asked Jackie. She threw down her pack. 'It doesn't look very safe.'

The log had been hollowed out, and it was balanced by a few uncut branches on either side. There was just enough room for Tembo and the girl. They waded through mud and got in. Jackie still clung to her basket, and the bushbaby sat on her shoulder, secured by the lead to her wrist.

The Masai touched their packs inquiringly. 'Keep them,' Tembo grunted. The moran grinned and handed each of them a crude paddle. From somewhere on the hillside came the faint squeal of the baby elephant.

'I hope he survives,' said the girl as they pushed off.

'He will if anything does,' said the man, slicing into the muddy water with short decisive strokes.

The hill had become an island fringed with thick belts of mahogany, matondo and mopani, and other trees that give the illusion from a distance of providing solid ground. For a time the girl and the man made poor progress through these obstructions. In many of the branches sheltered animals unable to cross the short distance of water to the hill itself. The girl identified genets and civet cats, cowering in the waving leaves, and dozens of hyraxes, or rock rabbits, their chisel-teeth bared unhappily. Once she saw an eight-foot black mamba streaking across the water ahead of them.

When they had cleared the submerged and partly burned trees the girl looked back and saw that the Masai was now standing with the old woman beside him. She looked again.

They were pulling into shore a second dugout, with another one linked to it by lianas.

'Did you say the Masai were not very clever?' she asked Tembo.

He brought his paddle inboard, and twisted round. The moran was loading the second dugout with their discarded gear. 'That's worth more than another Maria Thérèsa dollar,' said the girl, laughing, and the man grimaced and resumed his paddling.

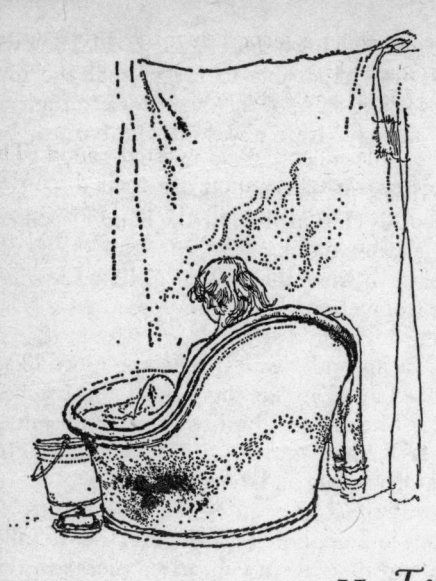

## 15. Tembo opens fire

The monoplane came swooping down from the northern hills, flying dangerously low between the new banks of heavy cloud and the rippling floodwaters.

'Make for the tree!' the girl said from her vantage point in the prow.

They had paddled the dugout some distance across the swift-running water, but until now they had kept clear of the clumps of tree-tops that formed islands along the way. These had become places of refuge for snakes and baboons. Even the more timid creatures, wildcats and porcupines, became aggressive in these conditions.

Tembo shot their crude dugout under a roof of branches. The aircraft passed them, a red light winking in its belly. It seemed to be following the railroad. The noise of its engine was reflected back from the overcast sky, and the echoes lasted long after the machine had gone.

'We've been lucky not to have more,' said Jackie. She was shaking a little. It was impossible to forget that the man hunched up in the leaking stern of the dugout was a fugitive. The words 'shoot on sight' were always at the back of her mind.

'It is the first and last plane we shall see. A new storm is coming.' He pointed his chin at the narrow band of yellowish light between the water and sky.

There was a splash behind them. The girl saw a small green monkey dive from a branch and disappear.

'I didn't know monkeys could swim.'

'Some can. They swim under water to escape crocodiles.'

The monkey bobbed up alongside the dugout and reached for Jackie's paddle. She moved hastily away and put a protective hand over Kamau nestling in her shoulder. The monkey chattered at her feebly and dived again.

As they moved out upon the water she saw a purple-rumped baboon slide off another branch. He was a fully grown dog baboon, and he tried in vain to submerge in the same way as the monkey. He was able only to duck his head, so that his bottom and tail stuck above the water like the conning-tower and periscope of a submarine.

The girl had started to laugh at this grotesque sight when there was a sudden swirl of water, a snapping of jaws, and the baboon disappeared.

'Crocodiles,' Tembo muttered, and remained silent again until they were within an arrow's range of the embankment.

The long ridge of artificially banked earth had become, in effect, a dam between the new lake of floodwaters and a shallow valley on the other side. Along the top marched the telegraph poles. Here and there the girl could see mounds of gravel and an occasional storage hut. Otherwise the embankment was as bleak and deserted as the hill. There had been no sign of a train all day.

A curtain of rain swept down from the north, followed by a wind that whipped the surface of the water into small waves. There was a fairly strong current now that seemed to flow faster as they neared the embankment. It had already carried them some distance south of the hill, and Jackie calculated that the effect must be to bring them somewhere close to the little station of Ndi.

She cuddled Kamau closer to her breast. The wind was cold and cut like a knife. It was accompanied by the renewed growling of thunder.

'Paddle harder,' Tembo called out. He was steering the dugout directly at the embankment now, although it seemed to be drifting sideways almost as swiftly as it progressed forward. The craft bobbed like a cork in the waves which were short and choppy. All along the embankment the water was piling up under the pressure of the wind, and the roar was like the pounding of ocean waves. Logs and uprooted trees formed a line of rubble that fell and rose against the earthen wall with the regularity of battering-rams. Water slopped over the girl's knees and the basket at her feet was awash.

There was a rumble like stones rattling down a metal chute. At first Jackie thought it was another thunder-crack until she saw rock and rubble cascade down the embankment. She remembered how floods in previous years had undermined sections of the railroad, in some cases flushing away the rail-bed so that the lines were left suspended in mid-air.

Tembo lifted his paddle and threw it away from the dugout. 'Get ready to jump!'

The girl crouched forward, one hand pressed against the front of her soaked shirt.

The dugout turned and tossed like a matchstick. There was another grumbling roar of collapsing earth. An enormous branch of a waterlogged tree loomed ahead. The dugout drifted sideways into it, and the man and the girl jumped.

Jackie found herself hanging by the arms from the stout branch, her feet under water. She swung her body so that her knee caught in smaller branches protruding from the

main stem; and in this fashion, wriggling feet first like a
tree cat, she made her way to the bank. She felt her arm
gripped by Tembo and allowed herself to be hauled to the
top.

'Look!' he commanded.

She saw that the two lines of railroad track descended at
this point into a shallow dip, protected on the flood side by a
stone wall which had previously appeared as a continuation
of the embankment. Rocks were scattered along this part of
the line and there were breaches in the wall where water
came seeping through.

'Which way is Ndi?' the man shouted above the noise of
wind and rain.

She pointed down the track, across the dip. They looked
at each other. Water dripped from the man's kepi. His cloak
was tight around him, like a cigar-leaf. The club still hung
from his wrist, and one of his trouser pockets bulged where
he had jammed the harmonica.

The girl felt the warmth of Kamau's body against her skin
under the cold wet shirt. Her boots squelched each time she
moved her feet and her jodhpurs seemed to have shrunk and
clung to her thighs and waist like a bandage. They had lost
everything else.

'Shall we run for it?' Jackie shouted.

Tembo ran his eye along the retaining wall. It protected
at least forty yards of the line, and he could see now that it
was extremely vulnerable to the pressure of floodwater piling against the other side. He took the girl's hand. 'Keep to
the track!' He pulled her after him, running in long easy
strides.

At the bottom of the dip, cut off from the wind, the girl
could hear the creak and grind of the big stones which had
been cemented as a facing to the wall. On the other side of
the track lay the valley, and she saw that already a small
river had formed, fed by water leaking through scores of tiny
channels under the rail-bed.

Chunks of stone and rock tumbled down the wall's face

and every instinct warned her that it was close to collapse.
Her feet were dragging. They no longer propelled her forward. All the strength for these last few yards had to come
from Tembo, whose energy was hampered only by the injury to his ankle.

They stopped at the top of the incline to catch breath.
Sheets of lightning provided a continuous illumination of
the wild scene. The newly formed lake had turned into a
storm-tossed sea and the wind drove wave upon wave
against the embankment. There was a loud rumble and
chunks of earth and stone tumbled into the dip, followed by
water pouring like coffee from a spout.

Tembo jerked the girl into action again, retreating a few
more yards.

'A washaway!'

A breach appeared in the retaining wall and widened
under the urgent onslaught of floodwater. The girl saw the
wall crumble piece by piece under her eyes. An aluminium
telegraph-pole was bent as easily as a pipe-cleaner. An entire
section of track vanished under the debris. With a tightening
of the throat she saw their dugout poised on the brink of the
waterfall and then tip end over end to the valley below.

Where the top of the wall had been visible there was
nothing but a line of foam and a flimsy black-metal pipe
supported on thick tripods that defied the flood. As the
breach widened, the flow of water became less turbulent and
broadened into a chocolate stream that bore upon its breast
all manner of dark and unidentifiable objects.

The girl and the man stood watching for a long time,
thankful to be alive.


The bushbaby was curled up beside the pot-bellied stove
whose radiance turned the tiny railroad station of Ndi into a
cosy haven from the storm. On either side of him stood
Jackie and Tembo, shaking themselves like dogs.

'If you are right, Ndi is cut off.'

The speaker was Gideon: station master, ticket clerk,

telegraphist, and signalman, and just lately gazetted by East
African Railways as sub-permanent-way inspector. He was a
small Chagga with fists like hams, a round polished face, and
a perpetual grin. He came from the prosperous coffee estates
of the Wachagga, high on the far side of Kilimanjáro. His
was one of the few African tribes who were rich enough to
finance their own schools, and this background gave him a
decisive and authoritative air. He took pride in his respon-
sibilities, and this was reflected in the way he wore his trimly
starched uniform of khaki. His eyes, slightly hooded, strayed
from the man to the girl and back again.

'You are lucky. Here the police cannot catch you.' He
directed this remark to Tembo.

'What do you mean?' demanded the girl.

'The road is impassable in either direction. The nearest
village cannot be reached, and all train services are suspended.'

'But why do you talk of police?'

Gideon picked up his wire-framed spectacles and peered
owlishly through them, first at the girl, and then at the wired
radio beside him on the table. 'Everyone is looking for you.
The police, it is said, will shoot this man if they can.'

'It is foolishness, all of it!' exclaimed the girl.

Gideon wagged his head. 'I believe you.'

He turned to the big table littered with exercise books,
rail-road maps, and a large old-fashioned telephone. 'If this
man had taken you by force, as the radio is saying, you
would not have come here holding his hand,' he said, opening his current log-book.

'Nevertheless, we must speak to those in authority,'
muttered Tembo.

By way of answer, Gideon handed him the phone. It was
dead.

'Do you have any men here?' asked Tembo.

'None.' The railwayman's small round face retreated into
the shadows, eyes restless. 'The men have all gone to their
shambas. I am left here alone.' He moved to a corner of the

room. 'But I have a shotgun and signal flares. When the storm abates we can summon help.'

'Does the radio work?' asked Jackie.

'When I run the generator. It provides the station with electricity. I closed it down to save fuel.' He turned to the girl. 'Never mind these serious matters. Would you like a bath? A hot bath?' He laughed at the expression on her face. 'Truly, I can arrange it.'

She was almost afraid to put his promise to the test. Nothing at this moment could have seemed a greater luxury.

'Please . . .'

Gideon picked up the log-book and handed it to her, not wanting to embarrass her Kamba friend who he guessed could not read. 'You may wish to see what I have written here,' he said with grave courtesy. 'It is the last report of conditions on the line. Meanwhile I will prepare the bath.'

She examined the open page with its ruled lines and the carefully pencilled words.

'What does it say?' Tembo asked when the door had closed on the railwayman.

'*At o800 hours a washaway was reported at Sultan Mahud,*' she read aloud. '*At Stony Athi, where the river-bed was still dry last night, water cascaded over the railroad bridge.*' Her voice faltered. '*A relief train ran into the breach at 1035 hours. The engine and three covered bogie wagons capsized. The fireman drowned.*'

'Wa! It is very bad.' He stood beside her, clenching his hands.

'*. . . at Mile 235 a forty-foot span girder bridge, together with abutment and wing-walls, were reported washed away along with twenty-five feet of embankment. Sections of track are without support . . .*'

She said: 'I wonder where my father is.'

There was a loud clatter at the door. Gideon entered with his head inside an inverted hip-bath. He looked so odd that she giggled. 'Where did you get that?'

'It has been lying in the yard for many months in a pile of settler's belongings.' His voice boomed inside the bath and he dropped it with a tremendous crash beside the stove.

'There are buckets outside in the boiler-room,' he said to Tembo. 'And hot water.'

After the Kamba had left, Gideon faced the girl. 'Are you sure this man has been – your friend?'

'Of course,' she said. Her face grew hot. 'He is the best friend I ever had.'

They spoke in English, the railwayman hiding his shyness by winding the big station clock that hung on the wall.

'Because,' he said slowly, 'the radio reported your father is coming in this direction with police.' He glanced meaningly at the shotgun propped in the corner. 'I could place your man under arrest. I have the necessary powers.'

'No!' Her indignation carried the ring of truth and Gideon's face relaxed. 'You must not do that. Truly, Tembo had nothing to do with my running away. I asked him for help.'

Gideon nodded. 'I wished to be sure.'

'What about my father?'

'He was travelling on a freight train, with another white man – Dr Crankshaw.'

The girl's face fell. 'Cranky! He will have told stories against Tembo.'

'There is no need to worry.' The railwayman moved to the door. 'The washaway that you saw – it will stop them.'

He opened the door and Tembo staggered in with two steaming buckets. The implication of Gideon's words took several seconds to sink in.

'Suppose nobody knows about the washaway?' asked Jackie. 'Won't the train . . .?'

'I have thought of it.' Gideon closed the door against the gale of wind outside. 'The freight should reach the washaway in about two hours, time enough for us to give a warning.'

He returned to the table and pulled his official cap over

the grizzled black hair. 'I am going to start the diesel. There will be a radio bulletin at two.'

Jackie was astonished to see that the hands on the big clock only pointed to a quarter to two. The day seemed interminable.

She heard the two men talking in Swahili, and she switched her attention to Kamau sleeping by the fire. The bushbaby was near the end of his journey. The idea oppressed her.

Then minutes later, behind a screen of old blankets rigged by Tembo, she lowered herself into the first hot bath in more than a week. The sensation was so unfamiliar that it seemed she had never enjoyed such a luxury before.

She heard the distant *put-put* of the generator starting up and stretched her legs, which were barely visible in the rising steam. Until this moment she had not realized how scratched and bruised she had been left by the past few days of travel. Now as the pains and irritations vanished one by one, she closed her eyes and sank to her neck in the hot water, making little islands of her scarred knees, pursing her lips, and blowing softly at the soapsuds gathering under her chin.

She heard the radio through a haze of voluptuous pleasure. 'A breakdown train, the Boulder Special, has left Nairobi for Mile 235.' Mile 235 – that must be somewhere close to Ndi.

'In a statement just issued by Flood Control Headquarters the following details were given for the information of repair gangs. The Boulder Special consists of two wagons of boulders, two forty-foot emergency bridge spans, launching tackle, two thousand five hundred timber sleepers, tools, welding equipment, and supplies of rations, together with engineering staff. The estimated time of arrival is 1900 hours. Because of washaways near Nairobi, parts of the train have been assembled *en route* with the assistance of army helicopters . . .'

She clambered out of the bath, sloshing water over the

concrete floor in her haste. There was a tattered towel hanging over the back of the little station's solitary chair and her mud-caked clothes were spread out on the floor before the fire. She dressed hastily, ignoring the discomfort of old clothes stiff with dirt.

'What are you going to do?' she asked, parting the screen of blankets.

'Get back up the line to the washaway,' Gideon said calmly. He was sitting at the rickety table, working on his log-book.

'Can we come with you?'

'Yes. I shall need your help.' He beckoned her to the table. 'When the bank collapsed did you notice anything?'

Tembo, joining them, said: 'The water flooded the line. It would be dangerous to try and cross.'

'Did you see if any telegraph poles were still standing?' Gideon persisted.

'No.' The girl's face lit up. 'But there was a kind of pipe – '

'Ah!' The railwayman spread his thick black hands palm downwards on a large Ordnance Survey map. 'Look here. See these broken lines? This is the main locomotive water supply from the slopes of Kilimanjaro. The water comes through a sixty-mile pipeline and reaches the railroad here ...' He put the point of his pencil in the centre of the map. 'Then it comes up the line here to Ndi to replenish the big water-tank outside. It might be possible to use the pipe to cross over. We can try.'

Standing in a siding, behind the station blockhouse, was a Land Rover converted for railroad use. It had steel flanged wheels and the back was cluttered with equipment that might be required in an emergency.

Gideon led them to it, explaining how the vehicle was driven like a trolley over the tracks. He brushed a pool of water from the driver's seat and squeezed behind the wheel. The wind drove the rain slantwise through the cutaway door. Behind the steel cab a canvas cover flapped and strained at the ropes securing it to iron bars. Jackie climbed stiffly into the cab and Tembo squatted in the back, balanced on tarpaulins and rope.

'We may need to use the lights as signals,' said Gideon, flicking switches.

The girl tightened her grip on Kamau when the headlamps suddenly stabbed the gloom ahead. The twin beams turned the torrential rain into silver bullets. She saw the windscreen transformed into an ochre-coloured screen as the wipers began to whine back and forth, flinging aside muddy gouts of water. She slipped her fingers inside the bushbaby's harness and thrust her booted feet against the floorboard as the vehicle jerked forward.

The scene of their recent escape from the flood was less than half a mile from Ndi. When Gideon saw the broken rails projecting like white bones from the rubble he jammed hard on the brake and the Land Rover's steel wheels squeaked in protest. The rails were greasy with mud and the vehicle skidded down the track until it bumped gently against a pile of stones.

'I know this piece of track very well,' said Gideon. 'Stay here while I take a look.'

He was gone a long time. Jackie, peering through the filthy windscreen, saw him scramble from sight down the embankment.

Tembo had climbed into the cab beside her. 'I see some men,' he said suddenly, his voice booming in the closed space. 'There, on the other side.'

She followed his pointing finger. Between gusts of rain she saw a number of dark shapes moving on the far side of the washaway.

She felt her heart constrict. Suddenly it was an effort to breathe. Her father was there! She knew this as surely as if she had seen him. She put one arm over the steering-wheel for support.

Tembo, unaware of this emotional crisis, scrambled out of the vehicle. He had the shotgun under his arm. Gideon's gun.

Dazedly she watched him go, stumbling over the rubble and then stopping at the edge of the crumbled bank.

The girl released her grip on the bushbaby's harness and looped the lead over her wrist. She could see the vague figures shifting position, as if seeking a way across the intervening torrent.

Tembo was standing on a mound, silhouetted against a patch of blue sky. Lightning still zigzagged across the hills to the west and there was an unending mutter and grumble of thunder.

'Tembo!' She ran to join him. 'Keep down until we know who they are.'

He made no move. His chest rose and fell with suppressed excitement.

'They will shoot you!'

He ignored her. The corners of his mouth were drawn back in what was almost a snarl. The lips were tight-drawn. A furrow creased the gap between his tufted eyebrows. He seemed to be carved from stone as he gripped the gun by butt and barrel.

She moved in front of him and saw the pale sunlight glint on a metal object carried by one of the men on the opposite bank.

'No, Tembo, no!' The child caught his elbow.

Something flashed on the other bank, and a quick sharp crack echoed across the water. In that same instant Tembo raised the shotgun and fired. Seconds later a vivid green flare burst overhead. The flare blossomed under the dark cloud-jumbled sky and as it fell earthwards it drew a charcoal line across the tiny patch of blue.

'Tembo!' The girl was shrieking now, trying desperately to pierce the man's trance-like mood.

Slowly he lowered the gun. His body, taut as a bowstring, quivered. He stared unseeingly at the girl and then his eyes seemed to lose their glaze. He blinked, and his body shook with a tremendous sigh.

'It was only a signal. Look. They were firing a flare pistol.'

She pointed to the ball of green light dissolving above them. 'They're our friends.'

Beneath them Gideon's anxious face appeared.

'Friends?' echoed Tembo.

'Yes. They're waving at us.' She stared until her eyes ached across the swirling brown waters. She could see men running. She prayed that Tembo's shot had gone wide.

He let the shotgun fall to his side, the butt resting in mud.

'What have I done?' His voice had dropped to a whisper. He had imagined himself cornered, hunted by men who refused to hear his explanations.

'Baba, did I hurt anyone?'

It was Gideon who answered. He pulled himself over the edge of the crumbling bank, his face angry. 'You probably missed. Give me the gun! And get back to the Land Rover.' He took Tembo and the girl roughly by the arms and spun them round. 'There are police over there – armed!'

## 16. Good-bye to Africa

Gideon backed the vehicle until they lost sight of the agitated group of men lining the distant shore.

'That was very foolish, *rafiki*,' he growled, twisting to face Tembo. He had taken the gun, resting it across his knees.

'It was my fault.' The girl spoke quickly. 'I told him the men might shoot.'

The railwayman grunted. 'It is necessary to get a message across to them with all speed. There will be great trouble otherwise. I saw police with guns – and dogs.' He leaned over the wheel. 'Also there is this matter of the relief train – the Boulder Special. It will reach here shortly after dark. Those men' – he pointed across the washaway – 'they will need to be told, in order to place warning lights.'

Tembo said: 'It would be best if I try to cross. There are ropes here. If I tie myself to the pipe – '

'It is too dangerous,' Gideon interrupted. 'The water is too deep and you would be swept off your feet. And you might be recognized. The police will not risk having you shoot at them again.'

The girl stretched her legs through the open cutaway door

of the vehicle, dangling her feet and craning her neck to look at the sky. 'The rain's stopping again. Can't you signal with lights?' She lowered herself to the muddy rail-bed, leaning back into the cab. 'I'm sure my father is over there.'

She saw the look of alarm on Tembo's face. 'Perhaps I hit him,' he said with a groan.

'*U puzi!*' snapped Gideon. 'Nonsense!' He climbed out of the cab and joined the girl. 'When I inspected the breach,' he said pedantically, 'it appeared that only the water-pipe connects the two sides. It remains standing because the supporting pylons have separate foundations. The distance across the washaway is very great.' He added for Tembo's benefit: 'Too wide to shoot with accuracy.'

'Could someone climb across the pipe?' Jackie asked.

'The pipe is fifteen inches in diameter exactly. It would not support a full-grown man.'

'But I'm only a girl, and not heavy! Let me try. I'm sure I could do it.' Her voice grew more excited. 'If I could climb across I could explain everything. My father would listen.' She was thinking of Tembo, anxious to reassure him, aware of his gathering fears. 'Please. Let me try. I'm a good swimmer, if I should fall . . .'

'It is impossible.' Tembo spoke now, mustering his full authority. He turned to Gideon. 'There is no means of using the wires?' He indicated the telegraph lines that coiled and looped alongside the tracks, their supporting poles broken.

'None.'

Tembo rummaged around his pockets and pulled out the harmonica. He slapped it against the palm of one hand and blew an experimental note or two.

'Do you remember our game of Do-you-remember?' He was leaning across the cab seat now, facing the girl, who stood with one foot resting on a flanged front wheel.

'Yes,' she said impatiently. It seemed a strange time to exchange reminiscences.

'Then you remember how Kamau climbed into the trunk of a tree to look for grubs?'

'Of course.'

'And how we made him come out?'

'By blocking one end? Yes.'

Tembo clambered out of the cab and stood beside the railwayman. 'Is there water in the pipe?'

'No, of course not. The pipe is broken.'

'And a small animal could climb through it?'

Gideon's quick slanted eyes turned from the man to the girl. ' – er, yes!'

Jackie stiffened. 'You don't mean Kamau?'

'I mean Kamau.'

'No!' She tightened her grasp on the bushbaby. 'He might fall.'

'Not if he goes *through* the pipe.'

She looked at Tembo in outraged astonishment.

'We can tie a light line to his harness, make him climb through to the other side – '

'But nobody will see him,' she objected.

'It is only an idea,' said Tembo.

'The only idea that might work.' Gideon moved restlessly round the hood of the Land Rover. 'It is three hours before nightfall. It may get darker more quickly if another storm appears. It is essential that we get a message across the breach.'

He took the girl gently by the shoulders. 'You can write a note. Explain about your friend's innocence. We will clip the note in the galago's harness. I will also write a warning about the relief train. We will tie some fishing line to the galago. He will be safe.' He climbed into the cab and grinned suddenly. 'I am going back to the station for the fishing line. I would not wish you to report this in Nairobi, but I like this post at Ndi. It allows me to fish a great deal.'

He was back from the station in ten minutes. Sparks flew from the Land Rover's steel wheels as he screeched to a halt on the rails. There was only a slight drizzle now, although a strong wind continued to howl across the torn track.

Jackie and her companion emerged from their shelter behind a pile of rubble. The girl was pale but determined.

'Here is a pencil and pad,' said Gideon.

She leaned against the back of the vehicle, sucking the tip of the pencil, and then began to write:

PLEASE TELL MY FATHER IT WAS ALL MY FAULT. TEMBO HAS BEEN A FAITHFUL FRIEND AND HAS RESCUED ME FROM CERTAIN . . .

She paused, frowning at the melodramatic phrase, and finally added the word DEATH.

She rubbed the bushbaby's ears, slipping her hand inside the torn shirt, and then she wrote: IF YOU SHOOT AT TEMBO YOU WILL NEVER SEE ME AGAIN. She signed it: JACQUELINE RHODES.

Together they walked to the break in the embankment. Gideon handed the girl a large spool of looped fishing line. She read the card: '100 metres Luxor Kroic invisible nylon. Breaking strain: 37 pounds. Diam.: 0.0238 inches'.

She said: 'One hundred metres is not very much.'

'It will be enough. They will have ropes over there. Ropes to be reeled in, like fish.'

She disliked the analogy. It made Kamau sound like a piece of bait. She felt as if she were his executioner as she lifted the bushbaby from his nest on her shoulder and tightened his leather harness. His ears were cocked and his nose twitched as if he sensed her unease. She spoke softly to him, but averted her eyes from his trusting face, for she felt sure the plan was doomed to failure.

The washaway had broken the supply pipe, and the jagged end protruded near the top of a tubular steel pylon that stood near the edge of the broken bank.

She waited at the foot of the pylon, trying to discern the shadowy figures on the other side.

'I've written instructions here,' said Gideon, folding a piece of paper into her own handwritten note and pinning the messages to Kamau's collar. 'Now let me climb up with him.'

'No.' She hesitated, one foot on the bottom rung of the swaying pylon. 'It is better if I take the bushbaby.'

Tembo, full of sympathetic understanding, said: 'I will support you.' She felt his comforting hand under her elbow. She climbed the few feet to the top of the pylon. A spattering of rain made the rungs slippery, and she felt Tembo's shoulder behind her knees as he followed.

She could see now that water bubbled across at least forty yards of broken track. The pylon seemed to be swaying dangerously in the wind and sections of the pipe creaked and shifted at every joint. Just to look down at the swirling water made her head spin. The wind plucked at her body with icy fingers, whipping her flaxen hair across her eyes.

Beneath her, Tembo paid out the fishing line. She ran her hand over the line, clearing it of entanglements, and kissed Kamau quickly on the nose. Then she pushed him gently into the interior of the pipe.

Kamau crouched in the entrance, leaning forward on his widespread hands, legs folded like an athlete. He no longer heard the soothing sound of her voice, although he still felt the warm presence of her hand. He moved a few inches into the conduit and flattened his ears against the fearsome howl of wind blowing down the long black tunnel ahead. The darkness was a comfort to him. The pupils of his eyes grew large and round, and soon he could see a great deal more than most animals would have perceived in that damp and gloomy place.

He scuttled forward a few feet, and stopped. His body filled most of the narrow space and, as a precaution, he sat up and felt the wet cold curve of the pipe above his head. He could, if necessary, turn. Satisfied, he dropped back on to his hands and eyed the sludge and dead damp leaves ahead.

He knew little of fear, for his life had been entirely sheltered by the girl's love. Like all bushbabies, however, he had an overwhelming curiosity. He ran forward again, extending his ears to distinguish between the groans and mutterings of the jointed pipe. Every sound was magnified.

The bushbaby was endowed by nature with a variety of highly tuned senses. His ears moved like radar scoops, catching every small sound. His nostrils twitched in response to the rich feast of strange smells infesting the pipe. His eyes caught every glimmer of light and every hair on his body quivered. The fishing line tugged at his collar and harness, and instinctively he pulled forward against it.

The girl clung to the pylon and watched Tembo pay out the line. She was worried by the possibilities of disaster. What if a joint broke and the flimsy pipe collapsed under the wind's pressure! Suppose Kamau turned and ran back and became entangled in the line?

Worst of all, suppose a civet cat lay concealed within the conduit? It was just the kind of refuge such an animal would choose and against which Kamau would never stand a chance.

The girl took a tighter grip on the icy steel. Foot by foot, the slender nylon line disappeared into the broken pipe. She tried to drag her eyes away from it, but there was nothing else to hold her attention.

The minutes ticked by. The fishing line continued to move by jerks into the pipe. It seemed to her that it was more fragile than a spider's gossamer, this lifeline that could link her with her father.

'He should be there by now,' growled Tembo, two rungs below her. The spool was no longer jerking in his hand. Jackie gave the line a gentle tug. She could feel no resistance.

Her mouth had gone dry and she found nothing to say. If Kamau turned back now it would be so easy for the nylon to entangle and strangle him.

Suddenly she heard dogs barking, and in that same moment the line between her fingers jerked convulsively. She peered along the sheathed pipe, eyes watering with the strain. She could see nothing at the other end except blurred shapes. The barking grew louder.

'Police dogs!' Gideon shouted from below.

Of course! The dogs would have caught the bushbaby's scent as he emerged from the far end of the pipe. Jackie put her ear to the pipe, but any other sound was drowned by the wind.

Then came a sharp tug on the fishing line, repeated three times. This was the signal Gideon had prearranged in his note. It meant someone had unpinned it from Kamau's harness. The sharpness of Jackie's relief was blunted by anxiety for the bushbaby and she listened to the dogs' barking with growing concern.

Again the line was tugged.

'They tugged five times,' she shouted down to Gideon.

'That means they've got rope at their end.' He stood at the foot of the pylon, waving excitedly. 'When you get another five tugs begin to reel in the line again.'

Everything, the girl thought bitterly, was going in accordance with Gideon's plan. He must have realized that the dogs would draw attention to Kamau emerging from the pipe. He was not concerned with what might happen after that. She began to relax her grip on the pylon's steel uprights.

'Mind you don't fall, baba,' Tembo warned her.

'I'm going down,' she said. 'You can pull the line back. I feel dizzy.'

He eased her down to the greasy mud surrounding the pylon, taking in hand her part of the line. He felt someone tugging again: three-four-five times.

The girl leaned on Gideon's arm and closed her eyes. She felt unutterably sick and weary. She closed her eyes and saw a mental picture of three or four police Alsatians with tongues hanging out as they waited for Kamau to tumble from the broken-ended pipe.

'The rope!' Tembo's voice reached her through a fog. She found that Gideon had picked her up and was sitting her in the driving seat of the Land Rover.

'There is also a message.'

The girl rallied. 'Quick. I'm all right.'

'You are sure?'

'Sure.' She waved Gideon away. She must have fainted, if only for a moment. She shook herself and saw that Tembo was descending from the pylon with the end of the nylon line tied to a thicker rope.

She joined him. A sheet of paper had been screwed up and pushed into the iron ring that linked the nylon and the rope.

'It is signed by your father,' said Gideon, handing it to her with a smile.

DELIGHTED YOU ARE OKAY, it read. POLICE ACCEPT YOUR DEFENCE OF TEMBO SO STOP WORRYING. WE ARE HOPING MORE RUBBER RAFTS ON BOULDER SPECIAL AND WILL RIG ROPES FOR CROSSING. MEANWHILE STAY INDOORS BEFORE YOU GET PNEUMONIA.

There was a P. S.: KAMAU WAS SCARED BY POLICE DOGS AND RAN BACK INTO PIPE. HOPE YOU'VE GOT HIM.

Jackie's head flew back. Only the rope issued from the mouth of the pipe.

She scrambled up the rungs and shook the rope. Later the rope would provide stability. The men on the opposite shore would attach the rafts to the pipe to prevent them floating away, and if the pipe should break under the strain the rope would offer extra security. Now the girl shook the rope, hoping to encourage Kamau to leave the shelter of the pipe. She imagined him stuck, half-way down, afraid or unable to go forward or back.

She heard Gideon hammering a steel rod between the railties. On both sides of the break the rope was being anchored. Feverishly she peered into the pipe and clucked her tongue.

The bushbaby emerged without warning. His tiny face appeared in the mouth of the broken piping and his large eyes sparkled like elderberry wine when he saw her. His fur was wet and knotted, his tail spiked like a nailbrush, and there were pin-pricks of blood spattered over the yellow apron of fur under his chin.

He came out chattering happily to himself, unaware of all the fuss he had caused, looking as if it had been his lifelong habit to dive into the mysteries and hidden hazards of loco-motive water-supply pipes. His ears crumpled back when the girl hugged him to her face, his rat's tail curled up con-tentedly, and he nipped her cheeks with tiny nibbling teeth that parted each time his long tongue emerged to rove be-hind her ear.

The sun made its last brief appearance, breaking through the boiling clouds, touching the landscape with a golden-tipped brush. The girl, halted in her descent, saw one of the most remarkable sights known to man: the sudden blooming of the dead earth after the African rains begin to fall.

Wherever the flood had left the land exposed there sprang a carpet of gay flowers and green shrubs. Where once there had been gnarled thorn and withered scrub there now ap-peared green buds and lush grasses. For two weeks this trans-formation had been in secret preparation. Millions of plants and trees had come unobtrusively into bud, sensing the ap-proach of the rain that within hours would splash colour across the landscape like a child's brush on a magic paint-book.

Jackie held the little bushbaby against her face and thought for a moment that she had stepped into one of those miniature Japanese flower gardens made of paper, that un-fold their pretty colours when dipped in water. To her right the freshly green foothills rose to the dark crests of Kili-manjaro. To the left the tawny plain rose out of the flood, stretching to the world's uttermost edge. If she had to leave Kamau – and she had every reason to believe that their parting was now imminent – then there were few better places in which to say good-bye.

And then the sun went out and it was darker than ever before. Kamau smelt the salt in her tears.

The first of the rubber life-rafts inched its way across the swift current. Jackie was unable to take her eyes from the figure huddled amidships. A slouch hat, pulled down as protection against the wind-driven rain, concealed the face that she was sure belonged to her father.

The raft bounced upon the rippling waters and was held to its course by ropes looped over the pipe. The ropes were secured to either end of the raft and manipulated by two other men who warped it as sailors might manoeuvre a small vessel. Each time they came to a pylon planted in the water the lead man threw out an extra rope which he secured to the next section of pipe, and in this way, slowly and painfully, they worked their way to a point in midstream where the flow of water hit its highest peak.

The pipe was now bending under the tremendous strain. A sudden sharp crack startled the silent watchers. The middle section of the pipe flew apart. At once the raft shifted several feet downstream until the powerful nylon rope inside the pipe could take the strain.

A series of mild explosions followed as the pipe began to break up. Gideon, standing by his end of the anchored rope, said: 'It will be easier if the rope holds.' And the rope did hold, despite some ominous thrumming noises as the raft neared their shore.

Trapper Rhodes was first to leave, splashing knee-high through water and mud, his red face creased with emotion, eyes wrinkled, laughing and waving his arms until he fetched up in front of Jackie.

She buried her face in his shoulders, and suddenly there erupted all the tears and emotion that she had bottled up.

'Hey, don't cry – Miss Squeakie!' He had not used the term since she was a very small child, and now she hugged him more closely. She rubbed her face against his rough cheek, and felt his fingers comb through her tangled hair.

'I'm sorry!' she kept repeating until he was obliged to pull away from her.

'Sorry?' He rumpled her hair. 'Whatever you've been up

to, honey, now's not the time to apologize. I get weak at the knees when I think what might have happened to you.'

He caught sight of Tembo standing ill-at-ease.

'Jambo!' He kept an arm around Jackie as he strode across. 'You made some powerful enemies,' he said, pumping Tembo's arm. 'Thank goodness we got that message. Even then I had a hard time convincing Crankshaw and the police – ' He broke away. 'But there's still work to be done. We'll talk later.'

The raft had brought its own linking rope from the other shore, and now another was tied astern.

'Then we can pull it backwards and forwards?' asked Jackie.

'Exactly,' said her father.

'What will you do about stopping the relief train?'

Gideon, who had already introduced himself to her father, said: 'I have signals and a field phone ready.'

But it proved impossible to use the phone, which, if the lines further north had been untouched by the storm, might have been connected to the further embankment. Instead, Crankshaw's men waited for the arrival of the Boulder Special, sending up flares and flashing signal lamps to halt it before the washaway. The big old-fashioned ML Class steam locomotive clanked to a standstill and soon its powerful searchlight played over the waters. At once men poured out of the wagons and began the work of repairing the breach before daybreak.

It was thus late when Trapper Rhodes found time to sit quietly in the station house at Ndi, to extract from Jackie the full story of the events that had brought together this odd assembly: Professor Crankshaw, apologetic but still puzzled; Gideon, tireless as ever, fussing around them with steaming cups of strong tea; and Tembo, waiting tensely while the girl explained how she had drawn him into her adventures.

'Honestly,' she said, 'I never *meant* to walk all this way. It was just one accident that led to another.'

'I can see Tembo never had a chance,' her father re-marked dryly. 'What shatters me is – you did all this for the bushbaby.'

They turned to look at Kamau, who squatted on top of his basket, head cocked on one side, ears pricked.

'I had to take him home to the baobab tree.' Her face reflected her distress at the thought.

'But why? I still don't understand – why?'

'Because,' she repeated patiently, 'I lost the permit. Don't you see, I had no choice.'

She began to cry again.

'Of course you had a choice, honey.' He was pacing back and forth in front of the stove, and she knew how shocked he was. 'All you had to do was tell me – or Mummy.'

'But I still needed the permit, Daddy. Otherwise I'd have had to leave him on the quay.'

'But, honey, the permit was in your mother's bag, along with the passports and health papers.'

She gaped. It was some time before she spoke again. 'Does that mean I really can keep Kamau?'

'I promise faithfully – you can keep him! Cross my heart.'

'And I can take him on the ship?'

'But of course.'

'And I don't need to take him to the Place of the Hip-popotamus?'

Jackie knelt beside the stove with the bushbaby clinging to her neck. Her eyes met Tembo's, and they smiled to each other, and between them flashed both sympathy and under-standing.

Aboard the *Thoreau* two days later Jackie stood at the deck rail with Kamau openly perched upon her shoulder. She had a scrubbed little-girl look again, which did not de-ceive Captain MacRae, watching from the bridge.

'Looks like butter wouldn't melt in her mouth, don't she, mister?' He nudged the Third. 'Who'd guess she's roughly equivalent in trouble potential to one major flood disaster?'

In another part of the ship Penny Rhodes said to her husband: 'Some stronger instinct made Jackie undertake that journey.'

Trapper Rhodes nodded. 'I was thinking the same thing. Sure, she wanted to save Kamau's life. But deep down she didn't want to leave Africa. She didn't want, at the last crucial moment, to say good-bye.'

'Have you?' asked Penny.

'Said good-bye?' He tipped his wideawake hat to the back of his head. 'Yes. For the time being.'

'And no regrets?'

The ship's siren wailed and the deck trembled beneath their feet.

'No regrets. I served Africa the best way I could. And Africa taught me a lot in return.'

'I know what I've learned,' said Penny a trifle bitterly. 'How to survive in the northern desert. How to raise kids on an animal farm in the middle of the bush. How to live without neighbours and doctors. How to speak Swahili, and a bit of Kikuyu, and a smattering of Turkana. But I'm blessed if I can see how all that's going to help me now.'

He laughed, brushing the tips of his fingers under her tired eyes. 'Africa taught us to throw the clutter out of our lives. That should be worth something. It's one place on earth where men still stand up tall, not hunchbacked under the burden of their own possessions.'

'That's the best lesson Tembo taught her.'

Their hearts ached a little, for they both knew that many difficulties and disappointments lay in store for the girl, and they were sorry to take her so soon to another world, where her feet would never feel the soft kiss of cobwebs and morning dew while the water-bottle bird sounded the dawn alarm.

A time would come when she might remember her adventure with astonishment, marvelling at the things made

possible by love and faith. Between that time and this must
lie a wide expanse of hard experience and distressing doubts,
and perhaps of this Jackie was not fully aware.

Jackie, standing on the deck below, did have an inkling of
the realities ahead. She knew, although she might have
found difficulty in formulating the idea, that the traffic of
the big cities could stain a man's soul, and she was glad now
that Tembo the Kamba would remain here, in his own Africa.

As she waited, knowing he would hesitate until the last
moment to take his leave, she thought: 'Soon this will be
only a memory. If only there was some way to capture it, to
hold on to it, because I don't want to look back some day
and feel I've lost it.'

Her mind travelled back over the past few days – a time
when life had balanced on a knife's edge, when the sun
seemed brighter in consequence and the birds sang more
clearly. New lessons had been learned, old ideas discarded,
and her life would never be the same again. It had been a
time without a real beginning, and no measurable end, when
simple bonds of loyalty and affection were forged between a
man and a girl and one of God's tiniest creatures.

The memory would survive the bruises and the knocks of
life, and instinct told her that it would be a source of
strength when the future seemed less certain and her own
place in the world less assured.

She peered down the ship's side and saw Tembo pick his
way through the dockside litter. Already he seemed to be
divided from her by a widening gulf. He mounted the gangway with his characteristic air of self-effacement, nervously
bending his head and plucking his chin as he explained his
business to the white-jacketed officer. He looked thin and
vulnerable, away from his own haunts. He was out of place
in the rusty squalor of the docks.

She saw, in a blinding moment of insight, that Tembo
could never occupy the world to which she must go – dead

cities built of dead concrete and dead steel, run by dead mechanisms constructed from dead materials. Tembo was touched at all times by life and freedom; he slept upon the living grasses of a living earth; his day was timed by the vibrant sun, his year by the changing seasons.

She was glad he could not stay long. They talked a little, but whatever remained to be said could not be put in words.

He fondled the bushbaby. 'The rains, it is said, will continue for many weeks.'

She nodded. 'I have heard the damage is very great.'

He shifted awkwardly from one leg to the other. 'I shall return to my village for a time.'

'I will send messages to you, through Nairobi, if we are to return.'

He stuck his hand out. '*Kwa heri*, then, baba.'

'*Kwa heri*, old friend.'

He fumbled with his wrist, and she saw that he was trying to remove the bracelet made from the hair of the lion he had killed as a very young warrior.

'I cannot –'

'Yes, baba. Keep it until we meet again. Keep it, as once I kept the galago on the hill.'

She let him place it on her own thorn-scarred wrist.

'May the gods of sea and sky preserve you,' said Tembo, and turned away.

'And God keep you safe, old friend.'

She watched him walk slowly away, knobbly knees under faded khaki shorts, shoulders far too thin for his badly tanned jacket of bushbuck hide, walking flat-footed on long horny heels and large splayed toes, the old desert kepi jammed tight on his grizzled head, and then she could look no longer.

She saw him again when the ship sailed. He was sitting on a bollard and he had the harmonica between the hard palms of his hands. Above the throb of the engines she heard the familiar notes: 'When the Saints go marching in'.

'Do you remember?' she whispered to Kamau. The bush-baby pricked up his ears, and she was sure that he did.